ful What You Wish For

Also by Lucy Finn

Careful What You Wish For

If Wishing Made It So

Lucy Finn

A SIGNET ECLIPSE BOOK

SIGNET ECLIPSE
Published by New American Library, a division of
Penguin Group (USA) Inc., 375 Hudson Street,
New York, New York 10014, USA
Penguin Group (Canada), 90 Eglinton Avenue East, Suite 700, Toronto,
Ontario M4P 2Y3, Canada (a division of Pearson Penguin Canada Inc.)
Penguin Books Ltd., 80 Strand, London WC2R 0RL, England
Penguin Ireland, 25 St. Stephen's Green, Dublin 2,
Ireland (a division of Penguin Books Ltd.)
Penguin Group (Australia), 250 Camberwell Road, Camberwell, Victoria 3124,
Australia (a division of Pearson Australia Group Pty. Ltd.)
Penguin Books India Pvt. Ltd., 11 Community Centre, Panchsheel Park,
New Delhi - 110 017, India
Penguin Group (NZ), 67 Apollo Drive, Rosedale, North Shore 0632,
New Zealand (a division of Pearson New Zealand Ltd.)
Penguin Books (South Africa) (Pty.) Ltd., 24 Sturdee Avenue,
Rosebank, Johannesburg 2196, South Africa

Penguin Books Ltd., Registered Offices:
80 Strand, London WC2R 0RL, England

First published by Signet Eclipse, an imprint of New American Library,
a division of Penguin Group (USA) Inc.

First Printing, July 2008
10 9 8 7 6 5 4 3 2 1

*To my sister, Corrine Boland.
She's the only sister I have—and the
best one I could ever want.*

"The rarer action is in virtue
than in vengeance."
—WILLIAM SHAKESPEARE, *The Tempest*, V, i

Chapter 1

Like a writ of execution, the light green sheet of copier paper announced the end of the world as Hildy Caldwell knew it. Her breath became shallow, her knees turned weak, and her feelings skittered toward panic every time she passed the place where it lay atop the old upright piano.

The invitation to the tenth reunion of her class at Lake Lehman High School had come in April, the cruelest month. On that day silver sheets of rain flattened the butter yellow daffodils to the ground, their bloom ending prematurely in the violence of an early-season thunderstorm. The omen could not be more obvious. The minute Hildy opened the envelope, the paper started shaking in her hand.

How could she go? How could she face her old classmates with the truth? They had expected so much from her that they had voted her the Girl Most Likely to Succeed.

She could lose the extra five (okay, it was more like ten) pounds she had gained since she had graduated. She could buy new clothes. She could get streaks in her long tawny hair. But how could she change her life? Look at the Girl Most Likely to Succeed now—the Woman in a Rut on the Road to Nowhere.

She faced the facts as others would see them. She still lived in the small town where she had been born. Although her older sister had helped out, the long illness of Hildy's mother had kept her living at home and commuting to college while most of her friends moved far away. She had never followed her dreams to become a painter in Paris, New York City, or Gauguin's Tahiti.

Instead, last year after her mother passed away Hildy had taken her small inheritance and put a down payment on an old white clapboard house with pink roses crawling up a lopsided trellis. The 1920s Craftsman-style home looked so romantic to her; it had such potential, but it needed paint, a new bathroom, plumbing work—the list was as long as Hildy's arm. And the rustic dwelling sat on a muddy lane so rural it was nearly ten miles from the nearest grocery store and had access only to dial-up Internet service.

As for her job—talk about a yawn! Hildy taught English at the same high school where she had graduated a decade ago. Nothing exciting or unusual had ever happened to her, unless she counted a blue ribbon at the Luzerne County Fair for her portrait of a neighbor's pet sow.

Worse, she had no kids; she had cats. As much as she adored Shelley and Keats, few of her old classmates would ooh and aah if she showed off their baby pictures on her camera phone.

Worst of all, she had no honey to handle her honey-do list—no boyfriend, husband, or for a while now, even a date. Her last serious relationship had ended when the admittedly gorgeous but neurotically neat Procter & Gamble engineer she had been seeing for months issued an ultimatum.

"It's me or the cats," he had demanded, looking down at the patina of Shelley's white fur on his black jeans.

Hildy chose the cats.

To tell the truth, the breakup had been a big relief. She resented spending her leisure time cleaning the house to his level of satisfaction. And as much as she had trouble admitting it, Hildy knew the real reason why the breakup was inevitable. The invitation to her high school reunion brought it to the fore like an avalanche of cold realization crashing down with chilling truth on her heart.

The reason was Michael Amante. Big Mike. Six feet tall, with auburn hair and eyes the warm amber of a good bourbon, Mike had been the best dancer in high school, the best athlete, the best kisser. All the girls went crazy for him.

Hildy should know. She had been one of them. He had been her first crush, her first steady boyfriend, and, she was beginning to fear, the only man she might ever love. How pathetic was that? Hildy shook her head at the thought. She was heading for the Big Three-Oh and she was still hung up on her high school sweetheart.

And Mike had been wild for her too, or so he had said. But then there was that one awful day—Oh, what was the use of remembering?! It all had happened long ago, and even if Hildy was still carrying a torch for Mike, he had no similar secret fire burning for her. Last she had heard, he had made a name in real estate, lived in Manhattan, and had become engaged to a famous celebrity photographer who looked like a supermodel. What was her name? Kiki? Tiki? Wiki?

Whatever it was, the name was a far cry from Hildy—short for Hildegard. What had her mother been thinking? All through grammar school she had been tormented by kids calling her Hildegarden, Hill-da-Garbage, or Hillygarter. Finally in seventh grade she had a teacher—he was young and handsome—who had volunteered at her tiny school to teach a class in writing. The first day of the semester, he glanced down at the class roster, saw her name, and said, "Ah, Hildy. Right out of *His Girl Friday*!" After that she was Hildy, and no one dared to call her anything else.

So, it was a particularly painful turn of the screw that Mike—once *her* Mike—had chosen a woman who lived a life of glamour and excitement *and* whose entire name was just one word, like Cher.

That wasn't my *world,* Hildy thought as she pried her eyes open first thing in the morning, climbed out of bed wearing her Penn State football T-shirt, and dragged herself into the kitchen to stick a cup of coffee made yesterday into the microwave. While she waited for it to heat up, she steeled herself to face scooping out the cats' box—a job best done when she was half-conscious.

After doing the dirty deed, she held the plastic bag of scooped poop at the end of her outstretched arm and ducked barefooted out the back door to put it in the trash.

No one would see her "half-nekked," as they said around here, except for the squirrels and birds. When she deposited the bag, her thoughts turned once more to what she would say if she ever ran into Mike again. She would act as if she barely recognized him. *Mike?* She'd furrow her brow. *Mike? Oh yes, Mike Amante, I remember you now.*

Poised outside the screen door, the sun pouring down on the budding leaves above her, Hildy let her thoughts wander to that well-planned moment. She would raise her chin and extend her hand coolly to take his. She would be wearing very high heels to show off her legs, always her best feature. And she might not be a supermodel but she still had bright blue eyes, a turned-up nose, and looked young enough to be mistaken for her own students when the class went on field trips.

Hopefully Mike would eat his heart out. And even if he didn't, he'd never know how much she ached inside whenever she thought of him.

A bloodcurdling scream from inside the house shook her from her reverie. Her heart beating fast, Hildy rushed inside and followed the cacophony of murderous yowling into the dining room.

Shelley and Keats had crowded together on the sill before the open window. Their fur stood on end, their tails swished back and forth in unison like two metronomes, and their full-throated voices let the neighbor's cat Chief—who was standing on the porch rail on the opposite side of the screen—know how much they despised him. They hated Chief especially much, Hildy thought, because he still clearly sported the testicles they no longer had.

All at once, realizing what was about to happen, Hildy sprang forward with an Olympic-class lunge. She reached the window while yelling "No!" to all three cats. Shelley and Keats got the message, jumping in opposite directions to land gracefully on the floor.

Not Chief. He had turned away from the screen and raised his tail. Then he began a little two-step with his hind feet as he assumed the dreaded spray position.

"No!" Hildy yelled again while she reached desperately for the sash to slam the window down. Too late. The warm, pungent urine arced through the wire mesh to catch her midchest, soaking her T-shirt.

"Oh no," she moaned, holding the wet cotton away from her body. She watched the neighbor's cat sashay away, pleased with himself. "Chief!" she called after him. "One of these days I'm going to neuter you myself!"

Even as she said the words, Hildy had an epiphany. She had gotten a wake-up call from Chief that she couldn't ignore. She looked down at her odiferous garment and wrenched it off over her head. She marched to the clothes washer and threw it in, and suddenly she was filled with the understanding that she was spending these precious days of her life cleaning cat boxes and dodging cat piss.

It was no one's fault but her own. Her world had gotten very small. She had accepted its being quiet and dull. She needed to find love, excitement, and adventure. She needed to get Michael Amante out of her system and stop living in the past. She had to take action.

As she poured detergent into the machine and turned it on, she knew she had to do more than wash her T-shirt. It was time she cleaned up her act and cleansed her soul.

Over the next few weeks, as the school year ground to a close with excruciating slowness, Hildy made a decision to take the entire summer vacation to plan the rest of her life. Sitting at her desk marking final exams in front of her third period senior English class, she looked up and gazed unseeing out the window at the school parking lot while her mind wandered far and wide.

She needed to break out of her comfort zone and make a sea change in her existence. *Sea change. Hmmmm.* She thought she might enjoy being by the ocean. She always felt that the blowing salt-scented breeze, the endless blue waters, and the crashing waves held a kind of magic. Yes, she decided, it was time to go down to the sea. She remembered the famous lines by John Masefield. She was an English teacher after all and knew her verse: "I must go down to the seas again, to the lonely sea and the sky, / and all I ask is a tall ship, and a star to steer her by."

Back home that very night, Hildy went on the

Internet and searched for a summer house near the Atlantic Ocean that was within driving distance of Pennsylvania. Not many pet-friendly rentals existed. After hours at the computer, her eyes beginning to blur, she found a small place—actually it was tiny—at the Jersey shore in the VRBO, Vacation Rental by Owner, listings.

The gray, shake-sided cottage was in an oddly named town called Ship Bottom in a place named Long Beach Island. Hildy had never been to that part of the shore; she was buying a pig in a poke. And the cost for the season took her breath away. But displaying a characteristic impulsiveness, she grabbed it, spending the lion's share of her savings on leasing it for the entire summer.

Two days after school ended in June, Hildy closed up her home, put Shelley and Keats in their carrier, and drove south to this town where she knew no one but where she secretly hoped she might find *someone*. Maybe what she found would be a summer romance; maybe she would find peace of mind; or maybe, just maybe, she would find a man waiting near the sea in this unfamiliar place, and he would be the one she was meant to love.

Chapter 2

But if a romantic meeting on the sands had happened as she had fantasized it might, Hildy would not be where she was a week or so later on an unseasonably rainy and cold late-June morning. She was walking with her sister, Corrine, past the larger-than-life statue, an exact replica of *Augustus of Prima Porta*, which held a commanding position inside the huge, cavernlike lobby of Caesar's Atlantic City.

Hildy's eyes darted back and forth. Firelight flickered from torches on the stone walls in the four-story-high atrium above her head. A sense of unreality, of being outside of time and space, overcame her as she hurried past a row of white marble maidens in togas. The faux-Roman decor of the hotel overwhelmed her senses and even became a bit frightening.

"You know," Hildy said, trying not to spill her Styrofoam cup of hot coffee as she hustled across the dun-colored stone floor to keep up with her older sister's brisk stride, "you could have driven down to see me instead of coming with the day-trippers from St. Vladimir's."

Corrine didn't look at Hildy as she hurried forward, explaining, "The bus from the church was cheaper. Twenty bucks. Plus you get a coupon for fifteen dollars from the casino. And the Ladies Auxiliary at St. Vlad's provides a paper bag lunch and a snack on the trip going home. They're trying to raise money to save the church, you know. It's for a good cause."

She didn't bother to tell Hildy that on the way from Edwardsville, Pennsylvania, to Atlantic City, Father John also said a prayer for their safety and to wish them luck at the casino. Corrine firmly believed this plea for divine intervention increased her chances of winning—not that she didn't hope that somebody at St. Vlad's hit the jackpot to repair the old Byzantine church, too.

At that moment they reached the casino floor. Corrine made a beeline toward a bank of slot machines labeled SLINGO PROGRESSIVE. Flashing lights above the slots announced JACKPOT $3,405.00.

"We're not going to hang out here long, are we?" Hildy asked in a pleading tone.

"No, not long. Unless I get a good machine," Corrine said, sitting down and inserting her casino players' club card with a practiced hand.

Hildy slid into the seat of the machine next to her. Her voice turned a little whiny. "I thought you wanted to spend some time with me on the beach."

"With my cellulite? Puh-leeze," Corrine said. She peered at Hildy over the top of her glasses. "Besides, it's only eleven o'clock in the morning, and all I really want to do today is see your summer rental and talk. I bet you're just moping around all the time. I cannot believe you have not found one eligible bachelor on the entire Jersey shore."

"I didn't say there weren't any on the 'entire Jersey shore.' I said the only people I've met in Ship Bottom are teenage surfers, old guys fishing for striped bass, and happy families buying hot dogs and Cokes at Woodies Drive-In up on the boulevard. Ship Bottom is residential; you know, quiet.

It's not a party town. Besides, I'm not looking for romance. I came here to think about my future, decide if I need a career change, that kind of thing. . . ."

Corrine knew her little sister Hildy better than Hildy did herself; she was sure of it. She looked at that sad little face and said, "That is utter and total bull, and you know it. You're dying to find a nice guy. We need to come up with a plan to improve your social life." She gave Hildy an appraising look and frowned as she noted the faded light blue hoodie, baggy capri pants, and beat-up flip-flops.

"Your wardrobe can use some help too. You need to be wearing something cute and sexy."

Hildy's cheeks flared red. She knew Corrine was right, but she didn't have "cute and sexy" clothes. She had staid suits and skirts for teaching, old clothes like these for hanging around the house, and not much else.

Corrine shook her head at her sister's attire. "I'll figure something out. Maybe we can go shopping— oh, don't start protesting. I know, you're on a budget. My treat. Remember, I married well." She smiled at that. Her marriage to Jack had been a love match when he didn't have a dime, but he had worked hard and brought home a lot of bacon. "Just give me a couple of hours here first."

Corrine turned away then, already sliding the bonus coupon from the bus excursion into the money slot.

"A couple of hours? What am I going to do for all that time? I don't gamble." Hildy's eyes roved dispiritedly around the huge room filled with clanging machines, gaudy lights, and little old ladies playing the slots.

"Risk twenty bucks, why don't you? Come on, sweetie, maybe you'll get lucky." Corrine's index finger poised over the MAX BET button. She pushed down. The wheels inside the slot machine spun. Corrine's rapt face was lit by the garish red and yellow lights of the Slingo marquee. She forgot Hildy existed.

"Oh, okay." Hildy sighed and stowed her canvas tote bag that said SAVE THE WOLVES on it between her feet. She then tried to set her coffee cup in the narrow space between the two machines. It hit something solid as she attempted to slide it back from the edge.

Hildy peered into the dim space and spotted a brownish bottle in the way. *Yuck,* she thought, *somebody left their beer.* She gingerly reached in and pulled out the glass bottle using just her thumb and index finger.

She planned to set the bottle on the floor to be picked up with the trash, but when she got it into the light—as much light as existed in the dimly illuminated casino—she saw it wasn't a beer bottle. Instead she held a graceful, cut-crystal decanter of amber-hued glass, about seven inches high, and beautifully decorated with blue enamel and gold leaf. She guessed it was antique, and it looked expensive to her.

"Hey, Corrine, somebody must have left this," Hildy said, nudging her sister's arm with one hand and holding up the bottle with the other.

Corrine glanced over for the briefest moment before her eyes slid back to the machine. "Probably a souvenir. Leave it. If it's worth anything, they'll come back."

"Maybe they don't know where they left it," Hildy said. "I'll take it to the Lost and Found when we're done. I think it's valuable." She put the bottle into her tote, cushioning it between a paperback novel and her wallet.

Then Hildy looked long and hard at the machine in front of her and muttered to herself, "I'm not a

gambler. I feel as if I'm wasting twenty bucks."
Thinking about how little she had to spend for the
entire summer, twenty dollars seemed like a great
deal of money. "Oh well." She sighed. "I'll eat
peanut butter for a week."

Thus Hildy resigned herself to the loss, and almost immediately scolded herself for the negative
self-talk. She read a lot of self-help books. She believed in the power of positive thinking. It was self-
defeating to focus on losing the money. What she
needed right now was an affirmation.

She ruminated for a moment, then came up with:
*I am fortunate in every way and I wish to be
lucky today.*

Now, that was pretty doggone good for an instant
affirmation, she had to admit. She repeated it
softly, delighting in its singsong rhythm. A warm
feeling struck her like a ray of sunshine penetrating
the casino's gloom. Her fingertips tingled. The slot
machine in front of her seemed to glow for a brief
moment.

Hildy smiled. She just loved affirmations; they
certainly did produce good vibrations.

She chanted her little rhyme ten more times. "I
am fortunate in every way and I wish to be lucky
today." She felt immensely pleased with herself.
Then she slid her twenty into the money slot,
waited for her "credits" to appear on the LED
display, and then imitating what she had seen Corrine do, she hit the MAX BET button.

She watched the spinning wheels. A single bar
appeared on the first wheel, then a double bar lined
up on the second wheel, and a triple bar came up
on the third. *Ten credits*, Hildy read on the display
above her credit total. *Hey, I won!* Of course ten
credits only added up to a whopping $2.50 since
this was a quarter machine, but at least she was in
the plus column.

She hit the MAX BET button again. When the spinning wheels stopped there were no bars, no sevens, nothing at all. Over the course of the next few spins she got a cherry (four credits) and another set of bars, but this time they were all triple bars and that meant she had won twenty credits!

Okay, that's five dollars in the plus column, Hildy thought, dividing by four in her head.

But then she didn't win for a while and her credits were back exactly where she started. She shrugged her shoulders; she was getting bored and a little depressed at the way the money dwindled away so fast.

Hildy glanced over at Corrine. Her sister had told her to play for a while. Did five minutes count as "a while"? Probably not. Hildy exhaled hard. She was ready to cash out and go for a walk on the boardwalk. But dutifully she hit the MAX BET button again.

This time a funny oval icon with a laughing joker and the words SLINGO PROGRESSIVE on it appeared on the three spinning wheels, one after the other, starting on the left. A light on the top of the machine began flashing. To Hildy's utter mortification a siren started howling. She wanted to shrink up and sink through the floor.

Oh, Lordy, she thought miserably. *I've broken it.*

Her sister stared at her with a look of astonishment.

"Oh, Corrine, I'm so sorry—" she began.

"Sorry? Little sister, you won! You won!" Corrine stood up and started waving her arms wildly in the air. "Over here! Jackpot over here!" she yelled, as if the uniformed attendants couldn't spot the slot machine with a light going off on top like a police car's.

Other players started to crowd around behind Hildy's seat.

"How much did she win?" an elderly lady with large pink glasses and a flowered blouse asked no one in particular.

"Only three thousand and change. Some jackpot," a potbellied man griped. "These casinos don't want to get off a dime."

Three thousand dollars! Hildy thought. *Oh my! I won't have to worry for the rest of the summer! I can buy a new bathing suit. I'll buy a tube top and shorts. Maybe I'll get my own bicycle instead of using the funny one with the fat tires and wicker basket from the rental place.* Hildy had never had such a stroke of good luck in her entire life. In fact, she had never won anything before. To her, three thousand dollars represented a fortune and an entire summer free from financial worry.

After being escorted to the cashier by guards as if she had won a million bucks and needed protection, Hildy had to fill out tax forms before getting her winnings. Given a choice, she opted for a check, not cash. As soon as the cashier handed over the check, Hildy stuffed it in her hoodie pocket and hurried back to where her sister still sat at the slot machine, mesmerized by the spinning wheels.

"I'm back," Hildy announced. She felt dazed, probably from the excitement. She stood there near Corrine. The winning machine sat empty but Hildy had no desire to revisit it. The experience of hitting the jackpot had been exciting, but altogether, she thought, a bit odd, an anomaly that didn't fit in her quiet, ordinary life. "I hope you don't mind, but I don't want to gamble anymore, okay?"

Corrine smiled. "Smart move, little sister. Me, I'd like to play for a while. I'm breaking even. How about you take a walk or something? Buy me some taffy to take home. Give me until"—she paused, giving the matter some consideration—"hmmm, lunchtime maybe to try my luck, then come find me, okay?''

That was just fine with Hildy. A light-headedness had overtaken her. She longed to be outside in the fresh air. She headed toward the nearest exit. She was pushing through the heavy doors that opened onto the Atlantic City Boardwalk when she remembered she meant to go to the Lost and Found with the odd brown bottle.

She paused and decided to go to the Lost and Found later. Right now she urgently needed to emerge from the dark casino and get into the light.

Gulls wheeled overhead as Hildy began walking. The rain had stopped but pearl gray clouds still raced across the sky as if trying to close up any small slice of blue that appeared between them. A brisk breeze caught Hildy's long hair and threw it forward, making it a wild mess of tangles.

Hildy didn't care. She had just won three thousand, four hundred, and five dollars. She had been lucky—even luckier than she wished to be. She fingered the paper check deep in her pocket. She was grinning so hard, her cheeks hurt.

Holding her hair out of her eyes with her hand, Hildy ducked into a store that sported children's swim wings and fuchsia flamingos in its display windows. She quickly found a bright yellow cap with a visor that had ATLANTIC CITY in red on the brim. She looked at herself in the mirror on the counter. The hat was terrific.

Then she picked a pair of wraparound sunglasses from a rack and tried them on. She peered into the mirror again. With the visor and sunglasses, she appeared kind of sporty, almost hip. She put the items together on the counter. She added a box of salt-water taffy for her sister to take home. She was rapidly accumulating a small pile of goods.

Last, she splurged on a large beach towel. TO-DAY'S YOUR LUCKY DAY IN ATLANTIC CITY was printed on the terry cloth between an orange sea horse and a purple starfish. It so perfectly described her experience that Hildy figured she just had to buy it.

It felt good not having to watch every cent she spent!

"You must have won today," the young Asian clerk said as Hildy handed over three twenties to pay for her purchases.

"How can you tell?" Hildy asked and retrieved the cap as soon as the clerk had rung it up. Standing in front of the mirror again, she twisted her hair into a knot and secured it with her new hat.

"You have the look of a winner," the girl replied. She leaned forward across the counter and whispered conspiratorially, "Don't give it all back. Stay out of the casino!"

"I agree." Hildy smiled so widely that a dimple appeared in her cheek. "I'm just going to take a walk. I feel lucky. Maybe this is the day I'll meet my Prince Charming."

"You go, girl," the salesclerk said, and gave her a thumbs-up.

Chapter 3

Back outside the store, Hildy kept smiling. The sun was breaking through the luminescent clouds. Bright patches of light zigzagged down the wide wooden boardwalk. Open-sided jitneys rumbled past. Bicycle rickshaws filled with tourists traversed the distance between casinos. And with the sun, crowds had appeared as if from nowhere. Couples walked along holding hands. Mothers pushed toddlers in strollers.

A swift flow of melancholy welled up inside Hildy. She had no lover to hold hands with and no baby to take for a walk. For a split second, she wished she could see Michael Amante again. She quickly pushed the thought away. That was just the kind of foolish longing she had left her hometown to escape. She needed to savor her good feelings, not get all maudlin and weepy.

At the end of Michigan Avenue, she spotted a pathway to the beach. She thought she might find solitude on the soft sands that lined the shore. In any event, it would be a great place to sit down and think about the things she could buy with her winnings and still have enough money left to cover her expenses until September.

Once she came up over the dunes that acted as a barrier between the eroding effects of the water and the casinos, she could see the sea. She kicked off her flip-flops and carried them in her hand. It was easier to walk in the warm sand without them.

She strolled a short distance before stopping just beyond the tide line. She carefully put down her tote bag and spread out her new beach towel. She sat on top of the picture of the orange sea horse and folded her arms around her knees, gazing out at the Atlantic Ocean.

Contented, delighted, she looked seaward, a smile playing on her lips. She thought of Shelley's lines written more than a century ago: "I see the waves upon the shore / Like light dissolved in star-showers, thrown; / I sit upon the sands alone."

After a few minutes, the sun had warmed the air. Hildy peeled off her hoodie and stuffed it in her tote, mindful of the precious check in its pocket. Underneath the hoodie she had on a white Penn State T-shirt with a Nittany Lion in navy blue stalking across her chest. She looked down at herself. She had owned this shirt since she was a college freshman. It was definitely time for a wardrobe update.

As she stared at the vast ocean, her mind wandered and stopped paying attention to the dancing waves. She calculated how much of her winnings she could use for new clothes. She figured that five hundred dollars should buy her some nice sportswear, especially if she stuck to the sales racks. Then she'd take another three hundred and buy a sleek, light trail bike that was brand-new, not used and scratched up like the one she had rented. Satisfied with her decisions, she forgot about shopping and daydreamed for a while.

Keeping her eyes on the horizon, she thought how modern-day Rome lay about four thousand miles due east from where she sat. Strangely enough, Caesar's sat a few hundred feet behind her. The thought tickled her. She giggled to herself.

Suddenly she noticed how rough and wind-tossed the ocean had become. The tide must be coming in. She shivered. Murky gray green and filled with whitecaps, the Atlantic wasn't the placid blue sea of her imaginings. It heaved and roared with an immense power. The waves rolled in and crashed without mercy onto the wet sand. Sandpipers nervously skirted the frothy spume, careful not to be caught by the retreating water.

But the violent sea filled Hildy with a strange stirring. Everything was in motion around her: the rushing waves, the churning surface of the water, the gulls circling and crying overhead, the fierce wind that tried to pull the new cap from her hair. The sun went behind another cloud and the air seemed almost cruel, but in the next instant the sun returned and the wind tugging on her hat became only mischievous, not malevolent.

As the cap nearly flew off her hair again, Hildy laughed and grabbed the visor. This was life, sharp and tangy, filled with energy and possibility. *Is there danger here by the ocean?* she thought. *Yes,* she answered herself, *but it intensifies the moments of joy.*

She sprang to her feet and ran impulsively to the water's edge. A wave came up and encircled her ankles. Its coldness made her cry out. But the next wave felt warmer as it slapped against her feet. Like a child, she stamped up and down on the sand, watching the tan muck gush up through her toes. She moved deeper into the surf, letting the water soak the bottom of her capri pants. When a large wave receded, she bent over to pick up a pretty seashell—

And the next thing she knew a huge wall of

water knocked her down. Suddenly she was being tossed about, somersaulting in a crazy way underneath the surface of the water. She fought to find her footing, but which way was down? Which way was up?

All at once, she found herself sitting on the bottom, her head and shoulders above the surface, the wave receding. She coughed and tried to catch her breath. She went to stand but her wet clothes were heavy and made it hard to get her balance.

She had just gotten to her feet and started staggering toward the beach when another wave hit her hard from behind, knocking her down once more.

Panic chased all thoughts from her mind. She flailed about, trying to get back to the surface. Suddenly, she was being pulled into deeper water by the undertow. Then, just as relentlessly, she was being swept back toward the beach. She was overpowered and helpless. Her luck seemed to have run out in a very frightening way.

With a tremendous effort, she stuck her head up and broke into the air, gasping to fill her lungs. Facing the horizon, she couldn't tell how far from shore she had come. She had also swallowed a great deal of water and was terribly afraid she wouldn't make it back to land.

At that moment someone grabbed the back of her shirt, holding her firmly, keeping the waves from snatching her back to deep water.

With her T-shirt high up under her arms, Hildy choked and coughed as she did an ungainly crablike crawl backward, her fanny scraping the bottom, as her rescuer held her by the neck of her shirt. Finally her shoulders hit a pair of legs.

"I have you!" a man's voice yelled. "Stop struggling! You'll be out in a minute."

A strong arm reached down and encircled the bare skin of her waist, then lifted her up. She was carried toward the beach folded over the man's arm like a rag doll until she was dumped into a sitting position on the dry sand. She put her hands down to steady herself. She was trembling all over and felt weak with relief. She also noted that her bra and white T-shirt were practically transparent, but she felt too glad at being safe to worry about modesty.

"Are you okay?" the man's kindly voice inquired.

Hildy kept her head down and coughed, then sucked in more air. "I think so," she managed to answer.

"Here, I even grabbed your hat," the man said. "I think it will be good as new when it dries out."

A well-tanned hand extended her yellow cap toward her. She took it and looked up. The sun blinded her. She couldn't see her rescuer's face. She could tell, however, he was quite tall and his knees, also well-tanned, were about even with her line of vision.

"Thank you," she said. "I thought I was going to drown." She coughed again. She had swallowed half the damned ocean. Her throat felt terrible. Her stomach was churning. Wet strands of hair were plastered to her cheeks. When she peeled them off, she realized her hair and face were caked with sand. She must look like a drowned rat.

She turned to thank her rescuer again, tipping her chin back farther, squinting her eyes against the glare.

"Hildy?" the man asked then. "Hildy Caldwell? Is it really you?"

"Huh?" Hildy answered, totally confused. "How do you know my name?" She shaded her eyes with one hand and finally saw the face of the man in front of her.

"Mike?" Her voice came out as a squeak. "Michael Amante?" she managed to utter as her stomach gave a mighty squeeze. "Oh no—" she cried, and scrambled onto her hands and knees before, in a most unladylike manner, she retched up seawater onto the sand.

Chapter 4

Once she stopped retching, Hildy sat back on the sand. Feeling chilled in her wet clothes, she shivered. Goose bumps covered her still winter-pale skin. But that was the least of it. She had never felt so humiliated. She covered her face with her hands. She wanted to disappear from the face of the earth. She couldn't bear to look at Mike. Her shoulders began to shake as tears came unexpectedly, deepening her shame.

"Aw, Hildy, don't cry." Mike sat down next to her and gathered her into his arms. He pulled her against him. She hid her face against his bare chest. His skin was smooth, warm, and smelled so familiar her heart lurched. She began to cry harder.

"Shh, shh," Mike's voice said as if he were comforting a child. "You're safe. You're okay." He put his fingers under her chin and tipped her face up toward his. He used his thumbs to wipe away her tears.

Hildy could barely breathe when she felt Mike's touch. It crossed her mind that she had died out there in the water, and she had gone to heaven. She couldn't believe this was really happening.

"Oh, Mike," she said softly, and looked into his eyes, which were just as she remembered them, warm and amber, like fine bourbon.

His eyes returned her stare, and the two of them gazed unmoving until Mike leaned forward. Hildy squeezed her eyes shut as she prepared herself for the kiss she had dreamed about for ten long years.

Mike's lips landed on her nose. The caress was brief. It was friendly. It was not filled with love and longing.

"You're still a funny kid, the same old Hildy," Mike said, chuckled, and withdrew his comforting arms.

Hildy's eyes sprang open. "I most certainly am not!" she snapped, trying to hide the lump of disappointment that lodged in her throat. She sat up very straight and huffed, "I am not a kid. I happen to be a high school English teacher. I even have tenure."

"Whoa! I meant no offense. You always did get into crazy situations, you know. And you look exactly the same, that's all. Honest, Hildy, you haven't aged a day. I meant it as a compliment."

Hildy stole another look at Mike. He looked like he did in high school too, only better. His face had become more angular, laugh lines radiated from the corners of his eyes, and the boyishness in his features had vanished. He needed a shave and the auburn stubble on his dimpled chin and lean cheeks looked sexy, very sexy. Hildy's stomach fluttered. Her eyes started to dip toward his bare muscular chest, but she caught herself. She quickly looked away, out at the sea.

"You look like the same old Mike too," she said. "And I mean *that* as a compliment." The words didn't come out as she intended. They sounded sarcastic and bitter.

"Hildy, come on. You're mad, aren't you? Don't be, please." His fingers grasped her chin again and turned her face toward his. "Let me get a good look at you."

"Don't look at me!" Hildy protested, very conscious that her skin tingled where his fingers were. "I was just tossed around on the bottom of the Atlantic. I must be a mess." She tried to pull away from his hands, but he firmly held her face toward his.

"I just have to look at you. You're so doggone cute. Just like I remembered." His eyes dropped toward the transparent white T-shirt plastered against her now-transparent white bra that clearly revealed her small breasts. "In fact, all of you is just like I remembered."

"Don't be fresh!" she said, and quickly pulled the T-shirt away from her body, making it opaque again. She smiled. She couldn't help it. She felt so happy sitting here with Mike. With Mike! Her spirits floated upward like champagne bubbles, making her feel giddy.

"Come on, Hildy, smile, that's it. Let me see those dimples. That's better! I always loved your dimples. They just made me melt inside every time I saw them." He was staring at her. The air between them became charged with electricity. A funny feeling started low in her belly. Hildy could barely keep from throwing herself into his arms.

"Hildy"—Mike's voice got husky when he said her name—"you know, ever since I got the invitation to our high school reunion, I've been thinking about you."

"You have? I've been thinking about you too, but not just since the invitation. I've always thought about you. About you and me." Her voice was almost a whisper and it wobbled when she spoke. She felt like crying again, but this time from happiness.

Suddenly Mike broke eye contact. "No kidding! You've been thinking about me. Isn't that just something."

Embarrassment stained Hildy's cheeks red once

more. She had revealed too much of her true feelings. Mike's withdrawal had been immediate. It erased the moment of intimacy that had just occurred and put distance between them.

Hildy didn't know what to say now, so she didn't say anything. Mike didn't say anything either. Gulls cried out overhead with sad voices. The waves thundered on the shore.

"Well, maybe I better go," Hildy said at last, feeling awkward and wanting to escape. She started to stand up.

He put a hand on her shoulder, pushed her back down, and kept her from moving. "No, don't go. I have an idea."

He squeezed her shoulder, then brushed her neck with the tips of his fingers. Hildy's breath came out with an "Uh." She closed her eyes. His fingers kept stroking the place at the base of her throat. "Mike, don't—" she started to say, but didn't move. She kept her eyes closed tight.

"Hildy," Mike said, and touched her earlobe. A shiver of delight shook her from head to toe. "Let's get together. We can talk about old times. Catch up on what's happened in our lives. Are you staying around here?"

The realization raced through Hildy's mind that Michael Amante wanted to see her. He was asking her out on a date. Maybe she was dreaming. Maybe she should pinch herself. She finally opened her eyes and looked at him. He was staring at her. His fingers kept caressing her earlobe. She felt dazed.

"I have a summer rental in Ship Bottom. On Twenty-fifth Street, first house in from Long Beach Boulevard on the bay side. It's gray. It's got whales on it," she murmured. "It's easy to find."

"You'll be here for the whole summer? That's fantastic. I'm down here for the summer too. A big real estate construction deal. Condos. I'm staying at Trump Plaza." He paused and took his hand away from her ear. He slapped the pockets of his wet shorts. "Oh damn, no way I can write down your phone number. I didn't bring anything with me." Then his face brightened. "But you can call me. Just call the hotel. Really, Hildy, I want to talk with you. Will you call me?"

Hildy felt dazzled, lost in a dream. "Yes, yes, of course. I'll call you." She turned her head toward him. Mike's lips were so close. Her blue eyes gazed longingly into his brown ones. She felt as if she could see his soul. "When? When should I call?" Her voice floated on her breath, softly, seductively.

He answered at once. "Call me tonight—" Then his eyes slid away from hers. A shadow flickered across his face. He physically pulled away and when he spoke, a tentativeness muddled his response. "Wait, no, tonight's not good. Ummm . . . let's see. Call me tomorrow. Yeah, that's okay. But not in the morning. Call me—ummm, try after lunch, around one."

For Hildy, the spell had broken. First he came on to her, then he backed off. Then he came on to her, now he was hedging about what time she should call. Something else was going on here, and she didn't like her feelings being played with like this.

"You know, Mike—" she snapped. She was about to say maybe the whole phone call thing wasn't such a good idea.

Mike cut her off. "No, I mean it, Hildy. I do want you to call me." Mike picked up her hand in his and squeezed it. His touch sent a zing of electricity up her arm. "I really do." He said the words soft and low. He had started stroking her palm with his thumb. Hildy could barely think straight. His eyes sought hers again. "It's been too long since I've seen you. Promise you'll call."

It's been too long since he's seen me? She couldn't believe her ears. She'd walk across coals for him now. "I promise," she whispered.

"MIIIII-CHAEL! MIIIII-CHAEL!" A high shrill voice called from the distance. "MICHAEL!!! DARLING! WHERE ARE YOU?"

Mike dropped Hildy's hand as if it were a burning coal. He jumped up. He waved his arms. "Over here!" he called.

Hildy saw a woman coming toward them. As she got closer, Hildy could see that she was tall and slender, like a fashion model. A turquoise sarong hung low on her hips, revealing a diamond on a gold hoop through her pierced navel. She was holding a floppy-brimmed straw hat on her head with a bejeweled hand. Long black hair cascaded down over darkly tanned shoulders. And her ample breasts bounced with every step, nearly escaping the skimpy halter top that matched her sarong.

Hildy got to her feet slowly and stood next to Mike. He moved away.

"Kiki! You'll never guess who I ran into!" Mike's voice sounded too loud to Hildy.

The woman removed her dark sunglasses, revealing kohl-rimmed eyes so dark they looked black. She glared at Hildy as if she were seeing something repellent, like a cockroach. "You're right, Mike. I'll never guess. Who is this poor wet child?"

"Child?" Hildy sputtered. "I'm not—"

"She's only kidding, aren't you, Kiki?" Mike said, flustered. He quickly moved to the woman's side. "Hildy, this is my fiancée, Kiki. Kiki, this is Hildy, an old friend from high school. I've talked about her before. Remember?"

"No, I can't say that I do," Kiki answered, and extended a hand. Hildy felt obliged to take it.

Kiki's hand was cool and lightly perfumed. Hildy's was hot, sweaty, and covered with sand.

"Hildy, is it? What's that short for? Hildegard?" Kiki looked down her perfect little nose. Her smile never reached her eyes, and her red lips parted to show very white teeth.

Like a barracuda's, Hildy thought, and said, "It's Hildy. Just Hildy." She widened her stance, put her hands on her hips, and lifted her chin. She felt totally pissed off. This creature was odious. Whatever was Mike doing with such a witch? But even as the question formed, she knew the answer. Kiki was absolutely gorgeous.

Kiki turned to Mike, making a point of ignoring Hildy completely. "Michael, we have a luncheon with the governor in an hour. Darling, we really have to hurry."

Just then, wafting on the breeze, Hildy heard the *Gilligan's Island* theme song. She knew that ring tone. She had downloaded it herself to celebrate her summer vacation, and she had left her cell phone in her tote bag. She glanced around. Her towel and bag were just a few yards up the beach.

The jaunty theme song continued to warble about "a three-hour tour."

"Oh my, that's my cell. It's probably the pope calling. I simply must answer it." Hildy's clear voice rang out; it was very bright and very sharp. "Nice to have met you, uhhhm, what was your name? Kinky?" Hildy whirled around and began to stalk away.

"Hildy, wait!" Mike called out.

Hildy stopped and looked back over her shoulder. She gave him her best smile, the one that showed her dimples. "I really have to go, but thanks, Mike. Thanks for pulling me out of the water." Then the devil made her do it, and she added, her voice dripping sarcasm, "It's been just *great* seeing you. I mean that. I really do."

Then she turned away so Michael Amante—and his fiancée—wouldn't see the silvery tears already spilling from behind her eyelids and running down her cheeks.

Chapter 5

It was the best of days. It was the worst of days.

Hildy had never before experienced such extremes of emotion in such a short time. Even after she had walked away from Mike and answered her phone—her sister Corrine was ringing to find out where Hildy had gone—she felt confused about what had just transpired here on the beach by Caesar's.

When she finished the brief phone call, she thought she could feel Mike's eyes watching her, but she didn't look back. She couldn't bear to. With as much poise as she could muster, she held her head high and crossed the sand to return to the boardwalk. There, out of sight of the beach, she broke into a trot as she headed for the casino parking lot, level five, row eight, where she told Corrine to meet her.

Within seconds, a stab of pain radiated outward from the middle of her chest and scared her so badly she nearly stopped to call 911. But she realized this terrible hurt was just what happened when your heart breaks a little. Like a vase with a hairline crack in it, she was still in one piece, but definitely damaged.

After all, for a little while back there on the sand, all her wishes seemed to have come true.

Mike had behaved as if something special was happening between them. They both had been swept
up in a sudden passion; there had been magic in
the air. Hildy hadn't imagined the magnetism and
the desire.

Yet the rush of desire didn't mean Mike still
cared. Maybe the attraction that drew them so
swiftly together had been lust, although that seemed
ridiculous. Mike was going to marry a woman who
looked like a Hollywood star. *Why would he get all
hot and bothered over me?* she thought. *I'm the girl
next door, not a femme fatale. In the movies, I'm
the good girl who gets left behind when the hero
runs off with the naughty sex symbol.*

Just then, Hildy gazed upward. A huge statue of
the great Roman emperor Julius Caesar outside the
casino seemed to smile down on her, telling her to
consider the whole picture. As much as she ached
inside, Hildy felt a sense of wonder and awe that
it had been Mike Amante who pulled her out of
the sea. The coincidence had been so extraordinary
it must be some kind of miracle. It had to mean
something.

What did it mean? Hildy thought. Had her rescue
been a divine intervention? Or was some lesser
deity laughing at her right now, for behaving like
such a fool?

Hildy was so preoccupied that she reached the
casino parking lot without seeing the short man,
more stocky than fat, in a lime green sports jacket
who had been following her. He had spotted her
coming up the path from the beach at Michigan
Avenue. He hurried to try to get close to her, but
he couldn't believe how fast that young girl moved.
She was practically running.

The best the man could do was keep her within
view. Fortunately there was nothing wrong with his

eyesight. He might be fifty-something, but he had nearly twenty-twenty vision even if his eyes did protrude from their sockets like Rodney Dangerfield's. The problem wasn't his eyes. It was his thyroid; he'd had trouble with it all his life. It made him nervous. It kept his rage dangerous and his temper on a hair trigger. And those pop eyes had given him the nickname that even his parole officer called him, although not to his face—Jimmy the Bug.

And speaking of parole officers, Jimmy the Bug was trying to duck his. By the terms and conditions of his release from prison, he had been instructed to stay out of the casinos. But James O'Callahan Torelli, boss of a South Jersey crime family, hadn't been ordered to attend Gamblers Anonymous for nothing. Jimmy the Bug had a betting habit, one he couldn't kick.

So not having made a wager in a week and getting very antsy because of it, Jimmy the Bug figured nobody would look for him at Atlantic City in the daytime, when all the old folks came on the buses. He was cautious to the point of paranoia. He wore large black sunglasses. He had ordinary Nikes on his feet, partly because his bunions were killing him.

He was blissfully unaware of his idiosyncrasies. Nobody ever dared to point them out. He hitched his pants up when he walked, and he frequently talked to himself, muttering complaints and a steady stream of four-letter words. But since Atlantic City attracted a broad spectrum of oddballs and weirdos, nobody paid attention to the little man in the brilliant green sports coat.

Today he traveled alone. He told his crew, which is what he called the bodyguards, fellow criminals, and sycophants who stayed close to him at all times, that he had an appointment with his proctol-

ogist. Nobody volunteered to go along, which was
his plan. He didn't trust anybody unless he cut the
cards first. He had been betrayed before.

Jimmy the Bug had chosen Caesar's as the casino
where he planned to spend a few relaxing hours at
the slots, hoping it would settle his nerves. He
needed to get his equilibrium back after a week of
business disappointments, including a scam gone
bad and the arrest of one of his lieutenants. As it
turned out, Jimmy didn't even come close to mel-
lowing out. He had just settled himself at a Slingo
machine when who did he see pulling the one-
armed bandit maybe ten machines away? Mr. Ad-
derly, his parole officer.

Jimmy the Bug muttered two of his favorite
four-letter words, slid off the seat, duckwalked
around the end of the row of slot machines, and
made a beeline for the nearest exit. He gave a deep
sigh of relief when he made a clean getaway—until
he realized what he left behind: the very important
little bottle that he had put down next to his
machine.

"You scared me half to death, not showing up
by now," Corrine said when she walked up to the
red Volkswagen Beetle in the parking garage where
Hildy sat waiting. Then the slim woman with gray-
streaked hair bent down and squinted through the
open driver's-side window. "You're drenched. Were
you swimming in the ocean or something?"

"You're a regular Sherlock Holmes, Corrine,"
Hildy said. "Come on, get in. We don't have a lot
of time before your bus leaves."

"And whose fault is that?" Corrine huffed as she
sat in the passenger seat and buckled her seat belt.
She heard a funny little noise like a muffled sob
coming from Hildy's direction. She glanced over,

alarmed. "What's the matter? Did something happen? Are you crying?"

Hildy shook her head no. "I'm a little emotional, that's all. A lot happened today." Hildy refused to elaborate further. She put the car in gear, backed out of the parking space and drove toward the exit. She didn't check her rearview mirror, or she would have seen Jimmy the Bug pull out a pen and write her license plate number on his hand.

When Hildy reached the Garden State Parkway going north and traffic thinned out, she gave in to Corrine's persistent inquiries and told her the whole story of meeting Michael Amante—or not quite the whole story; she left out the part about him caressing her earlobe between his fingers.

"Naturally, I am not going to call him," she said.

"So you've told me three times." Corrine had listened very carefully to her little sister's every word. She twisted her mouth to one side and then to the other as she gave the situation some careful thought. "Let me see if I get the whole picture. Michael Amante, the same boy you dumped in high school for reasons you would never explain, shows up out of nowhere and saves your life. Then he acts all goo-goo eyes and asks you out—"

"Not exactly asks me out, but sort of." Hildy felt the need to clarify the point.

"Don't split hairs. The man asked where you were staying and practically pleaded with you to call him. Then his fiancée, this Kiki, shows up. Now I find that very interesting."

"Interesting? It was one of the worst things that ever happened to me," Hildy said, her fingers tightening on the steering wheel until they turned white.

"I don't mean her showing up, I mean that she's still his fiancée. When did they get engaged? Five

or six years ago? It was on *Entertainment Tonight*,
I think."

"I guess so. It was a while back. What difference
does it make? They're probably living together. She
let me know he's definitely not a free man. It was
humiliating. I get sick just thinking about it."

"Get a grip, Hildy. Stop letting your emotions
make you dumber than dirt." Corrine never did see
the point of wasting time being tactful. "When's
this wedding? I'm older than you"—Corrine regu-
larly reminded Hildy that she had been born a
good seventeen years before her sister popped
into the world, making her wiser about men,
money, and life in general—"and I've seen this
situation before. If there was going to be a wedding, it would have happened by now. One of
them doesn't want to get married—that's obvious.
This relationship is in the toilet. It's going nowhere except in two different directions. And a
man in love does not get stars in his eyes when
he meets an old girlfriend."

"I didn't say he had stars in his eyes. You're
jumping to conclusions. And you didn't see her.
She truly was beautiful." Hildy let out a deep sigh.

"And what are you, chopped liver?" Corrine
snorted.

"You're blinded by sisterly love. I'm sort of cute,
that's all. I'm not in Kiki's league, that's for sure."

"Look, Hildy, face facts. You've let yourself go,
but you were once the cutest girl in Lake Lehman
High School, and at that time Michael Amante was
crazy for you. Plus, and this is of critical importance, don't forget: You left him; he didn't leave
you. That makes it unfinished business on his part.
You're the girl who got away. You're a challenge.
You're what he couldn't get. Are you sure you
want him back?"

Hildy nodded, totally miserable. "If I learned

anything today it's that I'm never going to be happy without Michael Amante in my life."

"Well then, little sister, don't put your wishbone where your backbone ought to be. You need to fight for your man."

Chapter 6

Corrine emerged with some difficulty from the passenger seat of the cramped VW Beetle. She wrinkled her nose with disapproval at the gray cottage with a plaque of three whales cut from plywood cavorting over the front door. "I suppose it's quaint. You might stretch a point and say it's charming. But I cannot believe you spent your entire savings renting this tiny place."

"It *is* charming, and it's big enough for Shelley, Keats, and me." Hildy put her key in the lock and flung the front door open. A small enclosed porch furnished with white wicker furniture and chintz pillows was flooded with sunlight from windows that stretched along three sides of the shoebox-shaped building.

The cats ran up meowing. Hildy picked up Percy Bysshe Shelley and stroked his white fur. The other cat, the coal black John Keats, wanted no part of cuddling. He preferred sniffing the intriguing smells on Corrine's sandals.

Followed closely by the cat, Corrine walked into the adjoining living room and appraised the white bead-board walls, the old watercolors of Barnegat Lighthouse that hung on them in dime-store frames, the faded orange futon on a blond wood frame which acted as a sleeping couch, the tiny TV set with rabbit ears on top, and the bleached conch shells on the coffee table. She glanced down to where Keats wound around her ankles. "What do you suppose the original color of this rug was—green?"

Impatience skittered across Hildy's face. "It doesn't matter. It just gets sand on it anyway. Forget that. Look at the way the windows are filled with light all day long." She put Shelley down and shooed him away. She crossed over to the far end of the porch and began opening the sashes one by one. "Hmmm, there's a cross breeze too. Isn't that delightful? And just take a look out here." Hildy moved to the front door and opened it again.

Corrine was on the opposite side of the living room, peering through the door leading from this ten-by-ten foot space into the next room. It had probably been a little dining room, since it held an old red Formica and chrome table surrounded by four matching chairs. A bathroom sat off it to the left, next to the door for the only closet in the entire house. A postage stamp–sized kitchen was an few steps away, occupying the rear of the building.

"Corrine, you're not listening! Come on, look out here. If I go out my front door and turn right, I'm two blocks from Barnegat Bay, right at the public docks. I can rent a kayak or even a Wave Runner, although I haven't had the nerve to do either thing yet.

"If I turn left instead, I just have to cross Long Beach Boulevard and walk one block and there I am, on the beach. Can you believe that three minutes after I leave the house, I'm staring at the whole Atlantic Ocean?"

Her eyes were dancing now. She turned back to the miniscule front yard where her red VW Bug took up exactly half of the brick-paved surface. Corrine ventured a few steps closer, and Hildy grabbed her arm to drag her outside onto the front stoop.

"You see! It's location, location, location! That's what I have. I don't have to drive anywhere if I don't want to. Right over there, on the boulevard, I can get a Coca-Cola or a Red Bull from the vending machines. I mean if it's two in the morning and I get thirsty, no problem! What are they, one hundred feet from my front door? And look, next to that little store, there's a whole row of newspaper machines. Every morning I can buy the *New York Times, USA Today,* the *Philadelphia Inquirer,* or just about any Jersey paper.

"If I walk a couple of blocks, I can eat at Stewart's Root Beer, the Voodoo Steakhouse, Woodies Drive-In, or the Greenhouse Café. Sometimes I go out early in the morning and take a run down the boulevard toward Surf City. I get a cappuccino at the How You Brewin'? Internet café before I turn around and run back. And do you know what's five blocks in the other direction toward Brant Beach?"

"I couldn't begin to guess." Corrine freed her arm and went back inside. "Where do you sleep, on the couch?"

"Oh no, that's for guests." Then Hildy pointed to the ceiling. "Upstairs there's the cutest sleeping loft. And you didn't see the back deck, which is like having another room. I have my tea out there almost every afternoon—when it's not raining, that is. But as I was saying"—her voice was high and excited—"five blocks away is this great place to eat called the Dark Star Café. It's totally retro. The owner is a Deadhead and he's got a Jerry Garcia doll next to the cash register and all. The pizza is the best I ever had. They make their own mozzarella. Do you believe that! And the people who run it are so nice. They just opened up this season, and I hope they do well—"

"Whoa! I get the picture." Corrine held up her hand. "You like living in civilization and not at the end of a muddy lane in Lehman, Pennsylvania."

Hildy's eyes went wide. "I didn't think about it that way. I love living in the country, I do. But this place is like being on a whole different planet. The air smells like salt and ocean, and it's . . . it's soft. That's it, the air is soft."

She stood still, caught up in a thought. "But you know, the light is hard. Overly bright on clear days, I'd say. Maybe it's because there are no trees for shade and it bounces off the sand and water." Suddenly Hildy spun around, nearly knocking over a floor lamp, and caught her sister in a spontaneous hug. "You know, Corrine, sometimes I feel happy here for no reason."

Corrine proceeded to check out the kitchen, complaining that the refrigerator was an under-the-counter one and the stove had only two burners. It was also where Hildy kept her rental bicycle, next to the back door. Corrine noticed that she had tracked in a lot of sand on the tires and looked around for a broom. Meanwhile, Hildy returned to her car to bring in all the shopping bags. They had hit as many clothing stores as possible in the strip malls along Route 72.

She made a second trip to bring in her prize purchase, which was tied on the VW's roof: a brand-new trail bike, a red one, with all the bells and whistles, that was her own.

At the first store they hit on the way back, Corrine, who had generously added another five hundred dollars to Hildy's budget, had bought her pink-flowered Tommy Hilfiger pants and a matching cami, and insisted she wear them. Then they made a quick stop at a hairdresser where Hildy got a haircut while Corrine pampered herself with a manicure.

For the next two hours they had the best time picking out almost an entirely new wardrobe for Hildy. Some of the tops revealed more flesh than Hildy normally would consider exposing, but as Corrine pointed out, they were planning a battle campaign.

"You really think I'm going to see Mike again? I hate to think I'm spending all this money for nothing," Hildy dared to ask as she slipped on a crisp white eyelet skirt and lacy halter top to go with it.

"That looks great on you," Corrine said, "or it will once you get a tan. You're awfully pale."

"It has rained nearly every single day since I got here," Hildy protested. "But you didn't answer my question."

"Yes, well, since I am a betting man—or more accurately a betting woman—I'd place odds that Michael Amante will show up within forty-eight hours. I have one of my feelings. Something big's about to happen. I assume it has to do with you and him. As far as the clothes go, whether or not Michael appears, you needed them. You were looking . . . what's the word I want . . . *defeated*. Like an old maid, really."

"I'm only twenty-seven!" Hildy yelped.

"You were dressing as if you were fifty. How many times a week did you wear that brown tweed suit? The one that just hangs on you?"

"My classic from Talbots? I never wore it more than once a week, but I have another one that looks very similar."

"Yes, they're both classic all right. Classic 'I'm a single woman who lives with her cats.' Put this on next." Corrine handed over a silky turquoise designer dress for Hildy to try.

Hildy stared into the mirror. The dress hugged her curves seductively. "I don't think so. Look how low it's cut in the back. It almost goes to my waist."

"It looks gorgeous with your eyes. Stop being such a prude."

"I'm not a prude."

"Are too."

"Am not."

They both started laughing.

"Okay, you're right. I'm acting like a prude," Hildy agreed. "I'll buy the dress."

She didn't acknowledge what her sister suspected: Hildy was more than a prude; she was a virgin. She hadn't intended to be as chaste as a nun by this time in her life. She possessed all the hot desires of the heroines she read about in paperback romances. But somehow, whenever a relationship got to the point where the next logical step was the consummation of a growing intimacy, Hildy began seeing her boyfriend's faults in ever sharper focus.

Two years ago she had nearly succumbed in the brawny arms of an A-league baseball player for the Scranton Yankees. The six-footer with sun-streaked blond hair was a hunk and a half, but she began to notice that he sweated a lot, and he didn't shower enough. *It's so unpleasant*, she thought. She grew distant, and stopped answering his calls.

Last year, before she met the neat-freak engineer who demanded she give up her cats, she almost ended up in bed with a slim, green-eyed college professor. He was so sensitive to her needs that he willingly spent hours with her, sipping chai tea and browsing the shelves for bargains in the huge chain bookstore at the mall.

After several weeks of exchanging e-mails and going to every movie showing at the Dietrich Theater's Fall Foreign Film Festival together, Hildy finally made up her mind that he would be "the one." She didn't get all goose bumps when he kissed her, but she enjoyed his company, and she believed he'd be a gentle lover.

During a weekend in early December when the earth was frozen hard as steel, she accepted his invitation to spend a weekend at a brand-new ski lodge in the Poconos. It was a special package deal that included lift tickets. Neither of them skied. His intent was clear.

Snow was falling lightly when they arrived at the hotel. Hildy had been nervous, but she hid her anxiety well. He had ordered wine, a nice California Chardonnay. He spared no expense. They got cozy by the roaring fire in their suite. Hildy leaned back against the sofa cushions. The professor began unbuttoning her blouse, his lips trailing little love bites up her neck. Her breath was quickening.

"I've written some lines of poetry just for you," he murmured.

"Oh, how romantic," she sighed. "Say them for me." She closed her eyes to listen and willed herself to relax.

" 'Thine eyes blind me,' " he recited. Hildy's eyes flew open. The professor smiled, and he went on. " 'Thy tresses burn me, thy sharp sighs divide my flesh and spirit with soft sound—' "

Hildy sat up suddenly, and the professor's face slipped down to her breasts. "*You* wrote that?" she asked.

"Well, yes. Just last night," he murmured, having slipped his hands under her shirt and reached around to her back to unfasten her bra. He sounded self-satisfied; he thought she had been impressed.

"You! You!" Hildy huffed, her face turning red

with outrage. "Plagiarist!" He had committed the worst transgression that she, as an English teacher, could imagine. He had stolen those lines.

Hildy pushed him away. She stood up, straightened her clothes, retrieved her suitcase, fortuitously never unpacked, and marched to the hotel's front desk. The kind night clerk found a college student willing to drive Hildy home for forty bucks.

Had she not loved nineteenth century English poetry, she might not have known that Algernon Charles Swinburne had written the professor's lines, not last night, but over a hundred years ago. The poem was called "Anactoria," and to add insult to injury, the professor didn't seem to know that the lines were written by a woman, Anactoria—to her lover, another woman, the famous Sappho of Lesbos. The poem was long, obscure, and contained scandalous imagery of not just girl-girl love, but sado-masochism.

And to think she had almost given her innocence to a man such as that!

After Hildy had carried the bike and all the packages into the summer cottage, barely enough time remained for the sisters to have an early dinner. Hildy had to drive Corrine back to the bus in Atlantic City by six thirty. They went out on the rear deck to eat the spinach quiche and salad of baby greens that Hildy had bought at the Dark Star Café early that morning.

Under a lapis lazuli sky now free of clouds, Corrine admitted that even if the next house was very close and kept the deck in shadow most of the afternoon, the location was ideal and the cottage livable. Then the sisters talked about other things, reminiscing about growing up and remembering their mother when she was healthy and young.

They felt content to be in each other's company, something their busy lives didn't often allow since their mother's death.

It was only when Hildy cleared the table and brought the dishes back into the kitchen to rinse them off that she moved her tote bag off the counter. As she set it on the worn linoleum floor, she spotted something shiny inside. *Oh, damn! I have to remember to bring that bottle into the casino when I drop Corrine off,* she thought. She lifted it out of her bag and held it up, once again thinking how pretty it was.

Just then Keats jumped up and began sniffing a piece of leftover quiche.

Hildy squealed, set the bottle on the counter next to the sink, and quickly snatched the plate away from the potential pie thief. At that moment, Corrine walked in and said it was getting late, and that they needed to hurry. Hildy grabbed her tote bag and retrieved her car keys. The sisters hurried out the door.

The bottle, its amber glass glowing as if it had caught a ray of late afternoon sunlight, remained on the kitchen counter. Hildy had forgotten it again.

Chapter 7

The spindly French Provincial–style chair creaked when Michael Amante shifted his weight. Unable to get comfortable, he stretched his legs out under the table and sank further into misery. He didn't want to be at this boring luncheon for the lame-duck governor and the National Association of Realtors. He looked down at the slab of prime rib on his plate, the red juice congealing into little pools of fat. He picked up his fork and poked at it. He had no appetite.

He felt chilled too. He signaled a roving server and asked her to bring him a cup of hot coffee. He hoped it would warm him up. The air-conditioning in this hotel meeting room must be set at freezing. When he exhaled, Mike swore he could see his breath.

He had complained about the low thermostat to Kiki. She responded with an edge to her voice, acting as if he were incredibly stupid. She told him that the governor, a heavyset man with an oily face, must be kept cool so he didn't sweat in the public-ity photos she had been hired to take.

Mike shivered, sure that the air-conditioning duct must be right above his seat. He didn't feel well at all. It crossed his mind that he might be coming down with a virus. He had this heavy feeling in his chest; it almost hurt to breathe. But he knew that wasn't what was wrong with him. His condition reflected the state of his life; it hung around his neck like an albatross—a dead thing, a burden, something he didn't want anymore. For the past few years, he had drifted along, making lots of money, but finding his job increasingly meaningless and his mood ever more bleak.

He knew he was bored with real estate. He had contemplated a career change for a long time now, but recently he had discovered a passion for an occupation that was worlds away from anything he had imagined he'd do.

The seed of the idea sprouted when he became friends with Jake Truesdale, the head of the private security company he had hired on one of his building projects. He liked Jake. The middle-aged black man from Newark and the young white guy from Pennsylvania had a lot more in common than anyone looking at them could have guessed.

But they were amazingly alike. They both ran to stay in shape, liked dogs and 1950s cars, and had the collecting gene. Jake poked through antique stores looking for railroadiana, a natural interest since his grandfather had been a Pullman porter under Eugene Debs. Mike searched for first editions of children's books, especially those of Virginia Lee Burton who wrote *Maybelle the Cable Car* and his own favorite, *Mike Mulligan and His Steam Shovel.*

Since Mike was at the construction site a lot, they started eating dinner together most nights. Mike had became fascinated with Jake's stories. He relished every detail about protection services, investigations, surveillance equipment, and crime detection.

When a backhoe and a skid steer were stolen

from the building site, Jake brought him along to try to find the missing machines. They never got the equipment back, but they nabbed the thief and even connected him to an organized crime family in South Jersey. Mike enjoyed every minute of it.

Jake thought Mike had a knack for investigation, and late at night, while Jake watched the security monitors at the high-end condo project, they had talked about going into business together. They had similar outlooks and strong ethics. They were both adrenaline junkies; neither of them liked to sit in an office. For the past few weeks, Mike had started working with Jake every moment he could get away from his office. They were having a blast together. They had written up a business plan to become real partners.

But Mike's new venture wouldn't go over well with Kiki, who believed he was about to become the next Donald Trump. He wondered if his job switch could become a deal breaker. He hated to admit it, but if she decided to end the relationship, it might be the best thing that could happen.

To tell the truth, Mike had begun to feel panicky about Kiki. During the last month, she had begun hinting that they should actually set a date. Marriage to her made less and less sense to Mike. His feelings for her were complex and confused. She was a beautiful woman, and she came with a lot of perks, like comps at four-star hotels, easy entree to government officials, and introductions to movie stars. But she traveled all the time, and they spent more time apart than together. She didn't want to start a family either. She made that perfectly clear. So what was the point of changing what they had and going ahead with a wedding?

The server poured coffee from a steaming carafe

into the cup in front of Mike. He drank it black. The first sip burned his mouth. It was bitter. It fit his mood perfectly.

Then he thought back to what happened on the beach today. He smiled as he remembered. He couldn't help himself. That Hildy had always been such a firecracker—one hundred twelve pounds of blue-eyed dynamite. She had been in everything in high school. Always on the move! Could not sit still for a minute!

He had been so crazy about her, but he had screwed up their relationship—a royal screwup, the worst one ever for Mike Amante. He really would like to talk to her, apologize for what happened all those years ago, and try to make it right. Fat chance of that happening now. She probably would never speak to him again.

He drained the last of the coffee. He felt better. Hildy was so doggone cute, even cuter than he remembered. And the spark was still there. The attraction he felt instantly had shocked him. It must have shown too. Kiki really had her claws out when he introduced her to Hildy.

The leaden feeling started in Mike's chest again. What should he do about Kiki? It would be a hell of a mess to break up with her. Besides, he wasn't sure he wanted to. They even owned a Park Avenue apartment together.

He stole a look at his watch. He wished he had Hildy's phone number. He knew she'd never phone him tomorrow, not after Kiki showed up, and he had acted like such an idiot. Maybe he could sneak away and make some calls. He'd try his old football buddy George Ide back in Lehman, and he'd call his mom. Somebody up there must have Hildy's cell phone number.

Mike glanced toward the front of the room, at

the raised dais where all the VIPs sat. The way the governor was flirting with Kiki, he'd be hot and sweaty no matter how cold the room was kept. Mike watched for a moment. Kiki was bending over to pick up some camera equipment and making sure the older man could see her cleavage. She was playing him like a violin. She would never notice if Mike went outside for a while.

When Hildy and Corrine got to the bus departure area at Caesar's, the St. Vlad's crowd wasn't talking much. Nobody besides Hildy had hit a jackpot. Most of them had lost whatever they had. At six thirty sharp, the day-trippers shuffled slowly back into the Martz Trailways bus, heads hanging down. Father John, with his white dandelion-puff hair and apple cheeks, maintained an upbeat attitude as he stood by the bus door and helped the ladies with the step up.

Hildy knew all about St. Vladimir's need for money. The roof of the great old brick church with its gold onion dome needed replacing. The dome itself needed regilding at an astronomical cost. The carpets were old and worn. The appliances in the church kitchen had been new in the early 1960s. Worse, the church was going to be in violation of the fire code if the wiring wasn't entirely replaced by November first. With membership down to one hundred and sixty elderly parishioners, the doors of the century-old structure would probably close for good before Christmas.

"It will take a miracle to save the church," eighty-two-year-old Annie said, her eyes sad behind her glasses as she took Father John's hand.

"The Lord works in mysterious ways," Father John assured her. "Keep the faith. Somebody may hit the jackpot on our next trip."

"Yeah, when pigs have wings," Corrine whispered to Hildy as they dawdled at the end of the line, waiting until the very last moment to part.

"Can't they attract new members?" Hildy asked.

"Fat chance. The old Slavic neighborhood in Edwardsville is just about gone. Zerby Avenue isn't safe after dark anymore."

This subject bothered Corrine deeply. She and her husband had built a house in the more upscale community of Harveys Lake, but she still loved the old church and its parish, even though she didn't attend it anymore. She started talking rapidly, fire in her eyes. "Drugs and crime are making the old people prisoners in their own houses. It's the outsiders, coming in from Philadelphia and Allentown. They end up in public-assisted housing. No sense of community. And they aren't what you call religious. The town's not like it used to be when a bingo game happened every night of the week, and you could stroll down to Main Street for a pizza at ten without fear of being mugged.

"Now the police sirens wail all night. Edwardsville has become a place without hope. It's a shame about the church, but honestly—short of Father John's miracle—I don't think it can be saved."

Corrine stopped her tirade only when it was her turn to board the bus. Hildy hugged her sister hard, sad to see her go. The two of them were all that were left of their family, grown-up women, but orphans nonetheless.

Every bone in Hildy's body ached with fatigue when she finally got back to her cottage at twilight. She had stopped at the supermarket on the boulevard to pick up some cat food, a carton of two-percent milk, a half pound of honey ham, Little Debbie Swiss Cake Rolls, and Skinny Cow caramel-swirl vanilla cones. When she opened the front door of her cozy summer place on Twenty-fifth Street, she smiled, anticipating some quiet relaxation on the deck while she gazed at the stars and enjoyed the ice cream.

But immediately she felt puzzled. A glow radiated from the kitchen. Her first thought was *I don't remember leaving a light on.* The second was *The house is on fire!* Adrenaline poured through her veins. She dropped her grocery bag and ran toward the brightness, crying out, "Kitties! Shelley! Shelley! Keats!"

She flew through the kitchen door and stopped short. The golden light she had seen from the sunporch came from the bottle she had found in the casino. No longer sitting on the counter, it was on its side and open on the linoleum floor. Its stopper had rolled a few feet away. And inexplicably from inside it, a powerful beam of light pulsed and glowed.

Hildy felt perplexed. *Why is the bottle shining? Does it run on batteries?* But the questions vanished from her mind when she realized that a very large man sat on the step stool she used to reach the upper shelves of the cabinets. The cats, peering up at her with sleepy eyes, lay contentedly at his sandal-clad feet. The sandals, definitely not Birkenstocks, were held on by straps that laced up the man's muscular calves right to the hem—of his toga.

Hildy's anger exploded like an M-80 going off. The words flew from her mouth. *"How dare you come into my house!"*

The man smiled in a lopsided way. He was remarkably handsome even though his nose had been smashed, no doubt in a fight, and one cheekbone looked slightly flatter than the other. His hair, so dark a brown it appeared black, was a cap of short curls. Oddly enough, he was wearing what

appeared to be a wreath of real laurel leaves
atop it.

The man pointed to the bottle lying on the floor.
"You brought that here, no?" His accent was Ital-
ian; his voice seemed raspy, perhaps from lack of
use, but not guttural. In fact, he sounded like an
Italian count in movies like *The Garden of the
Finzi-Continis*.

A wave of guilt washed over Hildy. This man
must work for Caesar's. "Well, yes, yes, I did. I
was going to leave it at your Lost and Found de-
partment, but I forgot. I didn't know it was so valuable the casino would send somebody to get it—"
She stopped herself. She sounded apologetic when
she should be outraged.

Her hands went to her hips. "But that's not the
point. You had no right to just walk in here. How
did you get in, anyway?"

The man shrugged and pointed to the bottle
again. "You brought the bottle in here yourself.
You just said so. You left it on the counter. The
white cat knocked it on the floor. The black one
batted it around until the stopper came off."

Hildy felt completely confused. "How do you
know that?" A new wave of anger washed over
her, making her so mad her voice shook. "What!
Were you watching through the window? What are
you, anyway, a Peeping Tom?"

The man shook his head no and stood up. He
was well over six feet tall. His toga hung in graceful
folds from one shoulder where it was pinned by a
gaudy medallion with a Roman emperor's face on
it. Hildy recognized Caesar Augustus at once. After
all, she had just seen his statue in the casino. A
sword hung at the man's left side, and in his right
hand he held a gnarled wooden staff.

*How ridiculous that the casino makes its employ-
ees dress in costume,* she thought, remembering the

young cocktail waitresses in very short togas who wandered through the casino asking if anyone wanted a drink—at eleven in the morning, for heaven's sake. But Hildy hadn't seen any men dressed up. These brawny guys must be security for the high rollers in the evening crowd. Some VIP must have lost the bottle and complained to the management, she concluded.

The stranger took one step closer. A man as solid as a tree trunk, he loomed over her. She could see that long scars crisscrossed his chest, which was bare beneath his toga. And she could smell him, a strong but not unpleasant odor that might be patchouli, she guessed. But although he was nearly invading her personal space, Hildy, her anger still hot, stood her ground despite his bellicose appearance.

Unexpectedly, right at that moment, the man saluted her, thumping above his heart with his right fist. He bowed his head. "My name is Antonius Eugenius. I once was a centurion commanding a cohort in the Roman army. In the reign of Caesar Augustus I was stationed in Britannia before I was sent to Judea to subdue the Jews. But you asked what I am now."

Sadness flickered across his face. "I am what was in the bottle." He pointed to the amber glass container which remained eerily illuminated where it lay on the floor. Then he looked directly at Hildy with eyes which were a deeper blue and much older than her own. When he began to speak again, the glow of the bottle seemed to come into them, lighting him up from within. "What I am is a genie."

With those words he levitated off the floor and melted away into a plume of smoke which curled upward toward the ceiling and sparkled with a thousand tiny lights like a spray of golden glitter. Then the smoke whooshed downward and turned back into a human form. Once again the Roman centurion stood in front of Hildy, his flesh solid, his sandaled feet back on the floor.

Hildy's mouth fell open. Her head felt light and strange. The room began to spin around in a dizzying whirl. She cried out "Oh!" and tried to fight the darkness of oblivion that overtook her, but consciousness slipped away. She slid in a faint to the floor.

Chapter 8

Sometimes a transformation does not happen over time. It occurs in an instant, at the moment when fate delivers its lightning strike. A lottery win, a car crash, a rifle shot, a bomb blast, a heart-stopping medical diagnosis, a phone call in the night bringing bad news—these events happen in a blink of an eye. They divide a life instantly into two parts. And afterward, a person is never again the same.

So it was for Hildy.

When her eyes fluttered open, Antonius Eugenius was bending over her, fanning her face with a paper plate. She attempted to sit up too quickly, and faintness overcame her again.

"You passed out," he said, stating the obvious. "Keep your head down."

Hildy, staying prone as requested, stared up at the ceiling, which she noted had water stains in one corner. But quickly getting impatient with her vulnerable position and the strange situation, she complained, "I can't keep lying on the floor. How long do I have to stay like this?"

"A few minutes." His voice held the timbre of command. "You should practice some self-restraint. You appear to be an impulsive person; your anger overrides your caution. If you had been in my legion, you'd have been run through with a sword by now."

"If I had been in your legion, during the reign of Caesar Augustus or so you claim, I would have been dead two millennia ago. Tell me this isn't happening," Hildy said and squeezed her eyes shut.

"It's happening. Denial doesn't help. Maybe we need to talk."

"We are talking. That's what's upsetting me. I feel as if I have a unicorn in the garden."

"I don't understand," the man said, looking at her as if she were mentally deranged.

"It's a short story by James Thurber. I'm an English teacher. I tend to make literary references." Hildy thought for a moment, the linoleum cool against her back. "Here's a reference you should understand, if you are who you say you are: *'Omnia Gallia in tres partes divisa est.'*"

"Ah, you *are* a *grammaticus*. Are you testing me? That is easy; it's the opening of Julius Caesar's commentaries on the Gallic Wars. 'All Gaul is divided into three parts.'" His voice became annoyed. "I am an educated man. Did you assume I was born a plebeian or a slave?" His chin lifted, his pride evident. "My father was a Roman citizen."

"I really need to get off the floor," Hildy murmured to herself. Aloud she asked, "What did you say your name was?"

"Antonius Eugenius. You can call me Tony G. Should I call you master?"

Hildy moved abruptly into a sitting position. Her head swam but she remained upright. She put her fingertips to her forehead. "Master is the wrong gender and quite inappropriate."

"Mistress, then?"

"Absolutely not." She adopted the voice she used for dealing with wiseacre teenage boys. "You shall call me Ms. Caldwell."

"As you wish, Ms. Caldwell." A pained expression crossed Tony's face. As a Roman centurion, he led a cohort, nearly one hundred and sixty Roman soldiers. Now he had to obey this slip of a girl. But he accepted the cards dealt by fate. He had no choice. Some battles are best left unfought.

"Now, Tony, if you will offer me your hand, I want to stand." He did, and she did, swaying slightly. As soon as she felt steady on her feet, she dropped his hand. She tipped her head back and looked up at him. Her eyes narrowed. "You look familiar. Are you sure you don't work for the casino?"

"I am positive that I do not," he said.

Hildy remained skeptical. She suddenly knew who this man resembled: Tony Curtis in *Spartacus*. His name in the movie was Antonius too. Her suspicions grew that she was the target of a scam, although she couldn't imagine for what purpose someone who worked at Caesar's would pretend to be a genie in a bottle. She decided on another test for this Tony G.

" '*Arma virumque cano, Troiae qui primus ab oris Italiam fato profugus Lavinaque venit litora,*' " she recited.

The Roman's face lit up with delight. "You do know Latin! Shall we speak it then? It has been centuries since I've conversed in my native tongue."

"No, we shall not speak Latin. To paraphrase your own words, 'I am an educated person.' I had four years of Latin study, but I'm far from fluent. And if you really are an ancient Roman, as you say you are, I would like you to identify the line and give me a translation." Hildy's voice was arch.

"You really should choose a more obscure quotation," Tony commented. "Every boy at the gymnasium must memorize the first line of Virgil's *Aeneid*. In English, the line would be something like, 'I sing of war and the man'—he meant the hero Aeneas, you know—'who, exiled by fate, first came from the coasts of Troy to the shores of Italy and Lavinia.' "

But as Tony finished his answer, his voice caught in his throat. The light in the room dimmed. And the Roman who had stood so solidly in front of Hildy began to fade away, his outline softening and his body first becoming insubstantial, then transparent, until only a wisp of smoke remained where the large man had been.

"What's happening? Where are you?" *Something must have gone terribly wrong,* she thought.

Only a moment passed, although it seemed much longer, before the brightness returned. Tony G. changed again from smoke to flesh and blood. His eyes held a great sorrow, his mouth turned down at the corners, his shoulders sagged. He sat down heavily on the step stool.

"I must ask your forbearance, mis— I mean Ms. Caldwell. I am a stoic man, but hearing you speak in Latin touched my heart, awakening such memories. Then the import of Virgil's words suddenly struck me, reminding me that I too am in exile, wandering farther from home than Aeneas ever did."

He shook his head, overcome by weariness and grief. "I am a warrior, but I am also a man. You might say I began to fall apart."

He sat there on the stool an arm's length away from Hildy. He wasn't a vision, a hologram, or a dream. Hildy felt confused. The situation was fantastical, but this man had feelings, a past, a life. He was undeniably real. She groped for an explanation. "Tell me again, you were in the bottle and you're a genie? How can that be?"

"I don't care much to talk about it," he said and sighed. "But to give you the short version of a long story: I was to be executed— You wish to know why?" He paused as Hildy made a noise and held up her hand like a stop sign.

"Yes, yes, I would. Why don't you give me the unabridged version? I think I need to hear it."

The genie gave another deep sigh, and his eyes got a faraway look. "It was a case of being blinded by love, I suppose. I had been in Judea for some time when I met a beautiful woman near a well where she waited for an elderly servant to fetch her a drink. She was a lovely thing with flashing eyes and a smile that made my heart race. Her hair was black and interwoven with jewels. She smelled of sandalwood and she dressed in silks." His voice trailed off and he smiled at the memory. Then he continued.

"I looked at her longingly and she looked back. I ventured a greeting. She responded in kind, and with her first words, I was smitten. I approached closer. I took her hand and brought it to my lips. She didn't resist. In fact, I felt her quiver when I kissed her palm. I suggested that, if she was thirsty, we could visit a nearby tavern and have some wine together. She giggled and said she couldn't possibly.

"I dropped her hand and bowed. I turned to leave. Her voice stopped me. Perhaps I could come back to *her* rooms, she whispered just loud enough for me to hear. She had some very fine wine there. I couldn't believe my luck.

"And I shouldn't have believed it. Her rooms were in the palace of Herod the Great, a blood-thirsty tyrant—"

"I've heard of him," Hildy interrupted. "He's the king of Judea who ordered every child under two who lived near Bethlehem to be murdered. He feared the Messiah, said to have been born there, would usurp his throne. What a monster."

Tony G. nodded in assent. "You don't know the half of it. He had an obsession with threats to his kingship. Just the year before my own, er, situation, he had executed two of his own sons because he thought they were planning to overthrow him."

Hildy's eyes got bigger. She urged the genie to get on with his tale.

"As I was saying, I retired to the rooms of this alluring young female. She ordered wine to be brought, along with some meats and fruit. We ate, we drank, we talked for a while. I told her of my life. She said little of hers, but I was too dazzled to notice her reticence.

"Finally she dismissed her servant, leaving us alone in her chamber. We kissed. We . . . well, we got to know each other better. Dusk fell. The room filled with shadows. I had stayed too long, but I lay there in a stupor. I was intoxicated with more than wine and careless when I should have been cautious.

"The lady's servant reappeared suddenly, throwing aside the curtains that surrounded the bed. The old hag warned that Herod was approaching. I must flee. I grabbed my sword and my toga. I was in the act of putting on my sandals when the palace guards crashed into the room and seized me.

"King Herod himself came in behind them. 'Kill him,' he said without any emotion. 'Bring me his head on a platter,' he added.

"The sweet lady's hair was a mass of tangled curls and her feet were bare—as was the rest of her, to tell the truth. She threw herself at the king, falling to her knees before him. I didn't see what followed because the guards were dragging me away. I fought like a madman although I knew escape was futile. I felt humiliated. I should have died on the battlefield, with honor, not because I was dipping my . . ." The genie remembered he was speaking with Hildy and stopped himself mid-sentence.

"I'm not a child," Hildy said, her voice cross. "I know what you two were doing. Go on, please, with the story."

Tony G. gave her a wink, some of his good humor returning. "I was more angry with myself than with Herod, to be honest. I had been drunk on lust and desire. Now I was determined to go down fighting, not be executed like a common criminal. I lashed out with my feet. I struggled with the strength of ten men, conscious of nothing but the need to break free."

Tony G. puffed up his chest as he spoke.

"Then in the midst of the melee, I heard the old servant's voice shouting at the guards to return me to the chamber. She screamed out that Herod had changed his mind. Bloody and battered, I was brought before the king and thrown down on the hard stone floor. A guard put the point of his sword in the middle of my back, its tip piercing my flesh. He put his foot on my neck so I could not lift my head to see, but I smelled the woman's perfume. I knew she was there.

"Herod began to speak. He was just a puppet ruler, appointed by Rome after all, and I was a Roman centurion, as the lady must have told him. 'You aroused my anger, perhaps too quickly,' the king said. 'You are a Roman citizen, I understand, and well-connected in the senate. Explaining your execution would be tiresome; you do have such bothersome laws in the empire. Besides'—his voice became taunting—'being served another head on a platter has lost its satisfaction.'

"He laughed then, a cold, cruel laugh. 'My lady here has suggested it would be more amusing to give you a different kind of fate, worse than death perhaps.'

"My heart froze at his words. I did not fear beheading, which would have been quick. I cursed myself and my stupidity as I wondered what vile torture he had thought up in the few minutes since I was seized. He soon told me.

" 'I have a visitor from Egypt, a famous magician, or so he says. So far his tricks have been rather ordinary. He claims he casts spells and enchantments. Let's find out if he can entertain me with your fate.' "

The genie looked at Hildy then, his eyes sad, his shoulders sagging. "The magician put on quite a show for Herod the Great. First he drugged me, assuring my cooperation. Then he produced clouds of rainbow-colored smoke and made marvelous music from invisible instruments ring through the ether. He opened a great book and began reading out a spell. Suddenly I was a few inches tall and imprisoned in a bottle.

"Herod himself was the first to pull the cork and request three wishes. As he already had great wealth and power, his wishes were grandiose, but frivolous. After his third wish—a golden chariot pulled by golden horses—I found myself back in the bottle, adrift in a vast blue sea, the Mediterranean, I believe. And that, Ms. Caldwell, is my tale."

"Is it the truth?" Hildy challenged him.

A twinkle lit up the genie's eyes, which were as blue as the sea he had just mentioned. "For the most part," he said. "I was not executed as you can plainly see. And I truly am a genie, created by enchantment and cast upon the waters to wander forever."

Hildy gave him an appraising look. This Tony G. was not a figment of her imagination, of that she was certain. She had always been a sensible person, not given to visions or flights of fancy. But her belief system most definitely had not included genies. "I always assumed genies were mythical creatures," she offered, feeling uneasy.

"People assumed Troy was a myth too," Tony pointed out.

"Yes, until Heinrich Schliemann followed the clues in Homer's *Iliad*, found the original city in Turkey, and dug it up." Hildy talked more to herself than to Tony. She looked at him then. Anxiety spread like a sudden frost inside her. The appearance of this genie had shaken the very foundations of her world. And right now she had other priorities in her life that she wanted to deal with. She straightened her shoulders, determined to dispose of the whole problem.

"I'm really very sorry, but this is absolutely one of the worst times you could have showed up. I may be on the verge of—" She stopped. She had no intention of revealing her deepest hopes. "Never mind that. In any event, I feel very uncomfortable having you here, even if you are a genie. What am I supposed to do with you?"

"Help me escape."

"From the enchantment? Of course, I'd be glad to." Hildy felt an immense relief. She'd do whatever she had to and this unusual man would be on his way or disappear, or whatever, but he'd be gone.

"Ummm." Tony cleared his throat and avoided eye contact. "Not from the enchantment. I need you to help me escape Jimmy the Bug."

"You need to escape a bug? What are you talking about?" A bad feeling started blossoming inside Hildy even before the genie began to answer.

Her misgivings grew progressively greater after Tony G. started talking. According to the genie, his previous master, who had found the bottle while vacationing in Miami, was Jimmy "the Bug" Torelli, a convicted murderer, thief, racketeer, extorter, and well-known mob boss. Earlier today Torelli had taken Tony G., riding inside the bottle, to the slots in Atlantic City so that the genie could help him win a jackpot.

That piece of information brought Hildy up short. She interrupted the genie. "You could do that? Make the machine hit the jackpot?"

"The machines are already programmed by the casino, you do know that?" Tony G. talked with hand gestures and body language. He turned his palms up and shrugged his shoulders. "If it was going to hit the jackpot it would without my help, but I can nudge my master to the right machine and help things along a little, you might say."

"I hit the jackpot. After I put you in my bag." Hildy became quite agitated. She never cheated at anything, ever, not even her income tax. "Did you? I mean, I didn't wish—"

Tony G. looked at her and cocked his head. " 'I am fortunate in every way and I wish to be lucky today.' I am quite sure I heard you say that." He spoke without guile.

"Oh no, I didn't mean . . . now I feel terrible. I won the jackpot because I wished it. I will have to return the money. It's only right."

Tony G. gave her a pitying look. "You do not have to return the money. You won it fairly."

"No, I didn't. I wished it to happen!" Hildy protested.

Tony G. laughed. "And don't you think that everyone playing the machines also wishes it to happen? How do you know that's not why they win?"

"Because—because—you just told me you did it."

"I said the machine was already programmed to win. You chose to sit there. I had nothing to do with that. And what would you tell the casino, 'I'm returning the jackpot because I wished I'd win and I did'? That's ridiculous."

Hildy felt confused. His reasoning was flawed

and self-serving, but she couldn't get her mind around exactly how to counter his argument. "I still think it was cheating somehow."

"You are definitely splitting hairs about this. Are you always so tiresome? Besides, worrying about that win is the least of your problems. You need to focus on what is really important here."

"What do you mean?"

"Your ownership of the bottle has put you in harm's way."

Hildy felt her heart start to race. "What exactly do you mean by that? How am I in harm's way?"

"Because the well-known South Jersey Mafia boss, my former master, Jimmy the Bug, who not only has eyes that pop insectlike from his head but is what you in this century might call 'one can short of a six-pack,' is going to be looking for me."

"How hard is he going to be looking?" Hildy asked, but thought she knew the answer.

"I imagine he's working on it already. He had big plans for using me to expand his territory, to become the boss of bosses. He sees me as his ticket to taking over Atlantic City, Las Vegas, and who knows what. The world? He dreams big."

The blood had drained from Hildy's face.

"You're not going to faint again, are you?" Tony G. asked, ready to grab the paper plate again.

Hildy shook her head no. "Could you do that? Make him that powerful? I'm afraid I don't know what you can do and can't do."

Tony G. nodded yes. "I can make him *capo di tutti capi*, boss of bosses. I don't want to. It goes against my nature, and to tell the truth I think he's an idiot, although a very dangerous one. But if he possesses the bottle, I have to obey him. He gets three wishes in any event—you've already heard about genies and the three wishes. Everybody knows that."

"Don't be patronizing. I heard about that in fairy tales. My life never depended on what I thought was a story. Please spell it out for me." Hildy felt agitated. She needed all the details she could get.

Tony G. gave her a little nod. "As you wish. As a genie, I have to obey whoever owns the bottle. I can do errands, grant petty desires, that sort of thing, and it doesn't count against the three wishes my master gets. Maybe I should call the three wishes 'big wishes.' A big wish might be if you said, 'Tony G., I wish to be president of the United States.' That's huge, a life-changing desire. Do you see?"

"Was my jackpot win a big wish? I mean, I didn't even know I was making a real wish at the time."

Tony G.'s manner became gallant, charming even. "No, it wasn't. You weren't asking me directly for anything. I just felt like giving you a smile. I like seeing those dimples, by the way. Just like that Mike fellow does—"

"Mike! Wait a minute. Wait a minute. I wished I'd see him—and I did. Don't tell me—"

Tony G. studied his sandals as he answered. "You might call your meeting him a coincidence, you know."

Hildy's face turned dark. "But it wasn't, was it?"

Tony G. looked up and his bright blue eyes begged for understanding. "This fellow Mike was already in Atlantic City. In fact, he was already down on the beach. I just had to get you down there—"

"And knock me over with a wave, and nearly drown me?" Hildy felt manipulated. She didn't like it.

"It turned out well, didn't it?"

Hildy's emotions churned. Her thoughts became chaotic. "I want to sit down. Let's go into the other room." She walked into the dining room and pulled out one chair from under the Formica table, motioned for Tony G. to take it, then sat down in another.

"Look, Tony, I need to know something. Did you have anything to do with—with what happened between Mike and me? After he pulled me out of the water, I mean." Her hands had started shaking and she pressed them down on the red tabletop to still them.

"Oh, you think I— No. Not at all. You didn't wish for anything beyond meeting this guy. Anything that happened between the two of you had nothing to do with me."

Hildy let out a deep sigh and closed her eyes for a moment. "Thank goodness. I suddenly felt worried that none of it was real, genuine I mean."

Tony G. gave her a look filled with compassion. "You're in love with this fellow, aren't you?"

Hildy nodded. "I am. I wasn't sure until I saw him again, but I am." She let out another shaky breath.

"Does he feel the same way?"

Hildy shrugged. "I don't know. I don't imagine he does. He's engaged to marry someone else."

"Ms. Caldwell, if you don't mind my saying it, I could take care of everything for you. You want this guy to fall in love with you, I can do it. Believe me, it's easy."

Hildy looked horrified. "No! I want Mike to really love me, because I'm me, not because of some trick."

The genie gave Hildy another look, this time one with more pity than compassion. "Didn't you ever hear that all's fair in love and war? I could make him love you with the same intensity, the same passions, as if he decided to all on his own."

Hildy pressed her lips together tightly. "No means no. Look, maybe it was okay that you set

up Mike and me running into each other. But stay
out of my love life from now on. I mean that."

"As you wish. I live to obey you. I belong to
you, at least at the moment."

"And I do not want you to belong to me." She
sat silent for a minute, then spoke her thoughts
aloud. "But it would be unethical to return you to
someone who intends to commit criminal acts with
your powers. No, that is out of the question. And
you did ask me to help you escape—"

"Ms. Caldwell, you need to understand what
you're committing yourself to. Mr. Torelli is a convicted murderer, and he is going to do whatever is
necessary to retrieve that bottle and get me back—
and that might include killing you."

The words burst from her lips. "Killing *me*!"
Hildy yelled loudly enough that she terrified the
cats, who ran as fast as they could out of the room.

"That about sums it up," Tony said.

Hildy began shaking from head to toe, partly
from fear, and mostly from being so mad she felt
as if she were going to explode. "Well, we'll just
see about that. This Jimmy the Bug has no idea
who he's dealing with."

Tony G. gave the girl credit. She had a lot of
guts, but the way she was trembling, her words had
to be more bravado than anything else. But he hid
his observations and gave Hildy an unreadable
look. "I'm guessing he doesn't," he said.

Chapter 9

At about the time the genie's appearance transformed Hildy's life in ways she could not as yet begin to imagine, Hildy herself had caused a profound alteration in the lives of two other men, each in a radically different way.

Since he had run into Hildy earlier in this extraordinary day, Mike Amante had become a clock-watcher, a fidget, a man caught on the horns of a dilemma—and left with the uneasy feeling he was about to be gored.

"Mike, what is your problem?" Kiki's voice had lost its public silkiness and become irritatingly high-pitched. "You have been sitting in front of the television and changing channels for over an hour. You're not even watching anything. When are you going to get dressed? We're meeting my friend Odelia and her boyfriend for dinner and then we have tickets to see the Foo Fighters concert."

He groaned. Visions of a hot, jam-packed venue full of the Foo Fighters' screaming fans appeared in his imagination. He'd rather get a root canal. Sitting on the sofa in their posh suite at Trump Plaza, comped by the hotel for Kiki of course, he kept staring at the television, manically punching the buttons on the remote control, scrolling through the stations. *Two hundred damned stations and nothing worth watching,* he thought. At the same time, he answered Kiki without looking in her direction. "My stomach's upset. I think I got food poisoning at that luncheon this afternoon."

"Don't be ridiculous. Nobody else got sick." Kiki walked over and stood between Mike and the television screen to get his attention. She was wearing only her bra and thong panties.

He averted his eyes, not at all interested in her near-nakedness, and threw the remote control on the coffee table. "I'm not feeling well. I'm not up to going out tonight."

"What!" The veins on Kiki's neck knotted up like twisted blue yarn. "You can't be serious! We have reservations. We can't just stand Odelia up. Michael, stop this nonsense right now. You have to go!"

Mike had never noticed before how harsh and irritating her voice was. Its sharpness cut into his brain like a buzz saw. He wanted to shout back at her, *I don't care about Odelia. I don't care about the Foo Fighters. I don't care—about you!* Instead, he replied in a calm and reasonable voice, knowing that diplomacy was the wiser tack to take with Kiki, whose temper was legendary. "Of course you can't stand up your friends. That's why *you* need to go. Really. I want you to go without me. I can't eat anything anyway. Plus, I feel so rotten, I'd spoil your evening."

Kiki took a long hard look at him. "You do look pale. If you're feeling that sick, maybe you do have food poisoning. I should call Odelia and cancel. I don't want to leave you here alone."

"No, no! I insist. You go ahead. I'm totally beat, that's all. I'm heading directly to bed. Why let this screw up your night out? I'd feel even worse knowing that you're sitting around here when you should be having a good time."

"Are you sure?" She was already moving toward the bedroom to finish dressing.

"Positive," he called after her.

Mike really didn't feel good. His neck had stiffened up. His back ached a little. His nerves felt as if little cartoon mice were doing a tap dance on them. But he had lied about his stomach being queasy. He actually felt hungry. He thought about ordering a pizza or something once Kiki left. Then his thoughts went back to what he had been mulling over for hours: how to reach Hildy.

He had called his mother earlier today. She didn't have Hildy's cell phone number. She had looked in the church member directory for St. Paul's in Lehman and reported that only Hildy's home phone was listed. She suggested that Mike leave a message for Hildy and when she got it— she must be checking her messages, his mother reassured him—she would call him back. And wasn't it lovely that he had run into Hildy again after all these years?

Then she fell silent. "And how's Kiki?" she asked at last.

His mother had tried to like Kiki, Mike knew that. They just didn't click. His mother never complained when they didn't come out to Lehman for her birthday, or even when they missed Christmas. They had invited her to go skiing at Aspen with them during the holidays last year, but his mother had said no, it was nice of them to think of her, but she always sang with the choir on Christmas Eve. She liked to be home. She'd go over to Aunt Letty's instead of cooking since Mike wasn't going to be there.

Mike's mother didn't get mad or complain, but Mike felt guilty. He told Kiki that they should go to Pennsylvania for Christmas Day and leave for Aspen the day after or even that night. Kiki had given him that look, the one that said he was an imbecile.

"Don't you ever listen? I told you a half dozen times." She was exasperated with him, obviously. "I'm shooting photos for *People* magazine's big feature, 'Brad Pitt's Christmas in Aspen.' We have to be there early on the twenty-fourth."

As it turned out, Mike spent most of Christmas Eve and Christmas Day alone while Kiki was busy "with Brad." He did some solitary skiing to pass the time and then drank martinis at a bar along with the other lonely people. Mike pushed the memory away and thought about Hildy again.

This afternoon, after talking to his mother, Mike had reached his old friend George Ide at his auto repair shop in Trucksville. Over the clanging of metal and loud banging of an air compressor, George yelled out that he didn't know who might have Hildy's cell phone number, but maybe one of her girlfriends did. He thought she was still friendly with Susan. Mike remembered Susan, the cheerleader, didn't he? She used to be Susan Jeremiah before she got married. He'd try to get her number for Mike, he said, and no, as far as he knew, Hildy wasn't seeing anybody. Why did Mike want to know?

Mike said he was just curious, that was all, and why didn't George mind his own business.

George laughed at him. "You still have something going for her, don't you, Mike?"

Mike told him to shut up. Didn't George remember he was engaged?

"Maybe you're the one who needs to remember, Big Mike," George said, laughed again, and hung up.

Afterward Mike called Hildy's home number and left a message on the machine, asking her to call him. Hell, he had swallowed his pride and pleaded with her to call him. But he was sure she wouldn't, not after meeting Kiki this afternoon. Mike lay down on the couch and put a throw pillow over his face. He felt miserable.

Then he heard Kiki's voice. "Michael? Oh, are you asleep already?"

He didn't answer. He smelled the heavy floral scent of her perfume as she walked over to the sofa. She stood there a minute. He didn't move. He made his breathing soft and regular. He added a snore or two to be even more convincing. Then he heard her walk away and go out the door.

The minute he heard the door click shut, Mike sat up and tossed the pillow onto a nearby chair. He had a brilliant idea. He couldn't believe he hadn't thought of it earlier. He'd drive up to Ship Bottom and find Hildy, to apologize to her. It was the right thing to do.

Hildy had told him she lived on Twenty-fifth Street, the first house from the boulevard. A gray house, she said, with whales on it. If he left right now, he'd be there in an hour. Maybe she hadn't eaten yet, and she'd go have a pizza with him. Kiki didn't eat pizza. She said it had too many calories.

Before he walked out the door five minutes later, he had brushed his teeth, combed his hair, and splashed on some cologne. He checked what money he had in his wallet, grabbed his car keys, left the suite, and headed for the hotel's parking lot.

Whatever had been wrong with him must have passed, he thought. He felt great.

Just eight miles south of Trump Plaza in the Victorian town of Ocean City, another man was also obsessing about Hildy Caldwell. Jimmy the Bug had spent most of his day trying to track her down too.

His hunt had started off well. It had been easy

to find out who had hit the jackpot on that Slingo machine, the one where he had left the bottle. The casino cashier wouldn't give up the winner's name or address, but for fifty bucks Jimmy had gotten a good enough description to spot the girl coming off the beach at Michigan Avenue: same clothes, same oversized tote bag with SAVE THE WOLVES on it, same blond hair. He knew right away it was the right chick.

He couldn't catch up with her, but he managed to get her license plate number. Even though it was a Pennsylvania plate, he figured he had it made. He'd have the genie back in no time. He got in his white Cadillac CTS and drove back to his summerhouse in Ocean City. Once there, it took him a few phone calls, but he got a state cop, the nephew of one of his guys, to run the plates. By late afternoon, he had her name and her address.

It turned out this Hildy Caldwell lived out in the sticks somewhere between Wilkes-Barre and Scranton, about three, three and a half hours from Atlantic City. Jimmy the Bug made a few more calls, and a friend of a friend from Scranton agreed to send one of his guys to her house. The guy was supposed to wait for this girl to get back from Atlantic City if she wasn't there already, grab her as soon as she got out of her car, and take the bottle. End of story. Only it didn't turn out that way.

"Puggy!" Jimmy the Bug screamed toward the kitchen from the lanai of his four-thousand-square-foot summer "cottage" with ocean view. As a rule, he didn't usually conduct business at home—he had an office for that—but this genie problem meant breaking his own rules. "What did the Scranton guy find out!"

John Pugiliese, a string bean of a man with a long sallow face, came to the sliding doors with a dish towel in one hand and a ladle in the other. "Nothing more than I already told you, boss. After he got to her house, it was all closed up. He talked to a neighbor. The girl's away for the summer. Rented a place for the season down here somewhere. Gone until Labor Day. The neighbor said another neighbor has the address, but is still at work. The Scranton guy is waiting around. I thought we'd hear by now, but he didn't call back yet."

"Sumofabitch." Jimmy the Bug reached for a cigarette and lit it. He was getting very worked up over this whole situation. He had to find out where this girl was staying. "You know how many goddamn summer rentals are at the Jersey shore?"

"I don't know. A million? Two million?"

"Shut up, Puggy. It was a rhetorical question. Maybe I need to eat something. The ziti done yet?"

"Just took it off the stove. Be out in a minute. I'll tell Joey and Sal." He disappeared back into the shadows of the house.

Ten minutes later Jimmy's lieutenants—twins named Joey and Sal—Puggy, who was both bodyguard and cook, and their boss sat at the artisan-made wrought iron and glass table out in the lanai. From there Jimmy liked to watch the fishermen casting into the surf about three hundred feet away.

Puggy put a big dish of ziti and meatballs on the table in front of Jimmy the Bug. "Salad?" Puggy asked, then held out a bowl of romaine lettuce topped with shaved Parmigiana Romano cheese.

Jimmy the Bug waved it away. "Pour me some wine," he said. "You guys, go ahead. Take what you want."

Sal and Joey filled their plates with ziti and started eating. They didn't make small talk, such as *Hey, you see who won the game?* or *Nice day, huh.* They never did, not around Jimmy the Bug anyway. It was safer to keep your mouth shut. You never knew what was going to set him off.

But despite the lack of conviviality, Jimmy the Bug never ate alone. Some of his crew and at least one bodyguard were always there. He didn't have a wife anymore: Teresa, God rest her soul, died of a heart attack when he was in Trenton State Prison the last time. It surprised him. He always figured the husband kicked first and the wives turned into tough old *nonnas* dressed in black who lived to be a hundred years old.

Of course, he had a *cumare*, an Italian word the Americans pronounced "goo-mah." In plain English, he had a girlfriend. He thought about Jennifer and what a pain in the ass she was. Her bra size was bigger than her IQ. Besides, the relationship was all show. He didn't have the urge to get intimate anymore. And no way was he going to start popping Viagra. *Old guys trying to get a hard-on for a young chick—what a joke,* he thought.

The genie could have fixed that problem too, if Jimmy had wished it. Would have been a waste of a wish, the way he looked at it. He didn't have time to put up with a woman right now. He had plans, big plans.

Or he did before he lost the goddamn genie.

He cursed himself, he cursed the parole officer, he cursed that stupid girl at the Slingo machine for picking up something that didn't belong to her. He put a forkful of the ziti in his mouth. He cursed that too.

"Puggy!" he screamed, sending a spray of red tomato sauce onto the tablecloth. His eyes bulged even more than usual, and his face went purple. "I told you, cook the ziti al dente. You know what that means. Firm. Right? You call this al dente?"

"It said twelve minutes on the box, boss. I set the timer."

"It's mush! That's what it is. Garbage. You have the balls to serve me this shit?" He picked up the dish of pasta and hurled it against the wall. Then he got up, kicked his chair over, and stomped into the house, wanting to shoot somebody just to make himself feel better.

Chapter 10

"Do you know anybody who drives an expensive sports car? I think it's a Mercedes Roadster," Tony G. asked Hildy, who was at the kitchen counter opening a can of Friskies Mariner's Catch for Shelley and Keats.

Hildy looked over at Tony G., who had been walking around aimlessly or sitting on the step stool just hanging out. Hildy had turned down his offer to wash the kitchen floor or clean the bathroom. He had taken offense at her refusal and muttered something like, *This place could use a good scrubbing.*

Hildy finally instructed him to think up a game plan for their "situation," just to give him something to do. His immediate suggestion was that he should conjure up a 9mm Beretta, she should shoot whoever came looking for the bottle—he'd do it himself but genies were unable to kill anybody, he explained apologetically—and the two of them could dump the body or bodies in the ocean with cement blocks tied to their feet.

Hildy had given him a look that would put frost on a bonfire. "Obviously you belonged to this Mafia person a little too long. *I* am not going around shooting people and disposing of their bodies."

"It would be in self-defense," Tony G. argued.

Hildy did not answer him, or even acknowledge him, until now, when he mentioned the silver car. She raised her right eyebrow in a quizzical way. "No, I don't know anybody who drives a Mercedes of any model. Why are you asking?" She put her fingers under the tap water to rinse off the fish smell.

"Because that car just pulled next to your VW Beetle in your front yard."

Hildy started. "How do you know that?"

Tony G. had in fact looked out the window, but he wanted to impress her and said, "I know these things. Oh, wait, you do know the driver. It's that Michael fellow."

Hildy's face went white as paper. "What? Are you kidding? Mike is here?"

"It appears that way to me—and before you ask, no, I didn't bring him here. He showed up all on his own."

Panic swept over Hildy. She turned toward the genie. "You can't stay here. I can't let him see you. How would I explain you? Go back in your bottle. Hurry!" Her voice was frantic.

Tony G., having been ordered to vamoose, vamoosed, turning into a wisp of smoke and disappearing into his bottle. Hildy grabbed it off the floor where it still lay, stuck the cork into it, and looked around wildly for a place to put it. The refrigerator caught her eye. She wrenched open the door and put Tony G. next to the two-percent milk. She thought she caught a glimpse of him shaking his head no, no, through the amber glass, but he'd have to cope. She hoped he had a blanket.

She ducked into the bathroom to run a brush through her hair even as she heard knocking at the front door. She forced herself not to rush, fling it open, and throw herself in Mike's arms. Instead she let him stand on the stoop and knock a few more times. Finally she heard him call out, "Hildy! Hildy! It's Michael Amante, are you in there?"

Only then did she open the door a crack, peer out before slowly opening it all the way, and say calmly (instead of squealing as if she was over the moon at finding Mike on her doorstep, which she was), "Well, my goodness, it's Mike. What are you doing here?"

She stood in the doorway. She did not ask him in.

It was not the welcome he had hoped to get. "Hildy, uh, I didn't have your cell phone number."

"That's right."

"And, uh, I wanted to talk to you?" He put his hands in his pants pockets and played with his change.

Hildy folded her arms across her chest and did not smile. She knew the old maxim that what is too easily won is too little valued. "Talk to me? What about? Old times—or your wedding plans to what's her name—Kinky?"

"Ah, come on, Hildy, don't be mad. I acted like a horse's patootie today. I wanted to apologize and . . . and talk—really talk. I thought maybe we could go get a pizza or something. Really, I'm sorry about today. Let's start over, okay?" His face lit up with hope.

"Why this burning desire to talk to *me*, Mike? You've managed pretty well not talking to me since spring of senior year at Lake Lehman High."

Mike's voice went from asking to pleading. Both guilt and yearning filled him. "I know. I know that. It was May fifteenth, a Friday, three weeks before graduation. I want to apologize for that too, for everything that happened that night. Please, Hildy, come on out with me. Just for a while. There's so much I want to tell you."

To Hildy, Mike suddenly looked younger, so

much like the boy she had known in high school that her heart melted. She hadn't eaten since she saw Corrine hours ago. She was a little hungry. How could it hurt to say yes to a quick bite to eat? It seemed so important to him to talk with her, it would be just plain mean to refuse to join him for a snack.

"For just a short while—for pizza and that's it," she answered. "Give me a minute to get my wallet and house keys." She closed the door in his face and ran back to the refrigerator. She reached in, removed the bottle, and pulled the stopper out.

Tony G. materialized in a puff of white smoke that was tinged blue around the edges. He was frowning and his bare arms were covered with goose bumps.

"That was cold of you," he said, his choice of words deliberate.

"You were only in there five minutes. I'm sorry, okay? I'm going out for pizza with Mike. What should I do with you?" Her words rattled along in a rush.

"Take me along." He took a wide stance and put his hand on the hilt of his sword.

"I can't do that. It would be awkward. Two's company and all that. Tell me where to hide you until I get back."

"Nowhere. If Jimmy the Bug or his guys come looking for me, they'd find me here. They could dismantle this tiny place down to the studs in the walls in under an hour. You need to take me with you."

Hildy shook her head no. "That's not going to happen."

"Look, I'll be in the bottle. Stuff me in the tote under a towel, I'll mind my own business." Tony G. extended his hands beseechingly.

Hildy thought fast. She did not want Tony G.

tagging along, but she didn't want the Mafia stealing him back either. "I'll take you if you give me your word as a Roman and a centurion that you will not eavesdrop, or God forbid, watch me tonight."

"If you order me not to, I have to obey you. You don't need me to take an oath," Tony G. said, but he didn't sound convincing.

"Pardon me, but I'm not up on genie rules and regulations. How do I know you don't just make them up as you go along? If you want me to take you with me, swear."

Tony G. rolled his eyes dramatically for Hildy's benefit. In truth, he thought she had gotten the best of him. He had intended to monitor every second of her date. It was damned boring in that bottle. He took his sword from its sheath, got down on one knee before Hildy, and bowed his head. "I swear on my honor as a Roman and a centurion that I will not listen or watch you"—he looked up and smiled—"unless you need me to, of course."

"I won't need you. I don't need a chaperon. Now get back in your bottle."

Once Tony G. had disappeared, Hildy jammed on the stopper and stuffed the bottle in the SAVE THE WOLVES tote, covering it with her IT'S YOUR LUCKY DAY IN ATLANTIC CITY beach towel. She checked to make sure her wallet and house keys were in there too, then ran back to the front door where she stopped, took a deep breath, and forced herself to take her time as she opened it again.

Mike still stood on the stoop exactly as she had left him. No, she decided, he wasn't exactly the same as when she shut the door in his face. He wore a wide grin and his eyes were sparkling.

"Come on, let's go," he said and grabbed her hand.

An electric shock shot up Hildy's arm from his touch. "Oh!" she yelped.

"What?" Mike asked. "You say something?"

She shook her head. "Stone in my shoe, I guess. I'll shake it out in the car."

He took her around to the passenger side and opened the door for her. She peered in at the napa leather seats and burled wood dashboard with its GPS screen.

"Pretty impressive, huh?" he said proudly.

"I'd be more impressed with a hybrid," she said truthfully. "I'm saving up for a Prius." She got inside, putting her tote at her feet, and glanced over at Mike in the open doorway. Disappointment clouded his eyes, so she quickly added, "But this car is very nice, beautiful. I'm sorry, Mike, I just never thought about owning a car that cost about as much as my house. I'm glad you're doing so well."

He started to say something, then stopped himself. Once he too had gotten in and started the motor, he asked her if she had any suggestions where to eat.

"I know where they make the best pizza this side of Italy. The Dark Star Café. You're going to love it. Just go out the boulevard and turn right."

Since the Dark Star was only five blocks away, they rode in silence except when Hildy pointed to the purple sign in front of the restaurant and said, "There it is." She felt so light and floaty, almost as if this were a dream. She didn't want Mike to see how excited she was, but she could barely contain the emotions churning inside her. She told herself he just wanted to talk and this wasn't a date and it wasn't going to lead to a relationship. Yet the crazy hope, the hope she refused to acknowledge even existed, was that it would.

* * *

"Hildy! *Come sta*?" The owner of the Dark Star Café greeted Hildy like an old friend, even though she had been coming there for only a week. A psychedelic Grateful Dead poster from Watkins Glen, 1973, hung on the wall behind the counter. "Keep On Truckin' " played on the sound system.

"*Va bene.* I'm fine, Chef," she said. "We're going to have a pizza, the Caprese, the one that comes with slices of prosciutto, chunks of roasted pepper, and is topped with the homemade mozzarella."

"That's the house favorite." From behind the counter, the chef smiled broadly at her and gave a questioning look at the tall, good-looking young man standing at Hildy's shoulder. "A personal pizza? Or a large for the two of you?"

"Make it a large. I have help eating it tonight. Mike, this is Chef Salzarulo, the owner. Chef, this is Mike Amante, an old friend."

"Ah, a *paisan*!" The chef spoke in a big voice even when he didn't have to be heard over a Grateful Dead guitar riff. He leaned across the counter and offered Mike his hand. "You have a special lady there. You're a very lucky man."

Hildy's face reddened, and she began to sputter he wasn't her boyfriend, but Mike cut off her protest. "She is very special. I couldn't agree more."

Chef Salzarulo winked at Hildy before turning away to make the Caprese.

When they sat down at a table to wait for their pie, Hildy could barely make eye contact with Mike because all he did was stare at her while he grinned like an idiot.

Unable to endure the intense scrutiny any longer, she pasted a smile on her face and said, "So, here we are." She felt that was lame, but she didn't know what else to say.

Mike just kept right on grinning. "You look great, Hildy. I like your hair like that. I couldn't really tell how you wore it when it was all wet and full of sand. It's shiny, real pretty."

"Um, thanks. You said you wanted to talk?"

"I'd rather just look at you."

Hildy's stomach did a somersault. Her pulse speeded up. Her fair cheeks turned rosy once more. His words pleased her and utterly confused her at the same time. "Mike, what are you doing? I don't understand. Really, why did you come looking for me?"

She thought she heard something like a snort from under the table issuing from inside her tote bag. She scraped her foot to cover the noise. She frowned. She was going to give that genie a piece of her mind if he was listening after he had sworn not to.

Mike saw her displeasure and become concerned. "I don't mean to upset you, Hildy. Believe me." His handsome tanned face looked open and honest. "I'm not sure why I came, and that's the truth. I just knew that after we met on the beach this afternoon, I had to see you again. I'm sorry for that, for the way I acted when Kiki showed up, I mean. Everything happened so fast and I felt guilty, and I don't even know why."

Hildy heard another loud snort from her bag. "Stop that," she said and kicked the tote bag.

Mike appeared taken aback. "Okay, so I do know why. The minute I saw you, I felt immediately attracted to you." He reached across the table and took her hand in his. He held her fingers lightly and stroked her knuckles. "I've missed you," he said.

Hildy snatched her hand away. "No, you haven't. You've been building a lucrative career, appearing on Page Six of the *New York Post*, and getting engaged to a supermodel."

"She's only a photographer. She just looks like a model."

"Oh, shut up, Mike. The point is, you haven't missed me, so what do you want?"

Instead of looking at all chagrined, Mike laughed. "Same old Hildy. You were always the firecracker." He leaned toward her. "Listen to me. What I just said is true. The minute I saw you again, it all became clear. I have missed you. There's been a big gaping hole in my life, and that's because you weren't there."

"Mike, please don't hand me a line. What you're saying is such bull. You're going to get married."

Mike looked away and sighed. "I know it doesn't make sense." Then he turned his warm brown eyes on her. "But tell me you don't feel anything for me."

Hildy didn't say anything. She just stared at him for a minute while she tried to control her feelings, which had just exploded like a supernova and were speeding out into empty space at the speed of light. "Mike, I'm not going to answer that. Look, the pizza's ready."

Chef Salzarulo put the steaming pie in front of them along with two plates, knives, and forks. *"Mangia!"* he boomed.

Mike stared, then leaned forward over the pie and sniffed. "Hmmm, smells good," he said. He remembered his manners long enough to put a slice on Hildy's plate; then he grabbed one as if he were starving and took a big bite. Bliss shone from his face. He devoured the entire slice, then grabbed another. He raved between bites. "This pizza is amazing. The flavors are intense; the cheese is fantastic. I've never eaten a pie that was even remotely this good. You weren't kidding about it being the best outside of Italy." He reached for his third piece.

Hildy laughed and finished off her own slice. "I better warn you, it's addictive. I try to have a salad when I come here to eat, because I know I can't stop eating this once I start."

Mike looked at Hildy wolfing down the pizza, a little slower than he was, but with equal gusto. He liked seeing a woman enjoy food. He liked seeing Hildy, period. While they ate their way through the entire pizza, he started telling her about wanting to get out of real estate and start a detective agency. He described Jake Truesdale and how much fun he had working with him.

Then he asked Hildy, "What do you think? I wouldn't make the kind of money I'm generating in real estate. Am I being foolish?"

"It would be foolish to keep doing something that is killing your soul," Hildy insisted. "If you can't wait to go to work with Jake, then that tells you something—really tells you everything, right?"

"I think so too. My career in real estate was always about the money. In the beginning, the profits blew me away. I started chasing bigger deals. I took risks, spent days following up prospects, and nights crunching numbers. I was the young Turk, the guy to watch. One day I said to myself, why am I doing this? I was nothing but a salesman and I was full of shit most of the time.

"I couldn't stand the things I said to close a deal. I started looking for excuses not to take on a hot property. I hated going into the office. Pretty soon the money couldn't compensate for feeling miserable every day."

"Reality check," Hildy broke in. "You told me not a half hour ago that you love your Mercedes. Did you think about that? Maybe you need to have expensive toys and the lifestyle wealth brings. Maybe you would be even more unhappy if you had to budget every dime and scramble to pay the rent."

Mike shook his head. "I could handle the finances. To tell the truth, Hildy, I'm tired of the lifestyle I have. I can't tell you how phony so much of it is. Sure, I like having a great apartment and nice car. I'd be lying if I said I didn't. But they don't make up for the"—a shadow passed over his features and he thought for a minute—"the emptiness. It's outside me and it's inside me, a dark void right in the center of my heart that threatens to swallow me up. At times I wonder what's the point of life, what's the point of me living."

The words struck Hildy like an arrow, piercing her with a sudden agony, and prompting her to do what she did—reach out and take Mike's hand. "Then you should start your detective agency, Mike. It's the right thing to do."

Mike squeezed her fingers. "I knew you'd understand, Hildy. But what about you? Are you following your bliss, as Joseph Campbell said?"

"Hey, I'm the one who goes around quoting literature!" She laughed.

"I read books. I can quote with the best of them. 'Shall I compare thee to a summer's day? Thou art more lovely and more temperate.' "

Hildy lowered her eyes. "You are so full of it, Mike."

"I mean it, Hildy. You are lovely, from the inside out. But you didn't answer my question. Are you happy?"

"You might say I'm at a career crossroads too. Unlike you, I don't know what I'm passionate enough about to quit my teaching job. I came down here to think and reevaluate. I realize I have to get out of my comfort zone, reach out, force myself to grow—" She stopped herself and laughed. "I must be watching too much Oprah. Does that sound too Dr. Phil to you?"

He shook his head. "No, it sounds genuine. And smart."

The pie was gone. Their meal was over. Mike

looked down at the few remnants of crust on the silver tray in front of them. "I am totally stuffed. I feel like a horse who will just keep eating until it dies. The pizza was so good, if there were any more, I would have kept going until I burst."

"I'm glad you enjoyed it," she said.

Mike held on to Hildy's hand. He gave it a squeeze. "How about walking some of this off? Let's go down to the beach, get some fresh air, listen to the waves?" His eyes asked more than his words did.

Hildy felt torn between what she wanted to do and what was the smart thing to do. "I don't think it's a good idea, Mike—" she'd started to say, when she heard a faint but persistent tapping issuing from her tote bag. She pulled her hand loose from Mike's and scraped back her chair to cover the sound.

"Excuse me a second." She smiled brightly at Mike. "I need to get something from my bag." She ducked her head under the table and whispered urgently into her tote bag, "Stop that!"

A tiny voice rang out, "Don't go. He just wants to get in your pants."

"Mind your own business!" Hildy pretended she was clearing her throat as she answered the genie. She shoved the towel down hard on the bottle. "Now be quiet!" she warned through clenched teeth, rapping the bottle hard with her knuckles as she did.

The genie yelped loudly.

"You okay under there?" Mike's bewildered voice floated down from overhead.

"Pinched my finger!" Hildy called out and started to sit up, hitting her head on the underside of the table and rattling the plates. When she reappeared, her hair was mussed, and she clutched her wallet in her hand. She put it on the table.

Mike noticed what she had retrieved from the tote bag. "Oh no, Hildy. This was my treat."

"Huh? Oh, the wallet. I figured we were going dutch. This wasn't a date." She improvised as she went along.

"Don't be silly. I asked you to come with me. I won't let you pay a cent. But you didn't give me an answer. Will you give me a little more of your time and take a walk with me?"

"I don't think it's a good idea, Mike." It was a weak protest and he heard the indecision in her voice.

"It's a *great* idea. Come on, Hildy, we need the fresh air. I still haven't heard all about your life. We have so much more to say to each other. How about just a short walk? Fifteen minutes, then I'll take you home. We'll just talk. Promise."

It wasn't talk that Hildy feared—and it wasn't talk that she wanted. "Okay, fifteen minutes," she agreed and gave in.

Chapter 11

Once outside, Hildy told Mike she wanted to leave her tote bag in his car. He opened the car door, and she leaned in to put it on the floor in front of the passenger seat. The genie's muffled protests sounded like a staccato of little drum taps. Hildy ignored them. She'd deal with the genie and his broken oaths later. She made sure Mike locked the car.

Then she looked at Mike. He smiled. She smiled. He reached out and took her hand. Her heart beat wildly.

They hurried across the wide boulevard that ran the length of the island and walked down Thirtieth Street, which dead-ended at the dunes. There, a sandy path led over a high hill covered with spiky grass to the broad expanse of beach beyond. Hildy and Mike stopped and slipped off their shoes, leaving them on the asphalt. They began walking up the path in the pale moonlight.

The sand was cool under Hildy's feet. Pieces of clamshell and bits of scrub pinecones dug into her soft soles. She winced and stumbled a little. Mike let go of her hand and offered his arm for support. She held it tightly, and he pulled her along. After a few yards, they came to the crest where a bench sat for people to look out at the ocean. They passed it by and descended the far side to the deserted beach where the sand was lush and soft.

Enough light came from the houses facing the water for them to see to walk. It wasn't bright enough, however, for anyone who peered out of their windows to see the figures of Hildy and Mike as anything more than dim shadows. In front of the hand-holding couple, the sea stretched to the horizon in a wide expanse of inky black. The crashing waves left a serpentine line of white along the water's edge. The wind blew in off the sea. The air was cool. The surf roared and hissed. Hildy had never felt so happy, reveling in the beauty of the night and the thrill of being here with Mike.

They walked for a while in silence. Then Mike dropped Hildy's hand and put his arm around her, drawing her next to him. She in turn put her arm around his waist.

The silence continued. Neither of them spoke; in fact, not one word had been uttered by either of them. They skirted the foamy edge of the waves that slid up the sand with the incoming tide. Sometimes it caught them, washing over their toes. Hildy felt the wet, flat sand beneath her feet, the chill of the breeze on her bare arms, and the heat of Mike's body where they touched.

They kept walking, their bodies flush together, their strides in tandem. After a quarter of a mile or more, they stopped. Mike pulled Hildy into an embrace, lifting her against him, and lowering his face to hers. The kiss that Hildy had dreamed about for so many years became real at last.

Mike's lips were soft and searching. Their tongues entwined, their breaths quickened. They explored each other's mouths. They licked and nipped, kissed and sucked.

At first, Mike's hands cupped her head, his fingers entangled in her hair. But soon they moved down her back, finding the waist of her Tommy Hilfiger slacks, then sliding up under her cami. His fingers were warm on her skin. Everywhere they touched sent sensations coursing through her. She didn't protest as he stroked her bare back. She melted against him, reveling in his touch.

After a few minutes his fingers moved from her back around her waist to her belly, sending a flutter like butterfly wings through her. When his hands tentatively began to move upward, Mike broke his kiss and drew back, whispering, "Okay?"

Hildy nodded, and he cupped her breasts with his palms. He groaned and squeezed his eyes shut. His fingers teased her nipples taut, and she moaned too. Then he lifted up her cami and leaned down. Kissing and nipping at her left breast, he made her moan more and her legs began to quiver.

They were alone on the beach and alone in the universe. A silver sliver of crescent moon hung in the sky. A few stars were bright enough to penetrate the faint glow of the house lights. For Mike and Hildy, the world seemed empty of everything except each other.

Hildy sighed as Mike pulled his mouth away from her breast. Where his lips had been was moist, and the air caressed her bud with its cool touch. She shivered and swayed against him. He lifted her then and sank down on the sand, she in his arms. He sat her down on his lap, and she turned to him. She teasingly unbuttoned his shirt, running her fingers lightly over his ribs, making him jump. She wanted to feel his flesh, and then she needed it against hers.

She slipped his shirt over his shoulders and took it off. Then she moved so her breasts pressed against him. He folded his arms around her, lying down on his back, and pulling her on top of him.

They kept kissing and kissing. Hildy stopped thinking of anything but how long she had waited to feel
like this, how she used to feel like this in his arms,
and how she had never felt like this with anyone
else.

He kept saying her name over and over. She
could feel his hard member pressing against her
through their clothes. He slid his hand down her
body, finding her waistband, unbuttoning her pants,
and working his fingers down over her smooth back
and ass until they touched her there, where it was
wet and warm.

His fingers rubbed into the wetness. She gasped.
He went farther. She moaned. He moved his fingers back and forth, stroking between her legs.
She clung tightly to his neck, her face buried there,
no longer kissing him, just holding on tightly as
he did things she had let no other man do. She
twisted and moved, loving the feeling, wanting
even more.

Then Mike gently pulled his hand away. He sat
up, Hildy on his lap, and encircled her waist with
his hands to turn her so he could lay her down on
her back in the sand.

"Hildy, I want you," he whispered.

He worked her pants down off her hips, and she
let him pull them off her legs. She lay there in
her panties. She dimly saw him in the low light
unbuttoning his jeans and pulling out his member.
He leaned toward her. She felt the satin smooth-
ness of his shaft move along her leg.

"I want you so bad," Mike said.

And at that moment the clock of time stopped
and reversed. He had said those same words so
many years ago—only that time he wasn't saying it
to Hildy, he was saying it to Darla, the head
cheerleader.

Hildy's eyes flew open. "No!" she said, and sat up.

"What's wrong?" Mike asked, his voice hoarse, and misunderstanding her protest, added, "I have a condom."

"You . . . you . . . What! Did you bring one with you, planning this?" Fury drove Hildy to her feet.

Mike reached out and grabbed her arm, holding her, bringing her back to her knees in the sand. She turned toward him with anguished eyes. "Let me go."

He did. She jumped up. He scrambled up next to her and put his arms around her, preventing her escape. She began to cry.

"What's wrong? What's the matter?" He sounded as desperate as he felt.

"What am I doing?" Hildy cried out. "This is all wrong." She tried to pull away from his embrace.

Mike kept his arms around her, forcefully holding her still, her back against his bare chest. "Tell me what's going on, please!" His lips were next to her ear. His voice was urgent. "Tell me what's the matter!"

Hildy's eyes spilled over with tears. She looked out at the water. "Mike, why are you doing this to me? You're with someone else. You're marrying someone else. This is wrong. It was wrong then, it's wrong now."

He turned her around to face him. Their nearly naked bodies were pressed together. He put his forehead against hers, closing his eyes. He knew what she meant. "It's not wrong. It's not. You want me as much as I want you. Please, Hildy, please. I want you now. I always wanted you. Let me explain."

Hildy shook her head. "What can you explain, Mike? It's too late for us."

He pushed her hair from her face with his hands. He stroked her cheeks. "Hildy, what happened years ago in high school—listen to me—let me tell you the whole story. Let me apologize."

Hildy turned her face away; her voice was choked with emotion when she spoke. "It was just the same as now. You wanted what you wanted at the moment, without thinking about the consequences."

"I know, I'm so sorry. I ruined everything. But you never let me explain."

"Explain what, Mike? I was supposed to be away for a week with the debating club, but I got laryngitis. I came home that Friday night and tried to call you. Your mother said you were at a party over at George Ide's. I couldn't wait to see you, so I drove over there. And then—"

"I know. George saw you come in. You asked where I was. He said he didn't know, but he did. He tried to stop you from coming to get me after one of the junior varsity girls told you I was upstairs in George's room—"

"With Darla." Hildy turned her head away, her heart full of pain at the memory of opening the bedroom door and seeing Mike standing next to the bed with the naked girl pressed against him.

"I had a few beers, Hildy. It's no excuse. I know that. But she told me she needed to talk to me, that her boyfriend—Frank, you remember, the fullback—had left her. She started crying. All of a sudden, she didn't feel well. She thought she was going to pass out. She asked me to help her go upstairs to George's room so she could lie down. It was all an act, but I didn't know that. She had a bet with some of the other girls that she could get me to go all the way with her."

Hildy stiffened. She had refused to have sex with

Mike even though she knew most of the other cheerleaders slept with their boyfriends. She was the only holdout. She felt she wasn't ready for it. She wanted to wait, and they had argued about it.

Mike finally said he respected how she felt. He agreed not to pressure her. But he couldn't agree with Hildy's wanting to wait until their wedding night. That might not be until they finished college, four long years away.

So they had compromised. She and Mike had planned to get engaged in June, after they graduated. They agreed they'd consummate their relationship when they made that formal commitment to each other. Hildy thought it set a good precedent for the way they'd solve problems as a couple. She felt proud that they had been so mature about it. And for Hildy, waiting was a special promise they made to each other.

But Hildy had realized, in the instant when she opened the bedroom door, that Mike couldn't wait for sex—and that he obviously didn't love her enough to wait to have it with her. "And Darla succeeded, didn't she," Hildy said, her voice hard.

"No!" Mike took her by the shoulders. "She didn't. She took off her clothes and she was all over me. She unbuttoned my shirt and my jeans. I let her. I admit it. But I kept telling her no. I wouldn't cheat on you."

Hildy, her eyes brimming with tears, looked into Mike's face. "But I heard what you said to her. And you did cheat on me. You wanted somebody else, even if it was just for the moment."

"Hildy, no. I was trying to leave when she came on to me, rubbing her body against me. I did say to her 'I want you so bad,' but that wasn't everything I said. You didn't hear it all. I had already said it out loud, not just once, but over and over. 'I want you so bad—*but this is wrong. I love Hildy.*' Then I turned my head and saw you at the door. I didn't have sex with Darla. I swear to you.

"I saw the hurt on your face. You turned and ran. I grabbed my clothes and got dressed. I felt terrible. I drove all over Lehman, Idetown, and Dallas trying to find you. To make sure you were okay, to apologize. To beg you to forgive me.

"I kept going by your house, but your car wasn't there. Finally I knocked on the door. Your sister looked daggers at me and said you had gone away. She wouldn't tell me where."

"I told her not to tell you, Mike," Hildy said, her head still turned away from his. "I didn't want to see you. I was devastated. My heart was broken."

"Hildy, I thought I'd go crazy. I called everyone we knew. I called your house a hundred times. You didn't come to school. I was sick with grief. Then two weeks later you showed up in class and wouldn't even look at me, wouldn't talk to me or let me explain. So I figured that's how it was. You didn't really love me or you'd at least let me tell you my side of it."

"I was only a kid, Mike," Hildy whispered. "I told you I wanted to wait. It was important to me. I know other girls did it, but it wasn't how I was raised. We had discussed it so many times, so you knew . . ."

"Yes, yes, I did. I respected you for it. I've always been sorry for going up there with Darla. But I didn't go there with the intention of having sex with her. She did try to seduce me, and I was tempted. I admit it. But I didn't do it. I've always wanted to tell you I was sorry." His strong hand cupped her chin and turned her face to his. "I am sorry, Hildy. I'm sorry for what I did that day and

I'm sorry you stopped loving me because of it. I'm sorry for ruining everything."

Tears ran down Hildy's face. "I never stopped loving you, Mike. And now it's too late."

"Hildy, why does it have to be too late? Why? We're not kids anymore."

Hildy pushed away from Mike. She was upset. She was angry. She was hurt. She leaned down and picked up her pants from the sand. "It's too late because you're marrying someone else," she said, thinking, *How can he be so stupid?*

A terrible feeling of desperation washed over Mike. He moved toward her and encircled her with his arms. "No, I can't lose you again. I can't. I'll end it with Kiki, I promise you. I don't love her, Hildy. It's you. It's always been you."

Then he was kissing her and she was kissing him. Their mouths merged, his tongue exploring hers. He broke the kiss suddenly, taking her face in his hands. "Do you want me, Hildy? Do you? If you do, show me, please."

Her hands moved to his jeans. They were still open and unzipped. Her small fingers reached inside, gripping his hard shaft. She was trembling, frightened but excited. Did she want him? More than anything in the world. She knew what she wanted to do.

She knelt in front of him and did what she had fantasized about doing with him, but had never done with any other man. She put her lips around the head of his member and took him into her mouth.

His hands found the back of her head. His knees were shaking. "Oh, Hildy," he groaned. "Oh, my Hildy."

She teased him and tantalized him with her tongue. She sucked and stroked. It felt heavenly, but Mike's groans made it clear he couldn't wait much longer. He gently pushed her back away from him. He lowered himself beside her. He again lay her down on her back in the sand, kissing her face, her nose, her lips. Then tenderly he pulled her cami over her head. He gently moved her panties down off her hips. Her naked flesh looked like ivory against the dark sand.

Mike slipped his own jeans down and took them off. He put his hand between her legs and widened her thighs. "Hildy, do you want me to do this?" he asked in a soft voice.

Hildy was twenty-eight years old now, not eighteen. She had waited all these years for the right man. She knew Mike was that man. Her heart was beating so fast she could barely breathe. She had never wanted anything, anyone so much. She opened her legs wide in response to his question. She gripped his hand and pushed it against her wetness.

"Yes, Mike," she whispered. "I want this."

He knelt between her legs and put on the condom that had been in his jeans pocket and was now in his hand. Then Hildy felt the tip of his member touch her there in the dark center of her being. She cried out in fear and expectation.

With one hard thrust, he pushed inside her and suddenly it was his turn to cry out. He felt the barrier still intact within her. He understood that he was her first. "Oh!" he yelled, then the *Oh* became a groan as the barrier broke.

Hildy gripped his shoulders. Mike buried himself within her. Whatever pain she felt vanished as, matching the rhythm of the waves, they began to move in the eternal ride of love. She was nearly delirious with the sensations. She mewed like a kitten and then as the most wonderful feeling began low down in her belly and rushed like lightning upward, she called out, "Yes! Yes!"

The night sky exploded in a rush of shooting stars.

Chapter 12

Pleasure has a price, and since it was Hildy's first time, the aftermath of this romantic interlude was just plain messy. Hildy overcame her embarrassment and told Mike she'd have to wait until he got some tissues before she left the beach.

Mike was full of reassurances and concern. He hurried off to get the car from the Dark Star Café's parking lot and drive it back as close as possible to the area of the beach where Hildy waited. He quickly discovered they had walked all the way from Thirtieth Street down to the next town of Brant Beach. He broke into a jog, a little worried about leaving Hildy alone.

But Hildy relished the time sitting on the sand by herself. She looked out at the darkness of the ocean, listened to the crashing surf, and thought about what had just occurred. She realized that Mike had a lot to get straight before any kind of serious relationship between them could truly happen. He still had other commitments and perhaps in the heat of the moment he made promises he'd regret in the light of day.

She'd be sorry if he did, but she wouldn't be entirely surprised.

She wasn't sorry about the consummation though. She smiled, a bittersweet but genuine smile. She had always wanted her first time to be with Mike, and against all odds it had been. *You can't escape your fate,* she thought. This could have occurred ten years ago, and didn't. Instead it happened when she could cope better emotionally with the intensity and the intimacy. She could even accept the love-making as a onetime thing, and that was okay.

No, it really wasn't okay, but she felt certain she could handle whatever happened, even if Mike and she went different ways.

She put her forehead on her knees. She could handle the hurt and disappointment, but would she ever get over it? She hadn't gotten Mike out of her thoughts or her heart in ten years. Now he was entrenched in both more deeply and more power-fully than ever.

But why was she contemplating letting him go before she even had him? She remembered what her sister said. *Fight for your man.* Okay, she'd take Kiki on, and may the best woman win.

When Hildy finally got back to the sleek, silver Mercedes, her tote bag stayed silent, much to her relief. Mike leaned across the center console and kissed her cheek before beginning the drive back to her summer rental. She noticed the time on the dashboard clock because Mike was looking at it so often. It was nearly midnight. The hours they had been together had flown by.

When the car pulled up in front of the house, Mike kissed her again. He made sure he had her cell phone number logged into his phone. He got out of his seat and came around the car to help her out. He walked her the few steps to her front door where she fumbled in her tote for the key, her fingers brushing the cool glass of the genie's bottle.

She stood there holding her keys as Mike leaned down to give her one last kiss. She had just begun to close her eyes when she detected something moving in her peripheral vision.

"Hey!" Mike yelled as a husky man wearing a ski mask grabbed him from behind and dragged him backward. Another man, his face hidden behind a mask as well, snatched at Hildy's tote bag. She held on to it like a bulldog. As he tugged, she started screaming at the top of her lungs, "FIRE FIRE FIRE CALL 911 FIRE FIRE FIRE CALL 911!"

The man threw a punch at her face. Hildy saw it coming and dropped to the ground, letting the fist sail harmlessly over her head. She landed hard on her butt in a sitting position. Without hesitating, she sank her teeth into the part of the man that was right in front of her, which happened to his crotch. He let out a scream that could be heard all the way to the Long Beach Island town of Love-ladies.

As she released her bite, she brought her elbow up into his kneecap while she grasped his ankle with the other hand and pulled forward. Her attacker went down hard on the bricks of her little front yard.

Hildy scrambled to her feet. She sensed rather than saw a fight going on behind her between Mike and the other assailant. Just then she saw four or five teenagers who were hanging out on the boulevard come running to help. An emergency siren wailed in the distance.

Her attacker got to his feet and ran off down the block toward the bay. The man fighting with Mike broke free as well. The teens, whooping and hollering, started chasing the two assailants. A police car careened around the corner and screeched to a halt. A big red fire engine pulled up right behind it.

The bottle was safe, at least for now.

*   *   *

Another half hour had gone by before the two Ship Bottom police officers finished taking Hildy's and Mike's statements about the attempted "purse snatching." Since this kind of street crime rarely happened in the quiet shore community, they asked Hildy and Mike over and over if they knew their attackers.

They both insisted they didn't, with Hildy mentally crossing her fingers at the fib. She didn't know the men but she felt certain they had been sent by Jimmy the Bug. The police finally concluded that it was a crime of opportunity: The muggers saw Mike's expensive car and targeted them.

Mike felt uneasy about leaving Hildy alone after the attack, but she insisted she was fine. He saw her into the little house, kissed her quickly and said he'd call her in the morning. Her unspoken question was, Where was Mike going? Back to the hotel room he shared with Kiki? If he was, would he sleep next to his fiancée in the same bed?

Her feelings must have shown in her face, because as he left, he said, "Don't worry, Hildy. I'll end it with Kiki—and I'll get a different hotel room tonight."

She nodded, wondering if things were going to be as easy as Mike seemed to think they would be. She also wondered what she was going to do about the genie and Jimmy the Bug. It had not been a random attack and she knew the thugs, or ones like them, would be back.

Hildy peered out the window to be sure Mike had pulled away in the Mercedes before she went to the tote and removed the genie's bottle. She quickly pulled out the cork and waited. Nothing.

She held the bottle up to the light. She could see the small figure of Tony G. inside. He was seated with his back to her. He definitely seemed to be pouting. Hildy put her lips close to the neck of the bottle. "Come out here at once."

A serpentine column of gray smoke slowly snaked out of the top of the bottle. Then Tony G. appeared and stood before Hildy, his face stern.

His mouth set in hard lines, his sinewy muscles tense, his manners gone, the genie spoke in a voice loud and accusatory. "I suspected you were a woman who didn't listen. Now you have proved it."

Hildy matched him in tone and velocity. "*I* don't listen! You gave me your word you wouldn't eavesdrop. Your word! You didn't keep it. I am outraged. I am appalled. I am . . . I am . . ."

"Wrong."

"Wrong? Are you out of your mind?" Hildy's hands were on her hips.

"Yes, wrong. I gave you my word not to listen or watch *unless you needed me to.* You clearly needed me to intervene, so I did. Not that it helped." Tony G. jutted out his chin, not giving an inch.

"What you do mean, I needed you to? Are you delusional? I most certainly did not need you."

"Hurrumph. The proof is in the pudding. You had sex with him."

"What? How dare you. What happened or didn't happen between Mike and me is none of your business. *None* of your business."

A vein throbbed on Tony G.'s temple. His voice became a bark. "*You* are my business. I am dependent on you. And you, you are an innocent. A babe in the woods. What you know about sex would fit on the head of a pin. And quite frankly, sex is something I *do* know about."

"Oh yeah?" Hildy really didn't have a good comeback since Tony G. was probably right.

"Oh yeah! Having sex with that fellow was the dumbest move you could have made."

The arrow hit home. Hildy did her best not to react. She had her own misgivings, but at the time, she did just what she wanted to do, and, at the time, she was glad. However, she wasn't conceding anything to Tony G. "I am not calculating or scheming! What happened with Mike wasn't a 'move.' Anyway, I don't think it was a dumb thing to do."

"I do! Didn't you ever hear the expression 'Why buy the cow when you can get the milk for free'?"

"You are totally offensive, do you know that?" A blush had stolen up Hildy's neck and she could feel her cheeks burning.

"Offensive or not, it's the truth. What did you have going for you?. What leverage did you have in this relationship? *You're the one that got away.* Now he's landed you, hook, line and sinker. You gave up your ace in the hole."

"What?"

"Okay, that came out all wrong. But you lost your major advantage."

Hildy wanted to believe that sex and love, in this case, were one and the same. She wanted to believe Mike had rediscovered his long lost passion for her. She wanted to think that in an hour or so, when he got back to Atlantic City, he'd be giving Kiki the bad news, that their engagement had ended. But she had this niggling doubt wriggling around in her brain that it was entirely possible that the genie was right.

Her feelings must have shown on her face because Tony G. said, "You aren't going to start the waterworks going, are you?"

Hildy looked up at Tony G. with tear-filled eyes. It was hard to remember he wasn't real, or at least wasn't human. She could see him breathing. She could see a light sheen of perspiration on his brow. She could smell the patchouli scent he wore.

"I'm okay." Hildy tried to smile, but her upper

lip began trembling. Exhaustion had suddenly overtaken her. Her emotions, fragile as glass, were in danger of shattering. Now, to top off the evening, a genie had told her that she had thrown away her best chance of making a go of it with Mike.

If she looked at the situation from an outsider's perspective, she had quickly surrendered to Mike's desire. He got immediate gratification, or at least had his curiosity satisfied. Why would he feel compelled to see her again? The hunt was over, the quarry taken.

"I guess you're right." She sighed and the sigh turned into a sob.

"Ah Hades." Tony G. reached out and pulled Hildy into a brotherly hug. He produced a tissue out of thin air and put it in her hand. "Look, mistre— I mean Ms. Caldwell, you're forgetting you still have an advantage left, and it's an unbeatable one."

Hildy blew her nose loudly. "What is it?" she asked in a trembling voice.

"Me."

Meanwhile, a full moon had risen over the Jersey shore, the weather pattern shifted from the northeast to the south, a Bermuda High blew in from the steamy Caribbean, the ocean churned white with the quickening breeze, and emotions in places other than the small gray cottage in Ship Bottom broke free to do mischief.

In his palatial summer home in Ocean City, Jimmy the Bug was busy smashing every plate he could grab from his kitchen. He would have wrung Sal's and Joey's necks if they had been stupid enough to get close to him. They weren't that dumb. While they weren't rocket scientists, they had enough smarts to call Puggy on his cell phone and tell him to make sure no firearms were within easy reach before they walked in with the bad news.

The news was worse than bad, they had to admit. Yeah, they told their boss, they had found the girl. No, they didn't have the bottle. They tried to explain how they had driven up to Ship Bottom just like Jimmy told them to, the minute he got the call from the Scranton guy.

They had hidden in the shadows, waiting for her to return, ready for a quick snatch of her bag. But at the last possible minute things went to hell. A whole gang of crazy teens—twenty or thirty young toughs, they insisted—appeared out of nowhere and attacked them. Otherwise, they would have had the bottle. Sal had his hands on it, honest to God. And despite the long odds against them and poor Joey getting bitten in the cojones, they fought like tigers and didn't run, at least they didn't run before the cops showed up. They had to take off then, now didn't they?

And no, they couldn't hang around for a second attempt because the Ship Bottom police were now cruising up and down the local streets looking for them. But on the positive side, they knew where this chick lived. Tomorrow, Puggy could take some firepower with him, and bang, she's dead. The bottle's theirs. She's a woman, there all alone. Who's going to stop them?

Jimmy the Bug's face went from fish belly white to puce as he picked up a tall water glass and winged it at Sal, who ducked behind a chaise lounge. "You morons!" he bellowed. "Who's gonna stop us?"

Then he grabbed a soup bowl and let it fly at Joey, who covered his head with his hands. A set of eight dinner plates followed like china Frisbees.

"You mental midgets!" he screamed. "She knows we're after her now. And who's gonna stop us? Don't you idiots have half a brain between you?"

He took aim with a salt and pepper set, then followed that with a sugar bowl and creamer. Smash, crash, broken shards rolled over the floor. "Who's gonna stop us? The goddamned genie, that's who!"

With his rage finally sated by smashed pottery, Jimmy the Bug sat in the lanai sipping a single malt scotch. He drank slowly. He stared out across the dark beach at the wind-whipped sea. He intended to get the genie back, but sending imbeciles after the bottle could only fail. He had to think this out. He needed a plan to get the girl to give up the bottle. Everybody had a price. Everybody had a weak spot. He intended to learn everything he could about this Hildy Caldwell. Then he'd know hers.

Pottery took to the air in the Trump Plaza too.

Mike returned to the suite he shared with Kiki around two thirty in the morning. If Mike had been a luckier man, she would have still been at the rock concert or having a late-night drink. She would never have known he left. And if he had been a wiser man, he wouldn't have entered the room with a big grin on his face.

"Where the hell have you been!" Kiki stood in the center of the hall, dressed in her sexy party clothes, her face not the least bit attractive when it was distorted by rage.

Mike's smile evaporated. "Ummm, out," he answered, having no quick comeback available.

"You turned your cell phone off!" She flung her accusation at him with the speed of a fastball pitch.

Mike felt confused. This wasn't quite the calm, serious talk about ending their relationship that he had planned. He had meant what he said to Hildy. He would end it with his longtime fiancée. He didn't know if he loved Hildy, but he felt maybe he could. And even if he didn't, he knew he didn't love Kiki anymore. He stood in the doorway looking perplexed. "Ummmm, yeah," he said. "I did."

"Who were you with?" Kiki had no doubts another woman was involved in Mike's evening. When a significant other of the male gender turns off his cell phone, two general reasons cover every specific situation: He's doing something he swore he wouldn't—or he's cheating.

"I went to talk. With an old friend. That girl you met on the beach today. That's all," Mike stuttered.

Kiki picked up a heavy ceramic lamp from the hall credenza with both hands and let it fly with deadly accuracy at him. He dove for the floor. It crashed into the doorjamb. The lightbulb exploded into a shower of glass shards.

"You bastard!" she shrieked. "I can smell sex on you." Then she strode over to where Mike lay on the carpet, looking up at her.

"Now you listen to me, Michael Amante. I don't care if you were with this pathetic little country mouse you knew in high school. I do care that I get what you owe me from this relationship. And after five years, Michael, you owe me a lot, and if you have any idea about calling off our engagement, I want you to know, I intend to collect every last dime."

"Ah, sure, of course." Mike nodded. Relief spilled over him. She was only worried about their stuff. Maybe the breakup wouldn't be so bad after all. "We'll split things fifty-fifty, or sixty-forty, I want to be fair."

Then Kiki's perfect face crumbled. "That's fair? Are you serious? If this comes out, I'll be humiliated. How could you do this to me?" she wailed.

She sank down on the floor next to Mike. He could smell her expensive perfume. Her smooth bare arm deliberately brushed his. She turned her huge brown eyes toward him. "After all the time we've been together. Oh, Michael!" she whimpered, not all that convincingly. "Michael, you can't go, not now."

Reluctantly Mike sat up and put his arm around Kiki's slender shoulders. "It will be for the best. You'll see."

Kiki buried her face against his chest, muffling her voice. She made her breath catch in her throat and let out a little moan. "You can't leave me, Michael. Not now," she repeated.

Guilt clutched its bony hand around Mike's heart. "Aw, Kiki, don't start crying."

Kiki made more noises in her throat, her breath catching in little hiccups. "Michael, please. You can't leave, because—because—I bought the prettiest wedding dress. A Donna Karan original. The picture is going to be on Page Six of the *New York Post*. Tomorrow. It was going to be a surprise. Oh, Michael!" she wailed.

Mike felt sick. What kind of a guy was he? He just took the virginity of the sweetest girl in the world—while he was formally engaged to a woman who depended on him to marry her. He felt trapped, panicky really.

"Look, Kiki," he said at last. "Don't get yourself all upset. We'll talk about this in the morning. Why don't you go on to bed. I'm going to sit up and watch TV for a while."

Kiki lifted her head, her long dark hair spilling like silk rain down her back. Tears like diamonds glittered on her eyelashes. She wiped them away with her fingers, no longer whimpering or even seemingly very upset. She kissed him on the nose, gripped his shoulders, her red nail polish very bright against his T-shirt.

She spoke to him as if he were a schoolboy. "Oh, Michael, you were very naughty, weren't you? I guess a man has to have a fling every now and then. It's how men are, no? I forgive you. There's nothing to talk about. I'm just going to forget this night ever happened, and you need to too. After all, my wedding dress will be in the paper tomorrow.

"And you know what else, Michael? I also told Liz Smith we set a date. I was so excited about the dress, and a September wedding sounded so lovely. I just couldn't resist telling her that she could announce the news in her column. September seventh is our day. Donald, that dear dear man, said he'd cater it all for us here in the Plaza."

Mike felt as if he had just been given a sentence by a hanging judge.

Kiki stood up and walked to the bedroom, turning as she got to the door. "But yes, you should sleep on the sofa tonight. Naughty boys do need to be punished, at least a little."

Michael thought his head was going to explode. He couldn't think straight. He settled himself in an easy chair and turned on HBO. A *Sopranos* rerun was playing. Mike didn't really notice. He was thinking that he couldn't deal with Kiki and the wedding. It was easier to push it out of his mind and focus on getting his new business going. He needed to talk to Jake Truesdale as soon as possible.

Then he thought about Hildy; he never meant to hurt her and now he was afraid he was going to break her heart.

Chapter 13

"It's another great morning on Long Beach Island!" The hearty, upbeat voice of Sonny Somers, the weather guy, issued from the radio next to Hildy's bed. The alarm had gone off at exactly seven a.m. Hildy stirred from sleep and put her pillow over her head.

Sonny's weather report penetrated through the goose down. "We've got the three Hs—hazy, hot, and humid. The Bermuda High I was telling you about—the one that had been sitting around eight hundred miles due east of Charleston, South Carolina—has moved in and intends to stick around for the rest of the week.

"Enjoy the sunshine. Expect temperatures of eighty-five to ninety by this afternoon with near one hundred percent humidity. A perfect day to get out your swimsuits and spend time at the beach.

"But bad news for you nine-to-fivers. Watch for rain this weekend. We have a tropical depression out in the Atlantic heading west. It could turn into Angie, the first hurricane of the season."

Linda Sue, the drive-time host, broke in, her chirpy voice darkened by alarm. "A hurricane! Sonny, is that something we need to worry about?"

Sonny Somers laughed. "No worry at all. The last major hurricane to hit New Jersey was the legendary Long Island Express of 1938, a borderline category four storm, hundred-mile-an-hour winds, and the fastest-moving hurricane on record. That's when the bridge to Brigantine collapsed. But even the worst hurricanes after that have only brought some heavy rain and beach erosion."

"Okay, Sonny, that's a big relief. So we're not in the line of fire, then?"

"This potential hurricane is sitting east of the Dominican Republic, a thousand miles away. It's those Floridians who need to keep on their toes. I'll keep you all posted."

"And that's it from Sonny Somers," Linda warbled. "Now let's go to Rusty Fender with today's traffic—"

Hildy managed to slap the OFF button on the clock radio, groaned, and sat up in the bed that was tucked under the eaves in the cozy sleeping loft of the cottage. Cozy? Hildy kicked off the covers. It was stifling up here. Even the cats, who had snuggled up next to her when she fell asleep, had sought a cooler location.

Two thoughts burned through Hildy's brain at lightning speed. She needed her coffee—and she needed it now.

Barefooted, her hair matted, her body covered by another of her well-worn Penn State T-shirts, Hildy descended the pull-down ladder into the living room. With her eyes barely open enough to see, she headed toward the smell of fresh brewed coffee which beckoned her thither.

She entered the kitchen. A masculine hand extended toward her with a steaming coffee mug.

"Ovid once wrote, 'A morning without coffee is like sleep,' " a man's voice said.

Hildy looked up in surprise and took the cup. "Ovid said no such thing." She shielded her eyes from the brightness of the blue-sky morning that streamed through the windows. She beheld the six foot four inch genie who had evidently come to stay.

Hildy had no desire for company of any kind. She managed to turn a sour look in the genie's direction. "I'm not used to having a roommate, especially one of the male gender. Why are you roaming around? Aren't you supposed to be in your bottle or something?"

"You didn't order me to return, nor did you replace the stopper. I was on sentry duty all night. I didn't think Jimmy the Bug's men would return, but I kept watch." He turned sad blue eyes in her direction. "I thought you'd be pleased, Ms. Caldwell. I fixed the coffee 'light and sweet,' just as you prefer."

"Great, thanks. Look, Tony, I like some time to myself in the mornings. I'm not sociable first thing. I don't converse with anybody before eight a.m., so give me a couple of minutes alone, okay?"

"Your wish is my command, Ms. Caldwell," Tony said with just the slightest trace of sarcasm.

"Stop talking like that," Hildy griped. Through bleary eyes, she noticed the cats' dish had been filled, the kitty litter was fresh, the windowpanes sparkled, the linoleum shone, and the kitchen was spotless. All that gleaming made it entirely too bright in there. She took her hot coffee into the little dining room where she sank down on a chrome and plastic-covered chair. This room too had been thoroughly cleaned.

"I thought you were a big tough Roman warrior, not a Merry Maid," she grumbled, realizing she should be grateful instead of feeling as if Tony G. had made a clearly uncomplimentary statement about her housekeeping skills. Her sister would be thrilled, she supposed.

With uncanny serendipity, Hildy's cell phone rang. She found her tote and extracted the phone, noticing it was the sister in question calling her at this ungodly hour.

"What's the matter?" Hildy said worriedly instead of saying hello.

"Now why would you think anything's the matter?" Corrine snapped back at her, clearly annoyed.

"You don't ever call this early. And you always get short-tempered when you're upset. Something's got to be wrong. So talk." Hildy's anxiety rose like a dark beast.

"Can you buy the *New York Post* in those news machines up at the corner?" Corrine said.

"The *Post*, the *Daily News*, the *Times* . . . Sure, why?"

"Go buy it, turn to Page Six, then call me back." Corrine hung up.

"That bastard!" Hildy shrieked as she stared at the photo of the wedding gown captioned, "A Donna Karan original for celebrity photog Kiki's September 7 nuptials to real estate magnate Michael Amante."

Tony G. peeked over her shoulder at the newspaper. "I hate to say it but—"

Hildy turned on the genie. "Don't you dare say 'I told you so.' Don't you dare!"

Tony G. retreated quickly to safer ground on the far side of the kitchen. He held up his hand in a placating way. "If I may make a comment?"

"What!" Hildy glared at him.

"The paper no doubt went to press before your . . . your . . . assignation last evening. Perhaps the situation has changed."

"Don't you dare make excuses for him! He had no right . . . no right . . . to sleep with me when . . .

when . . . he knew . . . he knew . . ." Hildy's throat closed up. "He knew I'd see this," she finished in a tiny voice.

"Indeed, but even when the spirit is willing, the flesh is weak," Tony G. said.

"I told you *not* to make excuses for him," she said, and stamped a bare foot.

"Okay, men are little better than hound dogs. I belong to a brutish, bestial gender. We have no scruples when it comes to getting some nookie."

"You can say that again," Hildy grumped.

"Okay, men are little better than—"

"Stop it! I wasn't being literal about that. But I'm going to kill him! I'm going to literally kill him. Where does he get off waltzing back into my life and playing with my emotions! Who does he think he is!" She started pacing back and forth between the sunroom and the kitchen.

Tony G. turned his head and stifled a smile. This Hildy Caldwell was a hellion when enraged. He felt sorry for Michael Amante, sort of.

Just then Hildy's cell phone rang. She figured it was Corrine. She snatched it off the table, about to flip it open. Hard muscular fingers closed around her hand.

"Don't answer that," the genie ordered.

"Why?" Hildy's puzzlement showed on her face.

"It's him."

"Mike? Really? Well, I want to talk to him." She tried to wrestle the phone away.

The genie didn't release his grip. "No. He must not know that you are willing to speak with him. Ms. Caldwell, think. Why is he calling? To apologize? To explain? To make excuses? To ease his guilty conscience? Or do you think it's to declare his undying love?"

"I don't know why he's calling, now do I?"

Steam could have come out of her ears she was so annoyed.

The ringing stopped.

"He'll call back. Believe me, he will call back. Let him stew. Let him worry. Let him think he's lost you. You need to play your cards right this time, *if* you still want him. Do you?"

Hildy stared into the genie's face. He stared back. She thought, *Do I still want Michael Amante?* Her heart said, *Yes*; her head said, *Hell, no.* "I'm not sure," she finally answered. "It depends—"

"That's absolutely right, Ms. Caldwell. It does 'depend.' It depends on the depth of his feelings for you. It depends on what he is willing to do to put things right between you. It depends on whether or not he breaks his engagement. Am I right?"

"Yes, you are," Hildy agreed.

"Then you cannot, you must not answer his calls and you absolutely must not call him back. Agreed?"

Hildy thought for a minute. "Yes. But I feel it would be a mistake to do nothing and just leave the field wide open for this Kiki person to steamroll ahead with the wedding plans."

"Ah, Ms. Caldwell, I was not suggesting retreat. I was about to propose a plan of attack. Would you like to hear it?"

"I most certainly would, but can you hold the thought for five minutes? If I don't call Corrine back, she will get in her car and drive down here."

The phone was ringing again. Hildy looked at the screen. It was Michael. She waited until it stopped, then hit the speed dial number marked SIS.

The first thing Hildy did was assure her worried sibling that she was not going to drown herself in the ocean. She explained that she was in a holding pattern with a wait-and-see attitude. She mentioned that Mike had just tried to call her, but she didn't want to answer, not just yet.

At that point a meaningful silence stopped the conversation. When Corrine spoke again, her voice was heavy with suspicion. "And why was he ringing you at that phone number? His mother called me this morning. I was pretty surprised about that, let me tell you. She was pretty clear that Mike had been calling everyone to find out how to contact you, but he never did get the number of your cell phone."

"Mike's mother called *you*? This morning? Why?"

"She called *me*—after phoning the church secretary who referred her to Father John who turned her over to Annie who handled the bus reservations for St. Vlad's. Annie had my number on the bus list and gave it to her. The poor woman was nearly hysterical. Mike phoned her right after dawn to break the news about the wedding day. He didn't want her to learn about it from the newspaper or from somebody else who saw the *Post* first.

"In any event, Mike's mother pleaded with me to contact you. She said her son is, and I quote, 'about to make the worst mistake of his life.' Then she said, and I will quote this as well because I never heard Mrs. Amante say a bad word about anybody before, 'That woman is a heartless bitch and she will destroy him.' "

"No kidding? Mrs. Amante said *that*? I can't believe it."

"I'm not done. Then she said, in so many words, that Mike has been carrying a torch for you for years. If there was any chance that you still cared about him, to please do something to stop this wedding. I said I thought there might be an outside chance you did still care. Then she started crying, 'Thank God! Thank God!' and made me promise to call you. She's afraid to meddle herself. She's afraid if she makes him choose between her and Kiki, she'll lose her son. So I'm calling you."

"Holy cow. That's intense." Hildy didn't know what else to say.

"Intense! It's tragic, that's what it is. So what are you going to do— wait a minute. You didn't answer my question. How did Mike get your number? Did you call him even after you promised not to?"

"No, not exactly."

"What *exactly*?" Corrine used that big-sister tone that worked better than truth serum on Hildy.

"I saw him. He showed up on my doorstep last night."

"He did! Why didn't you say so? Why didn't you call me and tell me?"

"Oh, I would have, I really would. But I came back here late and things had gotten . . . ummm . . . things got complicated."

"Complicated? How complicated?"

"Ummmm, we sort of, you know, did *it*."

"Oh. My. God. Then you see that wedding dress in the paper. You must be devastated. I'm going to kill him. I'm coming down there. If I leave right now I can be there by noon."

"No! Really, it's not necessary for you to drive back down here today. I'm fine. I'm thinking about what to do. I'll call you if I need you, I promise. Let me figure this out first, okay?"

Silence filled the line. Finally Corrine's voice came through the phone, loud and clear. "Hildy, you are all that matters to me. I don't want you getting your heart broken. To hell with Mike Amante. If he doesn't want the nicest, cutest, smartest girl in the world, to hell with him."

Hildy's voice sounded stronger and more confident than she felt when she answered, "Corrine, don't worry. I think he loves me. He just doesn't know it yet."

*   *   *

"You have a powerful ally in his mother," the genie observed after Hildy hung up. He had been shamelessly eavesdropping again. "You now have the superior force to carry out our battle plan."

"You mean with my sister, his mother, and you on my side? How can I possibly lose?" Each word was weighted with irony.

The genie nodded. Her sarcasm was lost on him. She decided to be direct. "Look, Tony, I don't believe you can make somebody love you no matter who is on your team or how brilliant a plan you concoct. I don't think love works like that."

"How old are you?" Tony G. demanded.

"Twenty-seven."

"And you think you know about love?" His hand rested on the hilt of his sword. He put one sandaled foot atop the seat of a chair. He looked as if he was about to give a speech. He was. "I've been on this earth for two millennia, Ms. Caldwell, and one thing hasn't changed. Love between men and women is an illusion. Men desire what seems out of their grasp. They long for that which other men admire.

"If I may wax poetic: A man aspires to be the hunter who finally captures the fabled snow leopard that few have approached and none have been able to trap. Is it love that drives him to face the treacherous peaks and murderous cold in pursuit of the leopard? No, Ms. Caldwell, it is not. It is ambition, passion, obsession, but not love. And the greater the obstacles, the more elusive his quarry, the more he cherishes the prize he obtains.

"You, Ms. Caldwell, must be Michael Amante's snow leopard."

Hildy did listen to the genie's soliloquy carefully. Despite her conviction that love cannot be forced, perhaps it could be coaxed along. The genie had a point. She conceded the round to Tony G.

"I think we must agree to disagree about the nature of love. But you're right about my needing to think before I act. I have to help Mike realize he loves me and see this Kiki for the selfish, self-centered witch she is. What happened between Mike and me last night wasn't lust."

The genie rolled his eyes at that.

Hildy saw him do it, as she had seen a thousand high school students roll their eyes when she announced something like, *Today we will begin our study of Shakespeare's* Macbeth. *I know you're all going to enjoy it.*

This time she reacted, something she never did in class. She snapped at Tony, "That's very rude, you know. Mike cares for me, I really believe that. But I am afraid he will go through with the wedding because he gave his word. That's how Mike is. That's why I would like to hear your plan."

Tony G. shook his head. "Why not do this the easy way? Just wish that Michael Amante loves you and cannot live without you. Make another wish that he sees Kiki as a repellent, hideous succubus that he must escape at all costs."

"No, I told you that before. Mike's love for me must be his own choice. Otherwise it doesn't mean anything, you know?"

"You're a romantic, Ms. Caldwell. Despite that, here's what I think we have to do." Tony set out his plan which, while neither brilliant nor complex, showed an astute understanding of human nature. After listening carefully, Hildy thought it might work and agreed to give it a try.

"Now," she said, when they had finished discussing Mike and her, "we need to address the six-hundred-pound gorilla in the living room: What am I going to do with you? I don't want to keep you.

No offense, but I'm not cut out to have a genie for a roommate. But as I promised, I won't return you to that disgusting criminal. What do you suggest?"

Tony G. shook his head sadly. "There is no easy answer. To get rid of me—and how it pains me to hear you say that you want to—you can make three wishes and I'll be gone. That's the traditional way. Or you can unintentionally lose the bottle as did Jimmy the Bug."

"Can't I just give you away?" Hildy asked.

Tony G.'s face fell like a collapsed balloon. "No, no, don't even consider such a thing. Think of the responsibility you would be taking on, Ms. Caldwell, should you give me and my powers to another person. Wishes are tricky things. Wouldn't you be at fault if a wish ended up backfiring for the recipient of your largesse? How would you feel if someone foolishly wished to live forever, but forgot to wish she would not keep aging? How would you feel if a person wished for a billion dollars and landed in prison because he couldn't prove a source for the income? I do not believe that giving a genie away has ever happened, and I am not sure it's possible."

Tony G. paused in his speech and looked at Hildy like a disapproving schoolteacher. "Genies are not puppy dogs or Christmas presents. Fate brought me to you. Fate, Ms. Caldwell. You can fight it. You can accept it. You can welcome it. But you can't give it away."

Chapter 14

Slipping out of the Trump Plaza and stepping onto the Atlantic City boardwalk later that same morning, Mike took a deep breath of the salt-laden air. He had on his running shorts and his Nikes, ready to do a couple of miles. The sun hurt his eyes. He winced. He put on a pair of sunglasses.

In the bright light of day, Mike Amante's troubles did not look any better. If anything, they looked even worse. In addition, he had a splitting headache and other pains he couldn't identify. They seemed to be originating in the left side of his chest. He figured it was indigestion. He had eaten a whole roll of Tums. Nothing helped. Maybe he was having a heart attack.

He had called Hildy a dozen times. She had not returned one of his calls. She must be deeply angry at him, and he couldn't blame her. She'd probably never forgive him for what happened last night. She was such a great kid. He had discovered he still had intense feelings for her. But the more he thought about it, the more she seemed to belong in his past. They lived in different worlds. Who knew if they could have made a go of a relationship? He couldn't even think about what might have been. He knew it was too late.

His guilt was killing him, that was the problem.

Kiki had been amazingly understanding, more than he would have been if the tables were turned. He had been with Kiki for what, five years? She had always been true to him. She was right, he did owe her a lot. What could he do at this point anyway? The wedding date was set. Kiki had been on the phone all morning with The Donald himself working out the details.

Yet his stomach churned at the very thought of the wedding. He pulled out a new roll of Tums and popped a few more. What a mess he'd made of things. He'd probably never get to see Hildy again, or at least if he did see her it wouldn't be like it was last night. *Last night,* he remembered, *making love on the beach, the ocean crashing behind us.*

Shit, he couldn't think about it. He'd probably break down or something. He'd try calling her again later, just to apologize, just to say goodbye. He left his cell phone back in the hotel room, or he'd never stop hitting the REDIAL button, he thought—then kicked himself for lying. He wanted to call Hildy, but the real reason he left the phone behind was so Kiki couldn't contact him. She had talked about the wedding since the minute she got up. He needed a break from the situation, and from her.

Mike began jogging down the boardwalk. He couldn't believe how hot and humid it had gotten overnight. He took a swig from his water bottle. He felt the sweat on his upper lip.

He saw Jake waiting for him near Michigan Avenue. When he had phoned Jake around nine, his future business partner said they should run for a while and then talk long and hard. If Mike seriously intended to go ahead with their detective agency, Jake had gotten the case that could make them a name in the business. Did Mike want in?

Did he ever. At least he could look forward to the future when it came to his job. He wanted to do this detective agency deal so much, he could taste it. He took another drink from his water bottle. He ran on.

"Why do I have to buy you new clothes?" Hildy complained. "Why not just conjure up some?"

"I explained that my powers aren't unlimited, Ms. Caldwell. I can't take a human life. I can't use my magic for self-gain or profit. I can't wish things for myself, you see. All I'm asking is for you to go over to the Ron Jon Surf Shop and buy me some walking shorts and one of those Hawaiian shirts. I like a lot of red and yellow in the print, maybe something with parrots. Get me a pair of flip-flops too."

"Wait a minute. You asked me if I had what, a thousand dollars, to spend on your clothes. Those things from Ron Jon's are going to cost under one hundred."

When Tony G. had made his request earlier, Hildy wondered if he understood how much money a thousand dollars was for her. Spending it would eat up a third of her winnings, money she needed to buy food and gas. But then she rationalized that she wouldn't have that thousand dollars in the first place if it wasn't for the genie helping her hit the jackpot. In the end, she said of course she'd buy him what he wanted.

"Right," he acknowledged. "I need the surf shop outfit because I can't walk around in a toga without getting a lot of attention. But what we planned is all about image. Once I get these everyday clothes, we're heading back to Atlantic City for me to get what I really need—top-of-the-line Italian designer slacks, a sports jacket, shoes, and a shirt. A men's shop in Caesar's carries exactly what I need. A thousand dollars will barely be enough. I need to look the part. But I explained all that."

Misgivings about the whole enterprise made Hildy shiver. "Right. You explained. You know, maybe we should forget the plan. Maybe I should answer Mike's calls and just talk to him."

Tony G.'s face looked fierce. He gripped her arm. "Stay strong. If you call him and talk to him, it will be the perfect opportunity for him to give you an apology and say something like, *It's been nice, but it was just one of those things.* Your whole relationship will have become a one-night stand. Is that what you want?"

"No, of course not. But—"

"But—stop worrying about the money. I can conjure up anything you need. And I can dress *you* with magic; won't cost you a dime."

"Why should you? I just bought new clothes. They're very nice. I don't need to have genie-made dresses, thank you."

"Ms. Caldwell, you can't look like the whole-some girl next door when you see Mike again. You need to take his breath away."

Hildy shrugged. "I am who I am. I can't change that. Mike has to love me as just plain old Hildy. Take it or leave it."

" 'Plain old Hildy'? You don't know what you've got, I'll say that much. Here, watch." The genie opened an empty hand and yet tossed something into the air in Hildy's direction. A soft cloud of golden glitter enveloped her. It tickled her nose. She sneezed—and felt her clothes moving. She looked down at herself.

"What! What happened?" Her very cute blue-flowered Ralph Lauren walking shorts and ador-able white cami appliquéd with yellow butterflies had disappeared. Instead she wore a coppery silk jersey dress with a deep neckline and a side slit that rose embarrassingly high. The dress draped down her body sinuously and ended in an asymmetrical hem. An extraordinary wide leather belt slung across her hips. A matching leather jacket, a lighter adaptation of a traditional motorcycle style, lay draped over a nearby chair. It was too hot to wear it. Her feet had been slipped out of her practical Teva sandals and were now in strapped, open-toed leather pumps with very high heels.

Tony G. looked immensely pleased with himself. "From Donna Karan's latest collection. Nothing like fighting fire with fire. You look—well, go look at yourself."

Hildy stepped into the little bathroom and peered at the mirror of the medicine cabinet. She gasped. The face looking back was definitely her own, but her hair had been streaked with shimmering highlights and cut so that it danced around her face. Gold and diamond earrings dangled from her earlobes. Her mouth was dewy, her eyes were blue pools, her lashes were longer than Bambi's. She looked like a real-life Barbie; she looked like a top model; she looked like a pop star . . . but she didn't look like Ms. Hildy Caldwell, English teacher.

"Now for the test," Tony G. said. "Go over to the surf shop and get my clothes. Let me know what happens."

When Hildy returned a half hour later, she wore a stunned expression as if she had walked through the looking glass into an alternate world. "I've never experienced anything like that before."

"Tell me about it," Tony demanded.

"First this stock boy looked up when I walked in and dropped a whole stack of boxes. Then two salesmen got into an argument about who would wait on me. The one who did fell all over me. The other guy kept asking if he could get me a soft drink or a snack. They acted so goofy. Did you put a spell on them?"

Tony G. took the shopping bag from Hildy's now perfectly manicured hand. "Nope. You're a knockout. I thought you had the potential. You look great. Now remember, you need to carry yourself like you know you look great. Understand?"

Hildy nodded. She straightened her shoulders and tossed her head, making her razor-cut hair shimmer.

"That's it. Now we're ready to roll."

Back in Atlantic City another plan of action was being made.

"Here's what we got." Jake pushed a file across his desk toward Mike. "Take this and read it over later. Basically, here's the deal. Remember the guy we nabbed for taking the skid steer and backhoe off that building site?"

"Sure. Marty Bisignano, also known as Marty Biz. That got him charged with grand theft larceny."

"Right. Obviously he wasn't acting by himself. He had a flatbed to pick up the equipment and he had somebody to take it to. He looked totally legit. He wore coveralls embroidered with the leasing company's name, and he had an order on the leasing company's letterhead to remove the equipment.

"It was unlucky for Marty that the foreman at the site got a hair up his ass when Marty explained, very politely I understand, that he was taking the equipment out for maintenance. The foreman started bitching that he needed that backhoe and stormed off. He also got suspicious. Marty didn't know the foreman went and called me, since I was working security on the project, to check it out."

Mike laughed, remembering what happened

next. "I had already gotten a skid steer and a bull-dozer stolen the week before, same scam. I'm sitting in your office at the time. You and I go flying down to the building site and park your pickup in front of the flatbed. We get in a screaming argument with Marty to keep him busy until the cops show up and arrest him. It was sweet." He grinned at the memory.

"Yeah, and once we had this guy's name, I was able to find out who he's connected to, a local mobster down here named James Torelli. Marty Bisignano is facing a lot of time, but he's not talking to the cops. *They* haven't found where the machinery is being stashed. And they haven't been able to get to Marty Bisignano's boss. But I figure we can."

"But why? What's in it for us—besides the glory and our name in the paper?"

"It's like this, Mikey, my man. A billion dollars of construction equipment is stolen every year in the United States. It's easy. Most manufacturers, take Caterpillar for instance, use this one-key-fits-all approach. Believe it or not, the same damned key turns on, you know, their whole line of back-hoes. You can buy a set of keys on eBay and drive off with almost anything you see sitting on a building site. And since construction equipment isn't licensed or registered, most of it can safely be resold in another state or shipped to Mexico and China."

"Any of it ever recovered?" Mike asked.

Jake fiddled with a pen while he talked. Now he wrote a number down on a Post-it notepad and flipped it around for Mike to see. "What's that say?"

"Six and a half to ten percent?" Mike said. "That's it?"

Jake tapped the pen up and down on the desk. "That's the average. It makes me think nobody's looking for the stuff. We're not talking Tonka toys here. You're telling me nobody can find stolen bulldozers, stolen backhoes? You can't hide them under a tarp in somebody's driveway.

"Yesterday I started contacting some of the other construction companies with projects in this area. And guess what? Close to six million dollars' worth of equipment has been taken from sites in and around Atlantic City in the past two months."

Mike sat back in his chair and whistled. "That's a helluva lot of machinery. Where is it now? That's the million-dollar question."

"A million bucks is right. I made some arrangements with these companies. They're all hurting because of the lost equipment. They're falling behind on their schedules. They get hit with big penalties if they don't finish on time. So here's the bottom line: We find the equipment and get it back, we get twenty percent of everything we recover. You do the math. If we can bust the people behind the theft ring, we'll get a hundred-thousand-dollar bonus from the biggest company I talked to."

"So what's your ideas for investigating this? Where do we start?"

"Marty Bisignano is out on bail. The court is making him wear one of those ankle bracelets so he can't make a move without them monitoring it. I know his address. He's sure to be home. And since he can't go visiting any of his old friends, I say we do what we do best: watch his place and see who comes calling. Maybe it'll just be the Papa John's Pizza delivery guy. Maybe it will be somebody interesting." Jake leaned forward, his voice turning serious. "Mike, you better think about how deep you want to get in this."

"You know I want to do this. Why are you even asking?"

"Because this James Torelli is a killer. He finds out we're snooping around, he's likely to come after us. If we're not careful, bang, bang, we're dead. Is the money worth it to you?"

Mike gave Jake a long steady look. His life was in shambles. He didn't want to go back to the hotel room and see Kiki. He didn't want to go to a bar to drink away his troubles and brood about how screwed up he felt. He didn't hesitate before he answered his partner. "The money *isn't* worth it. Getting our business started is. We can do this, Jake. I'm not afraid of this mobster. If he wants to kill me, he's going to have to find me—before I find him."

Jake gave Mike a broad smile, his teeth bright white in his dark face. "I figured you might feel that way. I brought you a present." He took a wooden case smaller than a shoe box out from under his desk and slid it across at Mike.

Mike opened the lid. A black 9mm Beretta lay in the blue velvet interior. "I'm going to need a license to carry this."

"No problem," Jake said. He threw a piece of paper on the desk. "I have friends in high places. I asked them to expedite your PI license and this permit. I also got a call from our lawyer, the one who drew up the papers to incorporate our agency. He's only waiting on one thing before he files in Trenton and we're in business."

"What's that one thing?" Mike said, taking the gun out of the box and holding it in his hand.

"Our company's name."

For the next half hour, Mike and Jake tossed around some ideas. The best they came up with was JM Detective Agency, Got-Cha Surveillance, Integrity Investigators, and Catch-M Private Investigators. Nothing hit them as being perfect. They decided to go out for breakfast before starting their surveillance of Marty Bisignano, aka Marty Biz.

While devouring his own plate of eggs, sausage, hash browns, rye toast, and black coffee, Jake watched Mike pushing a Western omelet around on his plate. Gloom hung over him as visibly as a black cloud.

"Okay, partner. Something's eating you up. You worried about this job?"

Mike shook his head. "Nah, it's personal crap."

"I read in the paper this morning that you and Kiki set a date. But you sure as shit don't look like a happy man. You want to talk about it?"

Mike did, but he didn't know how. He picked up the salt shaker and started to toss it idly from hand to hand. "Nothing to talk about. I met someone I used to know. Old girlfriend, cute as a button. Well, things got out of hand. I didn't keep my pants on when I should have. Kiki found out and went ballistic. But it's over and done with."

Jake took a swallow of the strong hot coffee, then set it down with great care. "Mike, my friend," he said with deliberation. "This situation involves two women. You screwed both of them in one way or another. I'd bet dollars to doughnuts this is *not* over and done with."

Jake reached one large brown hand across the table and delicately picked up a pinch of salt from the trail of white that had fallen out of the shaker Mike had been fooling with. "Bad luck to spill salt." He tossed it over his left shoulder. "You believe in luck, Big Mike?"

"No."

Jake snorted at that. Quick as a striking snake, he reached over, grabbed Mike's hand, and turned it palm up.

Mike gave him a puzzled look.

Jake dropped another pinch of salt into the up-turned palm.

"Son," he said, "you don't know shit about women. I suggest you toss this back and get Lady Luck on your side. You're going to need all the help you can get."

Chapter 15

Mike Amante had heard the old joke, "Why are New Yorkers so depressed? Because the light at the end of the tunnel is New Jersey." He knew people sneered and called the Garden State the armpit of America. He couldn't deny that the industrial North Jersey landscape along Route 1-9 looked bombed-out, gray, ruined, stark, and bleak. And it was true that the landfills next to the turnpike sometimes caught on fire.

But Mike had fallen in love with the Jersey shore. He intended to move there. He'd looked at a couple of houses in Margate and Avalon a month ago. He just hadn't gotten around to telling Kiki that yet, in the same way he had avoided telling her he had decided to quit real estate and go into the detective business with Jake in Atlantic City, or AC as the natives called it.

But Camden did not rank on his list of favorite New Jersey cities. In recent years it had taken over top honors from Detroit for having the nation's highest crime rate. It had become the new Murder City. Not surprisingly, Marty Biz called it home.

Mike and Jake decided to split up the surveillance of Marty into six-hour shifts each. If nothing panned out in two days or so, they'd come up with a plan B. They kicked around some ideas before

Jake got in his white, five-year-old Ford Taurus to make the forty-minute drive to Camden.

"Another thing, Mike," Jake said. "A hundred-thousand-dollar Mercedes Roadster isn't going to blend in real well in Marty's neighborhood. Maybe you better rent a car or something."

"It cost more like a hundred and fifty thousand. And I was thinking the same thing. I'm going to garage the Mercedes for a while and go buy something more practical." Mike thought for a moment. "A Toyota Prius maybe."

Jake shrugged. "Yeah, sure. But a Camry might work out better. More common, but it's up to you. Let's see." He glanced over at the dashboard clock. "It's getting close to eleven now. I'll grab some lunch to take with me and still get there around noon. You show up to take over around what, six?"

"Right. I'll phone you when I'm on my way." Mike thumped the top of the Taurus a few times with his hand and Jake drove off. His adrenaline was pumping. If it weren't for being miserable, he'd be a happy man.

Tony G. "cleaned up well," as they say. Hildy tried to view him objectively. Nothing could be done about the broken nose and smashed cheekbone. Yet, now that he was dressed in his designer clothes, his rugged face gave him an undeniable masculinity that the sockless Italian loafers and ivory silk shirt couldn't undermine.

She had to admit he turned heads. A pert, pretty, and very buxom green-eyed blonde, who had been standing behind them on the up escalator inside the hotel, had actually slipped a piece of paper with her name and room number into the pocket of his Versace sports coat.

Hildy, noticing the incident, had reached into Tony's pocket and handed it back to the embarrassed woman. "You seem to have dropped this," she said coolly. She prayed she could be as self-possessed when The Plan went into play. She checked her watch. Eleven o'clock. It was all about to begin.

Not entirely by accident, Tony G., with Hildy's hand resting lightly inside the crook of his arm, exited from Caesar's onto the boardwalk at exactly the same time Mike was jogging up the boardwalk from the direction of Jake's office.

Hildy spotted Mike when he was still a hundred yards away. Her heart began to race. She knew the way he ran; she had seen him hundreds of times on the football field. As a woman in love, she would have recognized his build, his posture, and the color of his hair even if he had been in the middle of a crowd in Yankee Stadium.

When the distance between them closed, Mike looked right at Hildy and broke into a small smile before quickly and politely averting his eyes. There hadn't been a glimmer of recognition in his face. He had seen and noticed a pretty woman, but he didn't know who she was.

Hildy felt poleaxed. He didn't know her? Her temper soared into the absolutely, positively furious zone.

Then, as he was about to jog past, Mike suddenly stopped running. He turned. He narrowed his eyes. He cocked his head. "Hildy? Hildy!" The name burst from his lips, a word that captured all the wonder and perplexity he felt. Joy leaped up as he beheld her. He was a man transfixed.

Hildy went still as a statue. Their eyes locked. The rest of the world disappeared.

Mike uttered her name again. "Hildy? Is it really you?" He couldn't quite believe his eyes. Hildy had always been an adorable girl. This—this was a woman whose beauty took his breath away.

Even though Hildy had hoped to keep rein on her emotions, a bolt of desire like a lightning strike hit her full force. Her eyes softened. Her passion flared. Her determination to be silent, to turn away, wavered. She would have answered, speaking Michael's name like a plea, like a prayer, but she didn't get the chance.

Tony G. had stepped between them, breaking the spell, and put out his hand.

"I do not believe I've had the pleasure," he said, his Italian accent making each word sensual and so European.

Mike noticed Tony G. for the first time. Shock replaced the wonderment on his face. He automatically took the offered hand and shook it. "I'm . . . I'm Michael Amante. Who are you?"

Tony G. gave a little bow. "I am Count Carmello Arigento. So, how do you know the enchanting Ms. Caldwell?"

Mike's eyes returned to Hildy; he couldn't look away. He wanted to hold her. He wanted to kiss her. He wanted her more than he had ever wanted anyone in his entire life.

"You didn't answer the count's question, Mike," she said, remembering as per The Plan to put ice in her voice.

"Huh? Oh." He looked at this Count Arigento who was clearly waiting for his response. He couldn't figure out what the man was doing with Hildy. He looked far too old for her. He didn't look her type. Anyway, she wasn't supposed to be seeing anyone, according to George Ide.

Mike frowned. He growled at the stranger, "Hildy and I went to high school together. And how do *you* know her?" He thrust his chin out at Tony G. and puffed up his chest.

Tony's eyes twinkled with mischief as he answered in mellifluous tones. "How? I know her with my eyes, my lips, my touch, my every sense, for she delights them all. But you perhaps mean how are we acquainted?"

Mike had to restrain himself from taking a swing at this arrogant ass's already flattened nose. "Yeah, how are you *acquainted* with Ms. Caldwell?"

"I am a business associate of her brother-in-law. I had the honor of escorting Ms. Caldwell in Rome when she visited earlier this year. She has generously agreed to return the favor now that I am in America, yes?" He turned and gave Hildy an adoring gaze.

Mike gazed at Hildy too. He wondered why he had never realized she could look so elegant, so sophisticated, so incredibly sexy. It must be her clothes. Outside of the senior prom, he had never seen her this dressed up. And this was no white chiffon prom dress with a corsage pinned on it. This woman was dazzling. She could be on a magazine cover.

His spirits plummeted. How could he have not seen it before? He was such a fool, such a frigging loser. This angel had been his. Just last night she said she loved him, that she had never stopped loving him. Now she probably hated him.

He kept staring at her. He couldn't help himself. Hildy's face revealed nothing of what she was thinking, but something in her eyes when she first saw him had given him hope.

At that moment, Hildy reached out her hand and touched the count's cheek lightly with her fingertips. All of Mike's hopes vanished and were replaced by an ice pick sticking in his heart.

"Carmello has always been a delight. I have such wonderful memories of the eternal city because of his kindness," she cooed.

Mike suddenly saw the world through a red haze of impotent rage. He wondered just what had happened in Rome to make 'such wonderful memories.' He knew Hildy never slept with the guy, that was some small comfort. But what did happen between them?

"I am such a lucky man to have a beautiful woman such as Ms. Caldwell willing to spend time with me," Tony G. responded, again beholding Hildy as reverently as if she were the Mona Lisa. "I am hoping she will consent to let me be more than just an occasional visitor in her life."

Mike's nostrils flared. He thought his head was going to explode. His hands tightened into fists. What a line this guy was handing her. Mike felt he had to say something. He started to speak, but before the words left his mouth he heard an all-too-familiar shriek from somewhere behind him.

"MICHAEL! MIIIII-CHAEL! Here you are! I've been searching the entire boardwalk for you. I'm putting together the guest list." Kiki bore down on the three of them from the direction of Trump Plaza, descending like a B-1 bomber in a dive, a piece of notepaper waving in her outstretched hand.

Kiki stopped in front of the trio and pulled off her sunglasses. She looked at Tony G. with interest. She glanced quickly at Hildy. She clearly didn't recognize her as the same girl who had sat soaked and bedraggled on the beach the day before. She returned her gaze to Tony. She batted her eyelashes at him, coquettishly. She held out her slender fingers in his direction and gushed. "Oh, are you a friend of Michael's?"

Tony G. brought her fingers to his lips and kissed them while holding her eyes with his own baby blues. "Count Carmello Arigento. I'm a friend of a friend, you might say. And you are?"

Hildy's voice broke into the tête-à-tête. "Count, you are holding the hand of Kiki, the famous photographer. She's Michael's *fiancée*." She looked directly at Michael with eyes of steel as she uttered the hateful word. He looked stricken.

"I must congratulate you both." Tony G. dropped Kiki's hand and clapped Michael on the shoulder. He exuded goodwill. Then he moved next to Hildy and put his arm possessively around her.

Mike stiffened when Tony G. made the move. He watched with horror as Tony's fingers lightly massaged Hildy's upper arm. He wanted to murder this guy.

"And I just had the most wonderful idea," Tony said, all smiles. "Why don't you two join us for dinner tonight? Perhaps I could convince Kiki to fly to Rome and photograph my villa. I have George Clooney coming to visit in August."

"Sorry, I'm busy," Michael snapped.

Kiki wound her slender, tanned arm through Michael's and overrode his refusal. "Darling, it would be lovely. We should go."

Michael didn't even look at Kiki. All he wanted to do was tear Hildy out from under this guy's hands. He glowered. "I have to work. You go if you want to."

"Perhaps you can join us for drinks afterward, sweetheart," Kiki pleaded. "What time will you be done?"

"Late. Too late." The words tore at his heart. What if it were too late? What if he had lost Hildy? Maybe she'd sleep with this count just because Mike had hurt her. The thought was unbearable. He needed to get out of here. Hildy wasn't even looking at him now. She was whispering something in the count's ear. Michael couldn't stand to watch any more of this.

Tony G. spoke up. "It's settled then. We will meet Kiki at nine, at Mía's, that lovely restaurant off the main lobby in Caesar's. With a little luck,

Mr. Amante will be able to join us for dessert and drinks. Somehow I believe he'll be able to be there." He winked.

Michael thought there was something strange about Count Arigento. He couldn't figure it out, but something was off. One thing he was sure of though—this guy was the most arrogant son of a bitch he'd ever met.

Chapter 16

A man sorely troubled in mind and spirit needs a diversion. Mike, shaking Kiki loose from his arm, told her he'd catch up with her later. Not bothering to change out of his running shorts, he jogged off the boardwalk to the nearest car rental kiosk. He quickly arranged for a weekly rental on a bronze-colored Ford Fusion that came with a radio/CD player and an air conditioner but not much more. He got in and drove it directly to a Toyota dealer.

When he pulled into the new car lot, the sun was beating down furiously on the black asphalt, making the air shimmer above the softening surface. A smiling salesman, the armpits of his dress shirt soaked in sweat, hurried over to Mike the moment he emerged from the Fusion.

The heat clutched at Mike with sweaty hands. He felt surly. He barely nodded at the salesman, then followed him over to a demo car sitting on the lot.

Mike wasn't sure why he was looking at a Prius anyway. He pretty much hated the styling of the economy car in front of him, which the salesman quickly informed him was painted in the latest color, something girly called Driftwood Pearl.

But when the salesman opened the car's hood and gave the spiel about "synergy drive," Mike forgot to be in a bad mood. Always a car enthusiast, he found himself fascinated—especially when he discovered the engines were placed under the body of the car, not under the hood. He also thought an average of forty-six miles per gallon sounded damned good, especially if he had to start budgeting his funds in the near future.

His spirits improved by the minute. He got in the small automobile and inhaled that new-car smell. The salesman handed him the keys, and Mike drove off the lot in the direction of the Atlantic City Expressway, where he zipped along at sixty miles an hour for a while.

He played with the JBL six-disc in-the-dash CD changer with nine speakers in seven locations. He turned up the bass when he popped in the Bruce Springsteen album he found on the passenger seat and started singing loudly along with the CD about being born in a small town. He felt duly impressed by the Bluetooth phone in the steering wheel, the GPS system, the sunroof, the heated mirrors, and the leather interior. He felt a rush of happiness.

Women shopped to feel better. Guys went to look at new cars.

By the time Mike got back to the dealer, he really wanted a Prius, preferably in metallic Barcelona red. However, he ordered one in magnetic gray metallic with a dark gray interior, which was a lot more practical for surveillance work. He added every option available, and the price still totaled less than a sixth of what he paid for his Mercedes.

Mike started whistling. He thought about the look on Hildy's face when she saw what he had bought. He fantasized about selling his Mercedes and buying her a Prius too. He'd get her the red one for sure. He'd still have money left to make a down payment on a house for them near the ocean, maybe one right on that street they had walked down together last night after the pizza at the Dark Star Café.

At that moment, a cloud passed over his sunny outlook. It was stupid for him to think about buying a house with Hildy or showing her his car. The only thing he had to look forward to was seeing Kiki's face when she saw what he had purchased. She'd be apoplectic. She'd probably refuse to ride in it.

By the time Mike signed all the papers, it was late in the afternoon. He had just enough time to get back to the hotel room and change before he headed to Camden to relieve Jake. His partner had called a couple of times, mostly out of boredom. Nobody had shown up at Marty's home, but Jake spotted Marty when he came out to pick up the mail and yell at some kids who were throwing firecrackers in the street.

Once he was inside the hotel room, Mike discovered Kiki was absent. According to a note she left, she had an appointment with a florist to decide on the bridal flowers. He had another bout of heartburn when he read that and reached for the roll of Tums.

He tried to contact Hildy as soon as he retrieved his cell phone. She still wasn't answering his calls. He felt frustrated. He wanted to hear her voice. Even that wasn't enough. He wanted to see her dimples when she smiled.

As he headed out the door, he made a decision. He would try to get back to that dinner tonight, just as soon as Marty Biz went to bed. He had to see Hildy, he just had to. Maybe he could figure out a way to get her alone for a couple of minutes.

"Is this really necessary?" Hildy asked unhappily, finding herself in a spacious hotel room in

Caesar's, arranged partly by Tony's charm but mostly by a touch of magic. Her complaint came when Tony threw another handful of golden sparkles at her, and she had found herself dressed in an entirely new outfit.

"I don't think Mike really noticed what I was wearing," she murmured as she stared at herself in the mirror.

The genie stood there, his fingers holding his chin, evaluating Hildy's outfit like fashion guru Tim Gunn looking at a style-challenged housewife on the Bravo channel. "He noticed. Trust me, he noticed. You're just upset because you're showing a little cleavage."

"A little cleavage! This off-the-shoulder neckline exposes everything but my nipples. I can't wear this!" She turned around so she could see the back of the sleek black dress with its filmy accents of gold gauze.

"You are exaggerating. Your breasts are completely covered, or nearly completely covered anyway. The dress is perfect, another of Donna Karan's new collection. It's daring but obviously couture. You look like a million dollars."

"But I don't look like I always have. I don't look like myself!" she wailed.

Tony G. offered no sympathy, just a sobering dose of truth. "Ms. Caldwell, you are not the same person you were two days ago. You have received, if I may be blunt, carnal knowledge, so like Eve after eating the apple, you are no longer a naive child. You have discovered that your belief system, one that did not allow for genies or magic, was totally in error. And you have gotten a glimpse of evil. You have emerged from the cocoon of your former, not very worldly, self. Who you choose to be will be up to you. But it will not be the same person you were."

Suddenly understanding the sea change she had undergone shook Hildy. Her old life was gone. Her innocence was gone. Reality was no longer quite so simple as she believed it to be. Nor was the world as benign. Tony G. was right, she was no longer Hildy Caldwell who lived in a cozy 1920s Craftsman house in a small Pennsylvania town. She was not the person she had been, but she had yet to figure out who she was.

She studied herself in the mirror. The sandals with their very high heels made her legs look extremely sexy. The amazing black dress elongated her torso and made her appear taller and more slender. Her shoulders had become two alluring, creamy mounds that begged to be stroked, and her breasts peeked out just a little at the very edge of the plunging neckline, tantalizing the viewer. Her hair had been pulled back off her face. A thin shining rope secured it before it spilled like a sheaf of golden wheat down her back, nearly reaching her waist.

"My hair was much shorter this afternoon," she noted.

"I'm setting Mike up for the coup de grace," the genie explained. "Long blond hair will make him lose his reason. But you must not lose yours. We discussed this. Do you understand what you have to do?"

Hildy sighed with resignation. "Yes. I have to remain aloof and out of reach. He hasn't suffered or sacrificed enough. He can't capture the snow leopard yet."

All during dinner, Hildy realized that Kiki never recognized her as the girl Mike introduced at the beach. In fact, Mike's fiancée didn't exchange more than a hello with her at the beginning of the evening before she bestowed all her attention on

"Count Arigento." At one point, after the appetizer and before the salad, Hildy whispered to Tony, "Are you positive Mike is going to show up?"

Tony responded, "One hundred percent positive," and moments later, as Hildy brought a forkful of penne pasta with rock lobster and white asparagus tips to her lips, she saw him come up the marble steps and walk into the restaurant. She froze. Their eyes locked. Mike moved like a man in a dream. Hildy thought the light shimmered around him.

Kiki didn't notice any of this. When Mike pulled out the chair next to hers, she squealed, "MICHAEL!" and turned her cheek to receive his kiss. Then she looked him up and down, noticing the turquoise blue Polo pullover and the jeans that rode low on his slender hips. She smiled. "Darling, you really could have gone back to the room to change. We would still have been here."

Mike sat down and signaled the waiter. "I thought you'd be glad that I made it."

"Oh I am, of course, I am. I've been arranging the most fabulous photo shoot in Italy with the count. We're going to start at Lake Como and travel to the south, to Ravello."

"Yeah, that's nice." The waiter arrived at the table. "Bring me whatever *she's* eating." He pointed to Hildy.

"Very good, sir. And the wine as well?"

"No, bring me a vodka martini, straight up, no ice. Olives." Mike tried to fight back the emotions that surged up inside him. It was so wrong that Hildy was here with another man. And despite the clear connection between her and Mike when he first walked in, she was now deliberately avoiding his eyes. Worse, the count had his arm draped around the back of her chair, one broad, blunt finger lazily doodling on Hildy's bare shoulder.

Mike reached for a breadstick. His teeth snapped it in two. It felt dry in his mouth.

He found himself staring at Hildy again. He had to admit that she looked amazing, even more beautiful than this afternoon. Having her this close made him break into a sweat. He picked up his napkin and dabbed his temples. His glance landed on her bosom. His body temperature climbed higher. He figured he must have a fever, and why was Hildy wearing something so low-cut anyway? That wasn't like her at all. Jesus, every man in the room kept stealing glances in her direction. Some of them openly ogled her.

The waiter brought the martini. Mike drank it fast. His pasta followed. He didn't even sample it. Seeing Hildy with another man had killed his desire to eat.

Kiki had returned to her conversation with the count. Mike noticed that Hildy didn't seem to have any better appetite than he did. She pushed the penne around with her fork, piling it up like a fort around the pieces of lobster. But no matter what she may have been thinking, she absolutely refused to look at him.

Mike had to take action. He reached across the table and touched her arm. She jumped and lifted her soft cerulean eyes to look at him at last.

"Hey," he said in a low, soft voice. "Don't you have to use the ladies' room or something?"

Hildy seemed puzzled for a moment. Then she stole a glance at Tony G. He didn't appear to be paying any attention to her, but continued an animated conversation with Mike's witch of a fiancée. Hildy really couldn't stand the woman.

Hildy nodded surreptitiously at Mike, and said to no one in particular, "Please excuse me while I use the ladies'." She stood and headed for the stairs, which she descended with as much poise as

she could in four-inch heels. She was lucky she
didn't break her neck, she thought. At the bottom
of the flight, she was out of sight of the table where
the others sat.

A minute later Mike came rushing toward her,
taking the stairs two at a time. Not saying anything,
he grabbed her arm and led her out of the restaurant into the hotel's cavernous lobby past the huge
marble statue of Caesar Augustus. He spotted a
dim corner and steered her toward it.

Every millimeter of skin where his fingers
touched Hildy's arm vibrated with an exquisite tingling. When Tony G. had put his hand on her
shoulder, she found it annoying, like a persistent
fly. When Mike touched her, she caught fire. As
they crossed the vast lobby floor, she knew she was
headed for trouble, and she steeled herself to resist.

She didn't have time to prepare herself, however,
before Mike's lips descended on hers. Caught unaware, she kissed him back. Swept away in a vortex
of released desire, she sagged against him, clutching
him as if she were drowning all over again and he
offered rescue. But her surrender lasted only seconds before she took both her hands and shoved
him away.

"What do you think you're doing!" Her eyes
went from blue flame to glacial ice. "How dare
you!"

Mike immediately apologized. "I'm—I'm sorry. I
don't know what came over me. It's just when I
see you, I can't think straight. I want—I need to
touch you."

"That's a bit awkward, don't you think, taking
into account that your *fiancée* is sitting a few hundred feet away."

"I don't care about her. All I care about is you.
Tell me you don't want me, Hildy. I can tell that
you do."

Hildy found she didn't need to pretend to be angry when she answered. She was genuinely furious. "Just who or what do you think I am? You have no right to play with my feelings like this. You have chosen to make a serious commitment to another woman. That eliminates any possibility of your seeing me, or touching me, or kissing me. Now besides accosting me in a public place, why did you want me to leave the table?"

Hildy slid farther away from Mike, out of his reach.

He moved toward her, closing the distance. "I needed to talk to you. You won't return my calls."

"So talk." She crossed her arms across her chest.

"I'm sorry about what happened. Last night. I wanted to apologize." He sounded so lame and he knew it. He wasn't sorry at all. He would do it again right now, if Hildy were willing.

"What a load of horseshit, Michael Amante. Look, I'm not sorry it happened, but I can tell you that it will not happen again. You blew it. You can have your Kinky, Kiki, Wicki Wacky fiancée."

"Hildy, please listen to me. I didn't know that announcement was going to be in the paper. I didn't have anything to do with it. Kiki went ahead and set a date for the wedding without telling me."

"You never discussed it? It sounds like a terrific relationship you two have. But I guess that's what you want."

"No! That's not what I want!" Mike surprised himself with the force of his response. He didn't want to marry Kiki, so why was he going along with it? He had no good answer except that the meeting with Hildy had been so sudden and unexpected it turned his world upside down. Their lovemaking on the beach had happened as if by magic. He felt caught up in something beyond the ordinary.

Mike didn't understand what was happening to him. He suspected he had fallen in love with Hildy all over again, only it wasn't the same feeling as when he was a teenager. Now he had become a man unable to resist her, he had fallen under her spell, and he was in thrall to this woman in a way he had never felt with anyone before.

Mike had stepped so close, Hildy could feel the air move with his breath. She looked directly into his eyes. She spoke very deliberately and carefully. "I thought I knew you, but I am beginning to think you've changed so much that I don't. And you know, Mike, you sound as if you're confused about who you want in your life. But I'm not. I know what I want. Now, I need to get back to the table."

She began to walk away, then paused and turned to Mike. Her heart urged her to go back and throw herself in his arms, but she lifted her chin instead. "And I need to get back to my date."

Mike never returned to the restaurant. Kiki never seemed to notice. But as soon as they had all finished the entree, Hildy said to Tony that she really wanted to leave *now*. Exhaustion had overtaken her. Doubts filled her. She had either made the right move or lost Mike for good. She didn't know which.

Hildy refused to accept the genie's offer of a magic carpet ride back to Ship Bottom. The less she had to do with hocus-pocus, the better, as far as she was concerned. So as tired as she was, she insisted on driving them back, going north up the Garden State Parkway to Exit 63 and then turning eastward on Route 72 until they reached Long Beach Island. All the way, the genie kept reassuring her that she had done the right thing, and she had done it splendidly.

"Alea jacta est," he said.

Hildy nodded solemnly. Whether it had been the right thing or not, yes, the die had been cast.

Hildy reached Ship Bottom without incident. But as soon as she pulled her little red Volkswagen into the paved front yard of her cottage, she felt something was wrong. Tony G. sensed it too. "Wait here," he ordered.

"No way," Hildy said, and sprinted for the front door. It was ajar. She pushed it wide and ran inside. "Shelley! Keats!" she cried frantically. No cats scampered to greet her.

She raced from room to room crying their names. Silence was her only answer. When she reached the kitchen, she stopped. Written in black Magic Marker on the door of the under-the-counter refrigerator were the words: *I got your cats. You got my bottle. I'll be in touch.*

Chapter 17

"Do something," Hildy demanded. "That maniac has my kitties and it's all your fault!"

Tony G. spread his legs wide. He crossed his arms in front of his chest like Yul Brynner in *The King and I*. He nodded and stamped his right foot. The air swirled in silver currents around him, as liquid as if it had turned to water. The temperature in the room dropped quickly. Hildy shivered in the chill.

When the air stilled, Tony G. again wore his toga. The laurel wreath sat on his head, its leaves bright green against his cap of dark curls. "*You* do something, Ms. Caldwell. You have the power. Just wish."

Hildy thought fast. Wishes were tricky. She couldn't mess this up. She had to be extremely careful in the way she worded what she wanted. If she just wished for her cats to be returned, they wouldn't necessarily have to be alive. She shuddered at the thought. "All right. I wish for my two cats, John Keats and Percy Bysshe Shelley, to be returned to me immediately, unharmed, healthy, alive, and unchanged in any way from their state before the abduction and with no memory of their terrifying experience."

As soon as the words left her mouth, the doorbell rang. Perplexed, she walked into the front room to see who it was. When she flung open the door, a tiny old woman stood there. A cat carrier sat at her feet.

"Oh, my dear," the elfin woman said, "I'm Joslyn Baier. I live right next door. I found your two cats outside my kitchen window a short time ago. They were having quite a conversation with my Henry; he's a Siamese, you know. I can't imagine how they escaped, but I knew you'd be sick with worry. I popped them into Henry's carrier and brought them over the minute I saw you had returned."

"Oh, how can I thank you, Mrs. Baier!" Hildy picked up the carrier from the doorstep and brought it inside. "Do come in. I'll let them free, and you can take your carrier back."

After taking care that the front door had shut tightly behind them, Hildy opened the wire gate at the front of the carrier and her cats popped their heads out, blinking their yellow eyes, hesitant to rush free, seemingly a bit confused.

Hildy took Shelley into her arms, hugging him so tightly he soon struggled to be put down. Keats strolled out of the case, rubbed his head against her high heels, plopped himself down on her toes, and instantly fell asleep.

"Oh, is this your husband, dear?" Joslyn Baier said, spotting Tony G., who had made no effort to disappear with her arrival.

Hildy's head spun around. "My husband? No, no, this is a—a student of mine. He's Italian. I'm teaching him English."

"That's nice, dear," Mrs. Baier said. If she thought there was anything odd about Hildy, dressed to the nines, giving English lessons to a huge man wearing a toga after ten at night, she was polite enough not to mention it. "I must be going now. They're very sweet cats. It was quite all right if they came to visit. Henry seemed to like them enormously. He could use some playmates. He's an only child, you know."

Hildy handed her the carrier and thanked her again and again. Only after the elderly neighbor had left did she turn to Tony to express what was bothering her now that her cats were safe. "I don't really understand why Jimmy the Bug took my cats. Didn't he realize that I would simply wish to have them returned? It seems rather stupid."

Tony shook his great head. "Don't underestimate the enemy. That's a basic rule of engagement. Of course Jimmy the Bug knew you'd use one of your wishes to get your cats back. He also knows you now have only two wishes left. He's going to find a way to box you in, where two wishes—or one wish if he gets you to use up another—won't be enough to stop him. He'll finesse you and make you return the bottle. Whatever his plan is, believe me, it's already in motion. Stealing your cats was only his opening move."

Hildy went to bed filled with anxiety. She wanted her cats to join her. She wanted them where she could watch them and reassure herself they were safe, but it was much too warm. The temperature hovered in the eighties; only the breeze from the sea kept the little cottage from being stifling. Even so, the humidity left her feeling sticky and uncomfortable.

She looked over the edge of the sleeping loft. She could see the cats stretched out, their bellies pressed against the cool surface of the kitchen linoleum. "Ingrates!" she called down to them. They didn't stir. She gave up, pulled the sheet over her, and switched off the light.

Tony had assured her he would keep guard. Hildy

knew she should feel safe, but as soon as she fell asleep she was chased in her dreams by a giant bug with great sharp pincers reaching toward her. She woke frequently, but each time she dozed off, the dream came back again.

Hildy was not the only one unable to get a good night's rest. Mike had finally returned to his hotel suite after the bars closed, barely able to stand after the four more, or perhaps five more, vodka martinis he had consumed.

When he stumbled into the bedroom, he discovered Kiki fast asleep. He called her name. She didn't wake, but made ladylike snoring sounds as she slumbered on. He cursed about getting back so late and mumbled to himself. By the second martini he had made up his mind to have it out with Kiki.

Seeing Hildy tonight had taken away any doubts. What was he waiting for? For some slick Italian count to snatch her up? As far as he was concerned the wedding to Kiki was off. He wanted Hildy. The only way to get her was to end this sham of an engagement. He wasn't going to be forced into marriage. This was the twenty-first century, not the Middle Ages.

Determined to make a clean break with Kiki as soon as she awakened, Mike stretched out on the sofa, putting his arm over his eyes. The room spun crazily. He vowed to never touch another martini. Alcohol never solved anybody's problems. He had been a fool to get so drunk. The mother of all hangovers would greet him tomorrow morning.

Within minutes, he had passed out rather than fallen asleep. His mouth fell open and he snored loudly. Sometime during what was left of the night, he got the vague notion that Hildy was lying next to him on the sofa. He smiled and reached for her.

She had taken off her clothes. *Wasn't that considerate of her?* he thought.

Somewhere in the still rational parts of his brain, he wondered how she had gotten into his hotel room, but he was too happy to care. He nuzzled her neck—at least he thought he did. He pressed himself against her and lost consciousness again. He didn't remember anything at all after that.

When he opened his eyes at dawn's early light, he moaned. His stomach felt raw. A sledgehammer rhythmically whacked the inside of his skull. He couldn't seem to move. He panicked that he had somehow become paralyzed. Then he understood there was some kind of weight on his left side pinning him down.

He gingerly opened one eye. The morning sun streaming through the window cut into his pupil like a laser. He turned his head to see what was immobilizing his arm. To his horror, he saw the long, glossy black strands of Kiki's hair spread across his shoulder, and there, unmistakably spooned against him with great familiarity, was the graceful curve of her naked back.

"Oh no," he groaned, feeling sick. "What have I done?"

Chapter 18

At about the same hour, along the eastern edge of Long Beach Island, dawn had broken over the Atlantic. A faint hint of vermilion softened the horizon line like a blush on the cheek of an angel. Black skimmers and common herring gulls wheeled against the brightening blue, their plaintive calls like a woman crying. A spotted sandpiper scampered at the water's edge. But this magical interlude between the end of night and the arrival of day ended quickly. The sun rose as if yanked up like a yo-yo on a string, promising to bring back the blistering heat and suffocating humidity even as the hour struck seven.

Hildy witnessed none of the morning glory. Jarred into consciousness by the strident tones of Nirvana, she slapped down the alarm on the clock radio, silencing Kurt Cobain's whining about a gun in midchorus. She had decided to get up early, meaning to run five miles when the streets were still empty and the day was young. But inertia kept her from moving. Her legs tangled in the white sheets, she lay on the bed, slowly collecting her thoughts.

How was she supposed to distinguish fantasy from reality when the dividing line had blurred? She reviewed the strange and wondrous occur-

rences of the past two days: Mike appearing like a
white knight to save her life. His night visit ending
with lovemaking on the beach. A violent attack by
mobsters. A total makeover with hair, designer
gown, and makeup courtesy of Tony G.'s genie
magic. A cruel catnapping. The inexplicable return
of those same cats courtesy of an old lady on her
doorstep.

Hildy had no possible way to predict what might
happen today.

She rose and climbed down out of the sleeping
loft to find her coffee poured into her favorite VIR-
GINIA IS FOR CAT LOVERS mug. It sat on the Formica
table waiting for her. Tony G., wishing only to
please, stayed discreetly out of sight. Hildy sipped
the hot liquid greedily. She immediately determined one important thing: She needed to take
control of her life again. It seemed to have slipped
away, leaving her spinning around like a towel in
the clothes dryer.

Her coffee mug in hand, she walked into the
enclosed porch and stepped into a pool of sunlight.
It bestowed warm kisses to her bare feet. She
smiled. She smelled the salt in the air. She loved it
here. She wasn't sure she ever wanted to leave.

She turned her attention to her current situation.
She created a to-do list for the day, to wit:

1. Wear her own clothes.
2. Answer her own cell phone if she damned
   well felt like it.
3. Be straight with Mike. No more games.
4. Eliminate the threat of Jimmy the Bug somehow, even if it meant making two more wishes
   so that Tony G. disappeared.

A pang of sorrow hit her in the solar plexus when
she contemplated the loss of Tony G. He was like

the big brother she never had. Nevertheless she
mentally moved on to the next item.

5. Go to the beach and get a tan. Alone.

She finished the coffee. She felt stronger. She
could see clearly now. She had her day in order.

Her cell phone rang. She fished it out of her tote
bag and answered. And her to-do list went the way
of many best-laid plans—straight to the crapper.

Issuing from the silver Nokia in Hildy's hand,
her sister's disembodied voice informed Hildy that
she was in Edwardsville, on Zerby Avenue, and
you wouldn't believe how much traffic there was.
She was at St. Vladimir's, which was running another excursion to Caesar's. Father John had a
dream about a huge pile of gold. He believed it
was a vision and they had to trust in God to pro-
vide. But by going to Atlantic City? Corrine just
didn't get it unless Father John's pile of gold came
out of a slot machine.

Anyway, Corrine said she was waiting to board
the bus right this minute. It was due to arrive in
AC at eleven thirty. Hildy had to pick her up.
Don't argue. Obviously Hildy was in an emotional
crisis and all alone. Corrine was riding down there
to straighten things out.

Then Corrine said to excuse her a minute. Her
voice addressed someone on Zerby Avenue, Hildy
assumed. "What? Of course, I'm coming, don't be
rude. This call is very important. I'm speaking with
my little sister who is being seduced and abandoned
nearly right this very minute."

Hildy sputtered and attempted to interrupt, but
Corrine, unaware of Hildy's protestations, was back
on the phone to tell Hildy they were insisting that
she get on the bus and she had to run.

Hildy tried to say once again that she was just

fine, tried and failed. Her words fell on deaf ears and a disconnect. Corrine was on her way.

"Mike hasn't even tried to call me this morning." Hildy's voice held just the slightest wobble. She gave Tony G. a sour look. "I thought my long blond hair was supposed to make him lose his reason. All he lost, evidently, was my phone number."

"Patience is a virtue." Tony G. busily scrubbed the kitchen sink. His laurel wreath slipped down over one eye. He pushed it back with a soapy hand. "You gave him a lot to think about. You have to wait it out."

"While I wait, he's still sharing a hotel suite with his *fiancée*. Kiki is probably naked and falling all over him." The very thought of that shrew touching Mike made her squeamish. The thought of Mike doing . . . doing anything with the shrew made her feel as if she were going to retch.

Tony G. reached into the cabinet under the sink and took out a bottle of blue window cleaner. He figured he'd tackle the sunroom. He could have done the job by magic, but he was bored out of his mind. He needed another Punic War to keep him occupied, or maybe a real job. He left the kitchen. He started spritzing. The cats hung around at his feet, curious. Hildy followed.

"I guarantee he's not feeling amorous toward her. The relationship is dead. It just needs a proper burial," he said at last.

"From your lips to God's ears. But I don't share your certainty. I'd like to know where Mike slept last night; then I might feel better. Or worse." Hildy's heart thumped against her ribs, heavy like lead. She went to the closet and scooped up her makeup kit in her right hand. Then she headed for the only mirror in the cottage, the one on the bathroom medicine chest.

When she got a look at herself, she discovered that her hair had returned to the razor cut and highlighting of yesterday afternoon. She took out the wand from a tube of mascara and leaned forward. Her blue eyes stared back at her, but something about them had changed.

Hildy had dressed in a pair of new white mid-thigh shorts, rope-soled espadrilles, and a light blue cotton top with spaghetti straps. There was nothing magic about them; she bought them on sale at Macy's when she went shopping with Corrine. It didn't matter. Even with her own clothes on, she didn't look like the same person she was two days ago. She—what was it?—*sparkled*. She supposed the genie had something to do with it.

"By the way," she called out to Tony G. from the bathroom, "my sister is coming to visit. I have to leave for the casino in a couple of minutes to pick her up."

Tony G. exited the sunporch and came to stand outside the bathroom door. "You're telling me this why?"

"You can't go. You need to guard the house and the cats. For all I know Jimmy the Bug will try to burn me out next. But Corrine's visit presents us with a dilemma. What do I do with you when we come back here?"

Tony G. shrugged. "You introduce me as Count Arigento. Your foreign student."

Hildy shook her head. "You don't know my sister. She has this sixth sense. She'll know I'm lying. She'll know you're a phony. It's not going to work."

"So what's the alternative? I can't leave the premises unless I take Shelley and Keats with me. And where will you tell your sister the cats are? Getting a tan? Visiting the lonely cat Henry next door?"

Hildy's face lit up. "Why, that's perfect! Let me ask Mrs. Baier if she'll catsit. I think I'll give her my spare house key too. Jimmy the Bug won't know where they are. They'll be completely safe. You take the day off. Really. Go to the beach. Whatever."

Tony G. kept a poker face. "That's a great idea." Suddenly he twitched his nose and tossed some glitter toward the ceiling. A lovely musical crescendo danced up some invisible scales and then slid back down again. A camera phone appeared to float in front of the genie. He plucked it from the air.

"What's that for?" Hildy asked, her eyes big as saucers.

"I think I'll drop in on Kiki while you visit with your sister. We can keep in touch."

"Why is it that I think you're not telling me everything?"

Tony G. winked at her. "Because I'm not."

The sound of coffee hitting the inside of the cup made Mike wince. He kept his sunglasses on. He declined the offer of a menu.

Jake told the plump Spanish waitress pouring the java that he'd have the usual: scrambled, bacon, rye toast, OJ. When she left, Jake said, "You look like shit."

"I have a headache."

"Hangover?"

"That too."

"Maybe you need the day off." Jake's annoyance soured his words. They were in the middle of a case. Mike needed to pull his weight, not be out partying until the wee hours.

"Don't get all pissy on me. I'm not taking any sick leave. In fact, I'd like to head back to Camden this morning. You go this afternoon. I just need an aspirin." Mike fumbled around in his jacket pocket for the bottle of pills he bought at the hotel's gift shop.

"What happened at Marty's last night? Anything shaking?"

Mike opened his mouth, threw back three pills, and gulped the coffee. "Nothing. The lights downstairs went out at eight thirty. I figured that meant he was taking in the welcome mat. The bathroom light upstairs shut down before nine. I guess Marty Biz needed his beauty sleep. I sat around for a while but nobody showed. So I left by ten."

Jake said he figured that made sense. While Mike took the morning shift, he'd start nosing around to see if any construction equipment had been spotted at a truck stop or highway rest area. He'd also check warehouses in a fifty-mile radius to see if the stolen equipment was being stored, although usually the buyer for the stolen machines was waiting somewhere to take delivery, no questions asked.

Then Mike and Jake kicked around the idea of setting up a van to watch Jimmy the Bug's house directly. They killed that option fast. First of all, Jimmy would probably spot them since he'd been spied on by one agency or another for the past thirty years. Two, the Feds were probably already there. And three, Jimmy was too smart to lead anybody to anything incriminating at his own home. Marty Biz was a better target. They considered tapping his phone.

Then Mike told Jake he bought a new car, was going to ditch the Mercedes, and would start looking for someplace to live down the shore as soon as he could.

Business taken care of, the food arrived. Jake began eating his breakfast and spitting out what was bothering him. "Mike, you going to be able to operate with half a head? You got something on your mind, and if I had to take a wild guess, I'd guess it's booty."

Mike reached over and snagged a piece of rye toast from Jake's order. "I'll get it straightened out. Don't worry about it. I don't know what's the matter with me. I see Hildy and I'm like a man in a trance. Then I make up my mind to break it off with Kiki, and go and do something stupid that digs me in deeper." With a sigh, he spilled out what happened last night when he returned to the suite.

"Let me get this straight," Jake said, forking down his scrambled eggs. "You were dead drunk. You have no clear memory of actually having sex. It's true you're young and you think you're a hot stud, but I doubt you could have, even if you would have. If you get what I mean."

Mike paused midbite. "I assumed I did. She was naked and looked pretty satisfied."

"You know what they say about *assume*. It makes an *ass* out of *u* and *me*. If you ask me, and you did ask me, I'd say you were being worked. You follow me? Kiki is shrewd. You weren't doing what she wanted about the wedding, so she manipulated it. She's going to keep manipulating, my friend."

"But I don't know for sure. What I do know is I'm acting like a dog, with both of them."

Jake mopped up bacon grease on his plate with the rye bread. "Now, my mama always told me that one thing I should never do is get between a man and a woman. So I should keep my mouth shut. But I have to ask you one thing. Do you see yourself spending the rest of your life with either of these ladies? From what I can gather, you're already hiding the truth from your fiancée about your job, your car, where you're going to be living, and what you're doing with an old girlfriend. What's that all about?"

Mike stared at Jake; understanding switched on like a lightbulb in his brain. "It's about me being an idiot," he said. Mike signaled the waitress. The aspirin must be working. Suddenly he wanted something to eat.

Chapter 19

Only one road led onto Long Beach Island; only one road led off. The Route 72 Causeway ran in a wide single ribbon across Barnegat Bay, linking the three small islands between Manahawkin and Ship Bottom in a series of bridges. For the past several hours, John Pugiliese had parked in the CVS Pharmacy lot, where he could see Hildy's car the minute she turned off Long Beach Boulevard onto the causeway. Jake and Mike weren't alone in running a surveillance operation. Jimmy the Bug had decided to keep tabs on Hildy's goings and comings. It was simple.

At almost exactly ten thirty a.m. on that hot, humid day, Hildy's bright red Volkswagen Beetle zoomed past. Puggy pulled his black Lincoln Town Car out of the lot to follow her.

Listening to the radio, switching channels frequently to avoid any sad golden oldie love songs, Hildy took the by-now-familiar Route 72 past the strip malls until she reached the Garden State Parkway. She entered the toll road at Exit 63 and headed south.

Puggy made an accurate guess that she was headed for Atlantic City. He phoned back to the boss, who sent Sal and Joey to watch for her when she exited the parkway onto the Atlantic City Expressway.

The two thugs got there in plenty of time. They easily spotted the bright red car. Their Nissan Pathfinder hugged it close as Hildy headed east toward the gambling mecca. The black SUV continued to stick right behind the VW Bug up the ramp into the Caesar's parking lot. Puggy's Lincoln rolled into the same entrance not one minute later.

Hildy saw no evil, heard no evil, spoke no evil. She had her mind on Mike and his lack of calls, not on her own security. It never occurred to her that she could be followed. Being stalked was not part of the sheltered, safe world she had always known.

She never looked around the shadowy garage when she parked her car. She didn't observe the two vehicles that had traveled right behind her and stopped around the next turn. She didn't hear the three men exit their vehicles. She didn't check behind her when she walked at a brisk pace from the parking garage to the bus drop-off area.

She was a victim waiting to be victimized.

When she reached stall six, the St. Vlad's bus had just pulled in. The casino representative hopped on the bus to distribute coupons good for fifteen dollars' worth of play at any machine or table. After the uniformed employee jumped off, Father John appeared in the bus door. He waved at Hildy before exiting to stand on the pavement, ready to help the less spry players down the bus steps.

First out after him was Corrine. She spotted Hildy and rushed toward her, grabbing her little sister in a tight embrace.

"Hey! What are you doing? I'm fine." The show of emotion surprised Hildy and embarrassed her.

It also further distracted her from noticing the three men positioning themselves about twenty feet away.

Puggy had taken a gun from his waistband and put it at his side. Sal and Joey looked at each other and grinned. This would make up for their screwup the other night. They could grab the girl *and* the other woman. From the family resemblance, the second female had to be the sister who their boss had discovered was Hildy's only close relative. They had hit the jackpot without gambling a dime.

As Hildy and Corrine started walking back toward the parking garage, Puggy moved quickly, coming in from the right. Joey came in from the left. Sal watched their backs.

"Don't scream or I'll shoot you right here." Puggy shoved the hard steel of a gun into Hildy's side and snarled, his rubbery lips next to Hildy's ear. Hildy froze and stayed silent. Corrine had started to say, "Wha—" when Joey slipped his hand around the back of her neck and squeezed his fingers just enough to let her know he meant business. She swallowed her cry.

"Just walk along with us quietly and nobody gets hurt," Puggy ordered. His voice was cold and cruel.

Hildy nodded and found herself propelled toward the parking garage. Her heart was racing. She had read that the worst thing a woman could do was get into a vehicle with her abductor. But she couldn't react. Not only was there a gun pressed into her side, but she saw how Joey held Corrine. She feared the burly attacker would break her sister's neck with his huge hand.

Hildy found herself trapped and helpless; her eyes went wild with terror. She didn't know how to save herself or Corrine.

*   *   *

As Tony G. had stated not long ago, one of the basic rules of engagement is to never underestimate your enemy. None of Jimmy the Bug's crew paid the slightest bit of attention to what they believed were the frail, elderly parishioners of St. Vlad's getting off the bus and gathering around Father John.

Among those who had hurried, as Corrine had, to be among the first to debark was an eighty-year-old, nattily dressed man named Roger Samuels. He stood impatiently near the bus, urging Irene, his wife of fifty-five years, to "get a move on it." He blew air through his lips, exasperated that Irene was so damned slow and she knew he had to get to a particular Wheel of Fortune machine before anyone else did.

"Always in a hurry, and where are you going? Nowhere, that's where," Irene answered, not looking at Roger. Under her breath she kept muttering, "You can hold your damned horses. I'm not moving from this spot until I'm good and ready." Irene could be just as stubborn as her husband. She decided to irritate him further by taking her time. She needed to dig her player's card out of her purse and put it on the spiral card chain before they went another step.

Annoyed at the delay, Roger looked around impatiently. He immediately saw something that caught his attention. It brought back memories of China, where he had been stationed with the merchant marines during the Korean War. He had seen men shot, robbed, and abducted off the street in Shanghai more than once. He had no doubt about what he was seeing here.

"Hey!" he bellowed. *"Hey! Those guys have Corrine!"* He pointed with his cane.

Like swarming ants, the parishioners of St. Vlad's surged forward, the few men among them yelling loudly, and the ladies screaming in the high-pitched tones of the Algerian women in the film *The Battle of Algiers.*

Far from being frail or aged in spirit, these were the rawboned, big-bodied sons and daughters of Slav, Czech, Pole, and Russian miners and factory workers. They shared an ethnic memory of suffering and injustice that went back generations. They weren't born with silver spoons in their mouths. They knew how to work. And they knew how to fight.

Sal turned to check out the sudden noise behind him. He found a screaming gray-haired mob closing in on him. He threw up his arms to protect his face as Annie whacked him with her purse. Simultaneously Roger jabbed Sal hard in the kidneys with the tip of his cane. Irene, meanwhile, whose godmother had owned a neighborhood beer garden and thus given Irene plenty of exposure to the art of the bar fight, leaped at Puggy with her house keys in her hand, raking them across his cheek.

Puggy would have gunned her down like a dog, he was so incensed about the scratch on his face. But he didn't have a chance. Father John, Scranton's Golden Gloves champ of 1954, rabbit-punched him in the back of the neck, then spun him around to give him a hard right cross that landed with enough force to send Puggy's nose sliding sideways with a sickening crack, deviating his septum with a vengeance.

Puggy howled and lost hold of his gun, which skittered into the nearby bus parking lane. With his nose already spurting dark red blood, he desperately tried to block the vicious uppercut which then broke his jaw and sent him falling backward.

At the same second that Puggy was meeting Father John's iron fist, Maria Sosnowski, two hundred and twenty-two pounds of good healthy adipose tissue created over the years from a diet of *haluski* and kielbasa, hauled off and kicked Joey so hard in the butt that he went to his knees.

By this time, about thirty enraged members of St. Vlad's had set upon the three men, bludgeoning them with purses, shoes, and Ed Rushinsky's crutch. Sal pulled Joey from the melee, Puggy dragged himself free, losing his blood-drenched shirt in the process, and the three men ran for their lives.

None of the old people were good at running anymore. They let them go, shaking their fists and hurling Slavic curses in their wake.

Annie gently took the arm of a dazed Corrine and asked her if she was hurt. Corrine said she was shook up but fine. She looked around frantically for her sister.

Hildy, drained of all color and white as paper, was safely standing next to Irene Samuels, who was patting her arm in a comforting manner. While Father John was dispatching Puggy, the cane-wielding Roger had grabbed Hildy and dragged her away from the fight.

Hildy had briefly struggled to return to the donnybrook, but Roger held her back. Now that it was all over, Hildy looked around, desperately worried that one of the seniors had gotten hurt because of her. She saw Janey Snoglachek sitting on the tile floor.

"Oh no," she cried and hurried over to the figure who was dressed entirely in black from her babushka to her orthopedic shoes.

"Are you injured?" She put her arm around the heavyset woman and helped her stand.

"I'm fine, dear," she assured Hildy. "I didn't fall. I gave my walker to my friend Franny so she could bean that fellow who was kidnapping you."

"Oh, I'm so sorry. You could have been killed."
Hildy wanted to cry, she was so distressed.

"Now, now, dear," Janey said. "I'm ninety-one
years old, but I'm not about to let those hooligans
get away with that kind of nonsense. And we
kicked their butt, now didn't we."

Hildy didn't want to talk to the police. She knew
very well why the men had attempted to abduct
her. The last thing she wanted to do was spend
the next several hours lying her head off to the
authorities. She certainly didn't want the incident
to get in the newspapers.

While the members of the St. Vlad crowd were
comparing stories and waiting for security to show
up, as they surely would any minute, Hildy slipped
next to Corrine and said, "Let's get out of here."

"Don't we need to report this?" Corrine asked,
clearly puzzled.

"We need to go. I'll explain later. Really, come
on."

Holding her sister by the elbow, Hildy moved
them at a fast jog to her car, but this time she
looked around carefully to make sure the garage
was clear of assailants. *Nothing like locking the
barn door after the horse is stolen,* she said to herself. But she had learned a lesson she'd never
forget.

When they were safely on the open road, and
she had convinced herself that nobody was behind
them, Hildy turned to her sister. "Are you okay?
I'm so sorry that happened."

"What do you mean, you're sorry? What's going
on, Hildy? You look as guilty as the time you bor-
rowed my green cashmere sweater without asking
me and somebody at the football game spilled a
Coke all over it."

"I'm sorry because I should have expected something like that to happen. I should have been more careful. I know why those men were trying to kidnap us. Two of them attacked me a couple of nights ago. I guess I'm in a lot of trouble." Hildy focused on the road as much as she could. It was easier to talk if she didn't have to face Corrine, who was shooting suspicious looks at her.

"So *why* did they try to abduct us?"

"Remember that bottle I found next to the Slingo machine?"

"Sort of. It was some souvenir thing."

"No, it wasn't a souvenir. It was really valuable and the owner wants it back."

"So he's going to kidnap you to get it? That makes no kind of sense. Why didn't he just ask you for it? You were going to take it to the Lost and Found anyway if I remember correctly." Suspicion now warred with confusion on her face.

"I couldn't return it to him because of the genie that was inside the bottle. The guy who wanted it back was a Mafia don, you know, like the Godfather, and he wanted the genie to make him boss of bosses. After that, he could use the genie's powers to take over organized crime in the entire country."

Corrine struggled against the seat belt to turn and get a good look at her little sister. "Did you hit your head? Do you have a fever? Maybe we better drive to a hospital instead of to your cottage." Corrine reached over and put the back of her hand on Hildy's forehead.

"Hey! I'm driving. I can't see. I'm not sick. I'm not crazy. I'm telling you what happened. You have to believe me on this."

"Believe you?" Corrine's voice came out in the high soprano range. "Should I believe you if you said you just visited Santa Claus at the North Pole or helped the Easter Bunny dye eggs? You're talking crazy. There couldn't have been a genie in that bottle. Genies are in fairy tales. They're not real. Seriously, Hildy, what's going on? What kind of trouble are you really in?"

"Look, I know it sounds impossible, but this genie—he's from ancient Rome, by the way—is real. He's the one who made Michael run into me on the beach, because I wished I'd see him again. Understand? Now he's trying to help with getting Michael to realize he really loves me, which I don't know is such a good idea."

Corrine was shaking her head. "I'm really worried. You're talking crazy, Hildy. It's scaring me."

Hildy let go of the steering wheel for a minute with her right hand and reached over to give Corrine a reassuring squeeze. "Don't get upset. Look, you'll see when you meet Tony. He's as solid as you and me, except when he changes into smoke and goes back inside his bottle."

Corrine put her face in her hands. "Oh, God help us. My sister has totally lost her mind."

Naturally, when Hildy and Corrine reached the cottage and went inside, the genie wasn't there.

"So where is he?" Corrine asked.

"I gave him the day off. I told him to go to the beach, but he wanted to go see Kiki. She thinks his name is Count Arigento and he wants her to do a photo shoot of him and George Clooney in Italy. He should be back soon."

Corrine continued to look at Hildy as if she were totally bonkers.

Hildy remembered she needed to check on the cats. "Just make yourself comfortable. I need to call Mrs. Baier next door."

"Why?" Corrine asked. They had just walked in the door and her sister had to call the neighbor? It wasn't like Hildy at all.

"She's taking care of Shelley and Keats. They're

over at her house playing with Henry so Jimmy the Bug doesn't steal them when I'm not home."

"Oh, that explains it." Corrine started looking around the little house, trying to grasp some clue about what the hell was going on. The kitchen floor shone with wax. The windowpanes sparkled. The sink had regained its original whiteness after years of yellow stains. The place was spotless. That wasn't like Hildy either. A cold chill dragged its skinny finger up her spine.

Hildy was on her cell phone, telling Mrs. Baier she was back. Then she said, sure, since Henry was having such a good time, the cats could stay for a while longer. Once she ended the call, she turned to Corrine. "You don't believe a word I've said, do you?"

"Noooo. How could I?"

"Take a leap of faith! Just for once, believe in me!" Her face started to crumple. She needed her sister to trust her. To Hildy, love should always trump reason.

Corrine plucked a tissue out of the box on the coffee table and handed it to Hildy. "Come on, don't get upset. Your mascara will run. I do believe in you, I'm simply having a little trouble understanding what's going on. Can you give me more information? Maybe it's a matter of interpretation, you know? Like a Rorschach test."

Hildy sniffed. "Look, Corrine, I'll give you proof. Do you notice anything different about me?"

Corrine studied her sister. "You are looking exceptionally pretty, except that the tip of your nose is all red. Your hair looks terrific. I didn't know that stylist in the mall gave you such a great haircut. Very flattering."

"Right. Only the mall stylist didn't give it to me. It was the genie who created it. He threw gold dust into the air and it happened. And wait, wait, look at this." Hildy hurried over to the large closet next to the bathroom and flung the door open. "Donna Karan originals. Now where would I have gotten them? How could I have afforded them? The genie conjured them up for me. He thought seeing me all dressed up would impress Mike. Maybe it did. I think it might have."

Hildy threw herself into one of the white wicker chairs. "That's what I really need to talk with you about. The whole thing with Mike is all screwed up. He didn't even try to call me today. Maybe he's not going to."

Corrine went over to the closet and inspected the two dresses Hildy had shown her. They appeared to be genuine couture clothes, but they could be knockoffs. They didn't resemble anything Hildy had ever worn though.

With one ear, she listened to Hildy rattling on about Mike Amante. In her mind, the problem of getting back with an old boyfriend paled beside the fact that her sister was being pursued by the Mafia. That wasn't her imagination. The two of them had nearly been kidnapped. Lord knows what could have happened. It was terrifying. She decided to speak her mind.

"Hildy, look, I don't want to be insensitive or anything about Mike and you, but I'm concerned about what happened back at the casino. You're in danger. I don't know why those men are after you, but I'm scared for you."

Hildy sighed. She had been as clear as she possibly could be about the situation. "Oh, Corrine, don't you understand? Those men are after you too!"

Chapter 20

Surveillance work is ninety percent boredom. The other ten percent covers the gamut of feelings from the exhilaration of nailing a target in the act to the sick-making stress that accompanies *Oh shit, I lost him.*

With the needle stuck firmly in the ninety percent column, Mike had a severe case of buttock paresthesia, more commonly known as tingling tush. He had been sitting in the rental car for three hours with nothing to do but listen to the radio.

Then a blue van pulled up in front of Marty's. A rush of adrenaline spiked through Mike's veins. He grabbed the cell phone. His partner answered on the first ring. "Hey, Jake."

"Yeah? What's cooking?"

"A contractor showed up at Marty's. His truck says he's from Fast Builders in Delaware."

"The guy's probably putting in an order for equipment. Let's hope he's a repeat customer. Some of the other stolen machines may be sitting on his lot. I've got a list of serial numbers."

"You want me to follow him back to his place?"

"No, just read me the address off the side of the van." Mike did.

Jake decided he'd drive down to the guy's operation in Delaware and snoop around. They would need to watch Fast Builders and be ready to follow when the contractor went out with a flatbed to pick up the stolen machines.

Mike got the picture quickly. "Right. We don't know where Marty's going to grab the machines or who's going to steal them, but we can be there when they make the delivery. Then we can follow the thieves who are making the drop-off back to the boss."

"Yeah. Hopefully their boss is Jimmy the Bug and not Marty. We have to wait and watch. Our best-case scenario is to identify some of Marty's other customers if we're going to make any money by recovering the stolen equipment."

Mike couldn't see how they were going to get the names of the other customers except to keep watching for contractors' vans to show up at Marty's. "I think we're going to need more manpower than the two of us. You and I can't keep sitting around in Camden."

"No problem. I'll call in some of the guys I use for security. We'll figure out how to pay them later."

"Agreed. Look, I need a favor. See if you can send one of those guys down here to watch Marty now. I've got some business to take care of later today."

"Yeah, monkey business. Well, do what you have to do."

One of the things Hildy loved about Ship Bottom was the proximity of everything she needed. Today, it turned out she needed ice. She walked a block up to the boulevard and she bought a large plastic bag of it from the big square machine. Then she used some to make a batch of homemade lemon-

ade. She added a sprig of fresh mint and dropped
a plump ripe strawberry in each of the two glasses
she poured.

She had put some of the remaining cubes in a
dish towel. Right now, the dish towel lay across
Corrine's forehead. Corrine was stretched out on
the chaise lounge in the sunporch.

Hildy's older sister had not reacted well to the
news that she was implicated in Hildy's problems
with the mob. Corrine had faithfully watched every
one of the eighty-six episodes in all six seasons of
The Sopranos. She had a vivid imagination. She
envisioned her and Hildy, each tied to a chair, their
eyes staring sightlessly, a dark round hole from a
deadly bullet in their foreheads. The image horrified her. Her knees weakened. She began to sway.
Her eyes rolled back in her head.

The Caldwell girls were what their relatives
called fainters. Corrine hit the floor with a crash.

Corrine's loss of consciousness had happened
some time before Hildy served the lemonade. At
present Corrine remained in a semiprone position
on the chaise and sipped the cool beverage. She
had had time to calm down and collect her
thoughts. "Look, the way I see it, the guy wants
the bottle, give it to him. It's not worth dying for."

Hildy dragged a wicker chair next to the chaise
so they could both put their lemonade glasses on
a little round wicker table. "I told you why I
couldn't do that. It would be unethical to hand the
means to build an empire to this remorseless criminal. Besides, I promised Tony I would help him
escape from Jimmy the Bug. He doesn't want to
go back to a life of crime."

Corrine moaned. "Hildy Hildy Hildy. If this were
the 1970s I'd think someone dropped a tab of acid
in your drink. But it's not. I don't know why you
keep insisting that there's a genie in the bottle,

except that you've become . . . you've become . . . eccentric. You're just like Elwood and the giant rabbit in that old movie *Harvey*. I suppose it's something I can learn to live with. But you need to make your peace with Mr. Big."

"He's not Mr. *Big*. It's Bug, and his real name is Torelli. I can't make my peace with him. He's a stone killer. I need to get him taken off the streets, arrested, thrown in the slammer. That's what I need to do." Hildy's eyes were on fire. She felt as if she were on the edge of an epiphany. "Yes! That's it. That's the answer."

Corrine shook her head under the bandana of towel-wrapped ice. She held the compress in place with one graceful hand. She kept her eyes closed. "Don't you watch any television at all? These Mafia guys keep running the Family from prison. John Gotti did. So did Johnny 'Sack.' You have this guy arrested and put away, and he'll get you for it."

Corrine reached out with her free hand and fumbled around blindly until she found Hildy's arm. She squeezed it. "Hildy, listen. Just give Bugs the bottle. The genie is a figment of your imagination."

"No, he's not."

"Yes, he is."

"No, he's not."

"Yes! Yes, he is!"

"No, he is not," a deep voice boomed.

Corrine bolted upright, her eyes wide open. A big man wearing a red and yellow Hawaiian shirt and walking shorts stood in the doorway. Her cold compress hit the floor. Ice cubes skated across the tile. "Don't kill us. She'll give you the bottle!" she screamed.

Tony G.'s eyes sought Hildy's. "Now I know who you take after. Your sister doesn't listen either."

"Corrine," Hildy said, quickly standing next to her sister and putting her hand on her shoulder. "Relax. It's okay. This is Antonius Eugenius. The genie I told you about. He likes to be called Tony G."

Corrine turned on Hildy. "Are you crazy! Are you out of your mind! He's just some guy off the beach. Those clothes are straight from Ron Jon's." Her expression changed. She looked at her sister with pity. "Hildy, what load of garbage did he feed you, you poor gullible child? Did you give him money?"

Then, bristling with outrage, she twisted her head toward Tony G. "Did you tell her you were a genie, you . . . you scam artist! I should call the cops, that's what I should do. Hildy, give me your cell phone!"

Tony G. smiled. He extended his camera phone toward Corrine. "Lady, here, you can borrow mine, but why don't you wait a minute." With that he tossed a handful of glittering particles outward. They formed a golden rainbow that turned into a shining arch above Corrine and Hildy and the chaise as well. The temperature in the room plummeted. The air around the genie became as liquid as mercury. It swirled and dipped in undulating waves. Then it disappeared. A warm breeze returned. Tony G. stood in the middle of the room with a laurel wreath on his dark curls, his sword at his side, a staff in his hand, and a toga on his magnificent body.

Corrine's eyes rolled back in her head again and she sank unconscious to the floor.

After a few minutes Corrine had regained her senses and her pugnaciousness. She insisted on pinching Tony G.'s arm to see if he was real. She examined the iron sword he carried. She queried the purpose of the staff. (Tony explained that it was called a *vitis,* a symbol of authority that some centurions wielded like a policeman's nightstick). She peppered him with questions. She demanded to see the bottle, which Hildy had been keeping in the refrigerator.

While Tony G. patiently bore Corrine's relentless questioning, Hildy left to get the bottle for Corrine to inspect. She had just walked back into the enclosed sunporch when she saw a bronze Ford Fusion parked next to her red VW Beetle in front of the cottage. Had the thugs come for her again? Her heart raced as she got ready to sound the alarm. Then she saw Mike emerge from the driver's seat.

She thrust the bottle toward Tony G. "Get in here, quick!" He complied in a flash, leaving a luminescent trail of silver that hovered in the air. The bell rang. Hildy handed the bottle to a dumbfounded Corrine and went to answer the door.

"You didn't call me," Hildy said in lieu of hello.

"You weren't answering my calls," Mike countered.

"Should I have?" she said, as icy as the cubes in the lemonade.

Mike couldn't understand why Hildy had to make this so damned difficult. He didn't understand women at all. "Yes, you should," he said. "Will you answer if I call you?"

"Okay, I will." She started to shut the door.

"Wait!"

"What? I thought we were done."

"Hildy, come on. I drove all the way up here from Atlantic City to talk to you. I really need to talk to you."

"Well, I have company."

Mike's face darkened. "Is that count fellow in there? What's he doing here?"

Hildy flung the door open so Mike could see inside. "No, Corrine is here. Mike, you remember my sister, don't you?"

Mike sheepishly nodded his head. "Hi, Corrine. It's been a long time."

"Come on in here, Michael Amante," Corrine ordered. "I would like to say something to you."

Mike stepped into the room. The air smelled like ozone after a lightning strike. "You visiting for a while?" he asked.

"Just the afternoon. But sit down, will you? Do you know that you are killing your mother?"

"Corrine!" Hildy gasped.

Mike's face paled. "Killing my mother? Is she sick? I haven't been back to see her in months. Maybe I should call home." He grabbed his cell phone from the holder on his belt.

"Hold it!" Corrine ordered. "Let me ask you something. Why haven't you been to see your mother in months? You can drive there in a couple of hours. She raised you alone after your dad died. She sacrificed plenty to get you through school. So what? You are too big and important to go home now that your name gets in the papers?"

Guilt kept Mike from meeting Corrine's eyes. "No, it's nothing like that. I've been busy, that's all."

"Too busy to see your mother? She's not getting any younger, you know. One of these days she may not be there for you to see her. Michael Amante, I'm really disappointed in you."

Mike felt terrible. He had missed Thanksgiving, Christmas, and his mother's birthday. He had sent her a present, but he knew in his heart that wasn't right. He stared at his hands. "My mother and Kiki don't get along very well, and Kiki doesn't like to go up to Wilkes-Barre. She gets bored. She says there's nothing to do. She says that my mother can come to us if she wants to see me."

"That's what Kiki says. Is that what you think?"

"No, I guess not." He finally looked at Corrine. "I didn't realize how deeply I was hurting Mom. I'll call her later and I'll get up to see her as soon as I can."

"Michael, I'm not one to mince words—"

"You can say that again," Hildy muttered under her breath. Corrine shot her a dirty look.

"But the next time you call your mother should be when you tell her you've broken off your engagement to this Kiki person. Any woman who tries to drive a wedge between a son and his mother is selfish to the core. It shows her true colors. And another thing—"

Oh-oh, Hildy thought, *here it comes.*

"If you think you're going to hurt my sister by playing with her emotions, you've got another think coming. Why, never in my life did I expect you, of all people, to—"

"Corrine!" Hildy interrupted. "It's between Mike and me."

Corrine shut her mouth, pressed her lips firmly together, and crossed her arms over her chest.

"Look, Corrine, I drove up here to talk to Hildy, so if she'll come with me, we'll go out for a while, and I'll tell her what's on my mind. I promise you I have no intention of hurting her." He stood up and extended his hand to Hildy. She nodded and took it. They walked to the door.

"Mike!" Corrine's voice was sharp as a razor's edge.

He paused and looked at her.

"Remember. The path to hell is paved with good

intentions. And I will personally send you there myself if you so much as give my sister reason to shed one tear. You hear me?"

Mike nodded, and he and Hildy escaped through the front door as fast as they could.

Chapter 21

"Where's your big car?" Hildy asked as she hopped into the Ford.

"I'm getting rid of it. I'm using a rental until my new car gets delivered," he said, looking like the cat that swallowed the canary.

"You seem so pleased with yourself. What did you buy? A Lamborghini?"

"No, better," he teased.

"Not a Ferrari?" She was thinking what a waste of money that would be.

"No, not a Ferrari." He grinned.

"What then? I give up. A Rolls? A Bentley?"

"A Prius."

"No! You didn't. Really? Why on earth did you buy a hybrid? The other day you didn't seem to care at all about your carbon footprint."

"A lot has changed since the other day, hasn't it?" he said, and looked at her.

"Yes. Yes, it has." Hildy glanced down at her hands, suddenly shy.

"You want me to park somewhere, and we'll sit in the car and talk?" Mike asked as he drove to the corner.

"Oh no!" Hildy cried, her high spirits returning. "I couldn't bear to sit in the car on such a beautiful day. Let's head down to Barnegat Lighthouse. It's a very special place. I want you to see it. We can talk there. Turn left and keep going until you get to the end of the island.''

"Whatever you want, sure." Michael started north past Ron Jon's and the junction with Route 72. In minutes, they had left Ship Bottom and entered the adjacent town of Surf City, as its onion-shaped water tower clearly proclaimed.

Hildy provided a running commentary as Mike traveled slowly down the boulevard. The first thing that he absolutely had to see, she insisted, was Woodies Drive-In. There it was on their left. She pointed at the vintage white building through the windshield. Didn't it look just like restaurants did in the 1950s? she asked. Maybe they should stop for a hot dog, a foot-long one just like they used to get at the Ranch Wagon in Dallas. Remember?

Mike absorbed her happy chatter like a sponge. Hildy didn't talk about her meetings with movie stars or European royalty. She didn't keep pulling down the visor mirror to check her makeup. She didn't take out her cell phone and start making calls when he was right in the middle of a sentence.

He gladly pulled into Woodies. They went inside and ordered hot dogs with everything and Cokes with lots of ice. Then they finished off their meal with cones of soft vanilla ice cream, which they carried back outside. In the stifling temperature that hovered around ninety, the ice cream soon dripped all over their fingers, so Mike challenged her to a race to see who could lick the ice cream down to the top of the waffle cone fastest.

No biting, they said together. That would be cheating.

After two or three big licks, Mike had to quit because he got brain freeze. He made the funniest faces. Hildy laughed and kept licking. She won. She stuck out her white tongue at him. He couldn't help himself; he grabbed her around the shoulders and gave her a quick kiss on the nose.

They got back into the rental car and a few blocks later, Hildy told Mike to slow down to see the How You Brewin'? Internet Café where she usually checked her e-mail and drank espresso.

"Can we stop?" she asked, her blue eyes so irresistible he couldn't say no. Inside, Mike hung around the front counter, while Hildy logged in on one of the computers and deleted all her junk mail. There wasn't anything else in her mailbox, she informed him when she rejoined him just minutes later at the counter. She paid for her time on the computer and bought them two huge chocolate chip cookies, "for the road," she said. Then they were off again.

When they were nearly out of Surf City and entering the next town of North Beach, she squealed and pointed to a store on the corner of an ordinary strip mall. "There's Ciao Bella. The owner makes wonderful jewelry, and it's not expensive either. And the clothing is really cute."

"Do you want me to stop?"

"Oh no! I have all the clothes I can use right now. I just wanted to show it to you. I liked it, so, you know, I wanted to share it."

"I don't think I can use a wraparound skirt anytime soon," he joked.

She gave him a little punch in the bicep. They both laughed, and then they exchanged glances and got very quiet. Mike reached over and put his right arm around her shoulders, pulling her toward him, like he used to when they drove around in his pickup truck. The center console got in the way, but neither of them cared.

They rode along in a contented silence for a while, while the island narrowed even more until it was barely a city block wide. Suddenly Hildy yelled at him to stop the car.

"Look! Do you see that!" She excitedly pointed at a newly constructed, grayish white house on the bay side of the road, nearly hidden by some scrub pines. The building was palatial. It had to cost more than a million dollars, but it had a giant plastic Slurpee container, or at least that's what Hildy thought it looked like, stuck right in the middle of its front. The oddly shaped "tower" was sitting on an angle, as if someone had tipped it slightly to take a sip. Its flat roof looked exactly like a soda container's lid too, and there was a round raised skylight smack in the middle of it that resembled the bubble where you'd insert a straw.

Mike leaned forward over the steering wheel, peering out of the car's windshield in disbelief. "It's definitely just like a big plastic soda cup. And that fence around the bottom makes it look as if it's sitting inside a cardboard take-out carrier. I've never seen anything like it."

"What were they thinking?" Hildy giggled.

"I think it's an homage," Mike suggested with great seriousness. "This must be the home of the 7-Eleven Slurpee inventor. His millions were made from blue raspberry ice."

Hildy nodded gravely. "I do believe you are right, professor. It's a brilliant and daring public tribute to one's roots." They looked at each other and smiled.

All the gloom that had been following Mike around for days, for months really, vanished. He looked at Hildy grinning at him, her dimples showing. She appeared even more adorable today in her shorts and simple top than she did all dolled up last night. He couldn't take his eyes off her. He realized he was in love, and he was, at last, a happy man.

* * *

At the very northern tip of the island, on the south side of Barnegat Inlet, "Old Barney" stood in the spot where it had been built in 1859, using a design created by General George C. Meade. For nearly a hundred and fifty years it had survived the eroding waves and the worst of hurricanes. It remained solid and stately at the edge of the sea, but was no longer a working light. Now it was open to the public.

Hildy showed Mike where to enter the state park's parking lot. They quickly climbed out of the car and walked toward the lighthouse. Neither of them knew how it happened but they were holding hands.

Painted white on the bottom and a dark barn red on the upper half, Barnegat Lighthouse rose 172 feet above sea level. A sign outside warned that there were 217 steps to the top, and visitors should not attempt the climb if they:

Have or had a heart condition
Have or had serious heart trouble
Have or had serious back trouble
Have or had recent surgery or illness
Are subject to dizziness
Are afraid of heights

They read the notice together. Mike kissed Hildy's temple and said, "I may have a heart condition, but I don't think it's medical."

Hildy's own heart skipped a beat at his words. "Should we go up to the top?" she asked. "I see a lot of people walking on the jetty, but I don't think anybody else is crazy enough to climb those stairs in this heat and humidity."

"So we're crazy, you mean?" Mike teased.

"Without a doubt. I really wanted to show you

the view from the top. But it isn't just the view. You'll see. There's history in the stairs. You can feel it."

Mike studied Hildy. She thrilled him, he had to admit it to himself. He was hooked but good. "You have a very vivid imagination, don't you?"

Hildy shook her head. "It's not my imagination. Mike, I've learned some things recently. One of them is that if you allow yourself to be open, you'd be surprised what exists in this world that most people think is just a fantasy."

"I know *you* surprise me," Mike said, pulling her close and gazing down at her. "You amaze me. You stupefy me. You dazzle me."

"And you are so full of it, Mike!" Hildy disengaged from his arms and tugged him by the hand to the narrow door that led into the historic structure.

As it turned out, Mike truly was overtaken by a sense of awe once he stood inside. The yellow metal staircase spiraled upward as far as he could see, like a wild abstract sculpture. Their voices echoed off the brick walls. They started climbing. The risers were steep and narrow. They were grateful that they could rest on a landing about every twenty steps.

Sweat glistened on Hildy's arms and legs by the time they reached the small chamber on the top where the famous Fresnel lens, six feet in diameter and ten feet high, once provided a beacon for ships sailing between New York City and Europe. Mike stopped to admire the part of it visible in the circular room.

Hildy waited a minute before pulling him away and leading him to a miniature door. It led to the widow's walk outside and Mike had to duck down to go through it.

In the open air, high above the coast, the green-gray sea stretching to infinity below them, the wind

howled with an unexpected ferocity. It whipped
Hildy's hair around her face. It rippled their clothing.

"This feels so wonderful, doesn't it?" she called
to Mike over the noise of the wind.

"It's cooler than inside, but that wind is pretty
strong, don't you think?" he yelled back. They
stood on a three-foot-wide ledge inside a cage
made of iron bars. No one could fall from this high
perch or be blown off by accident. It was easy to
imagine that the powerful wind could have swept
someone off if there were no bars.

Hildy had to shout to be heard over the rushing
air. "It's exciting! The energy just fills me up." She
spread her arms and let the wind encircle her.

Mike moved close to her and lightly kissed the
back of her neck. He turned her around and she
pressed against him. With the sun beating down on
them and the wind racing across their skin and tear-
ing at their clothes, they kissed as if they had never
kissed before. And they kissed for a very long time.

After a while, they realized the kissing was awakening deeper passions, and this wasn't the time or
place for them. They reluctantly broke their embrace and went back inside. Mike suggested they
descend to the first landing where they could sit
down. He did want to talk with her; they had to
discuss what was happening between them.

Hildy nodded her agreement and they settled
themselves in a small alcove and clutched each other's hands.

"First, I want to apologize." Mike lowered his
eyes and held her hands tightly. "I could give you
a dozen excuses about how this situation arose so
suddenly that I wasn't sure what to do. But that's
a lie. I knew from the second I recognized you on
the beach that I still felt the same about you. No,
I felt more strongly than ever about you. It took

me by surprise. I felt like a man put under a spell or something."

An uneasiness stole over Hildy as Mike spoke. She hoped love had been the cause of his reaction and not Tony G. "Was that a bad thing?" she asked.

"No! It was great, and really confusing. Honest, Hildy, my life was already coming apart. I told you that. I wanted to switch careers, I wanted to move out of the city, and I had pretty much made up my mind I *did not* want to marry Kiki. Sure, I cared about her, but as time went on I had come to realize we weren't in synch. Our values were too different. Our dreams didn't mesh either."

"So do you think ours do? We don't really know each other anymore." Hildy forced herself to be rational, although in truth she didn't care about reason. If Mike said he wanted to go sell ice to the Inuit in Alaska, she'd think it was great. They'd have an adventure doing it. They'd be together, and the certainty hit her that being together was all she really wanted.

Mike sat there thinking about Hildy's question. "Hildy, we grew up in the same small town. Our mothers knew each other. We were taught the same things. We went to the same church in Lehman. I know we share the same values. As for our dreams, I'm going after mine. But I want yours to come true too. I think we can work out a future that makes us both happy."

Hildy slipped away from his hands. She took her fingers and smoothed his eyebrows, enjoying the feel of him. She kissed his eyelids. She traced the line of his lips. "Being with you makes me ridiculously happy," she said.

"I'd like to have a family. What about you? Do you want children, or would they get in the way of your career?"

He sounded so PC and so dumb, Hildy thought. "Mike, I want children. I want as many children as we can afford and the good Lord sends us."

"No kidding?" Mike was astonished. "But look, I really want to live here, at the Jersey shore. I'm starting this detective business with Jake in Atlantic City. We already signed the papers to incorporate. It's going to be one helluva mess to go back and live in Pennsylvania. I know you have a teaching job at the high school. If you can't move here though, I'll have to figure out how to commute."

Hildy kissed Mike again. "Mike, I would love to live at the shore. Ever since I arrived here, I felt as if I were in a new world that I didn't want to leave." She paused, then spoke quickly. "Listen, I have a suggestion. It's off the top of my head, but I think it might work. We can keep my house in Lehman as a vacation home. It's near your mom. We can go up there on holidays and weekends, and the kids would love summers in the mountains where we grew up. It will be perfect—"

"It sounds great, Hildy." Excitement swept him up. Then he saw her face, which had turned worried and a little sad. "What's wrong?"

"You're still engaged to Kiki, aren't you?"

"Technically. I wanted to end things last night. I didn't get the chance. She was asleep when I got in and she was still sleeping when I left this morning." Thinking about the previous evening made Mike uncomfortable. He hoped there weren't going to be any unforeseen complications because of his stupidly getting drunk. He pushed the thought away. Why worry about something that may not have even happened?

"Maybe we shouldn't be making plans for *us* when there isn't any *us*, at least not yet," she said.

"Hildy, listen to me." He put his hands on each side of her face. "I love you. I love *you*. I always have. I won't let *anything* keep us from being together. I give you my word. From this time on, there is an *us*. Whatever happened before today, please let it be the past. We can deal with it. *Us*, you and I, are the future. No matter what, Hildy. I promise you."

"Mike, please mean that, because it would break my heart forever if it's not true."

"Hildy, trust me. I would never let you down."

Chapter 22

Flushed with happiness, Hildy returned to the cottage with Mike late in the afternoon, at an hour when the light turns golden, sounds diminish, and shadows lengthen. She had been given a halcyon day. No murmur of disquietude marred her pleasure at simply being with the man she had loved in secret for so long and now was loved by in return. She didn't realize that such a still, sweet interlude often comes before the worst of storms.

They found Corrine, a magazine in her lap, on the sunporch, sitting alone except for the presence of Shelley and Keats, who had finished with their "play date." The cats sprawled under the chaise lounge, lazy and content. According to what Corrine had learned from Mrs. Baier, their afternoon included Fancy Feast and fresh cream. Corrine added, "Your neighbor said she would be delighted to have your 'dear little kitties' visit again soon. 'They make Henry so happy.' Is Henry her grandchild? She seemed to think I knew."

"Henry is her lonely Siamese," Hildy responded, then spoke sotto voce near Corrine's ear. "Where's the, you know, the bottle?"

Corrine whispered back, "The bottle is in the hall closet. Tony forbade me to put him back in the refrigerator. He's a charming"—she choked on the word—"*genie*. Wait until you see what he brought you."

Corrine tried to wag her eyebrows. Hildy thought she looked as if she had developed a tic. She couldn't begin to guess what Tony G. had for her that would provoke that kind of response.

Then Corrine turned to Mike. She smiled sweetly and asked him where he was going now. Discovering that he was heading back to Atlantic City, Corrine suggested that he save Hildy the trouble of driving her back to the St. Vladimir's bus.

Mike looked at Hildy. She thought she detected panic in his amber eyes. She was going to override Corrine's suggestion. Then she thought that if Mike truly meant everything he said, he could handle Corrine's scrutiny. If he didn't measure up, Hildy would hear about it the minute Corrine stepped out of his car and could get to her cell phone.

"You know," she said to Mike, "I'd really appreciate it if you gave Corrine a lift. The ride is a perfect opportunity for the two of you to get to know each other better."

When Mike leaned over to kiss Hildy goodbye, chastely, on the cheek, he whispered, "I'll get even with you for this."

Corrine, for her part, winked at Hildy as she went out the door. Hildy's nephew and two nieces didn't call their mother the Interrogator for nothing.

Hildy stood in the doorway and waved. As soon as Mike's car turned the corner and disappeared from sight, she went back into the shadows of the house. She took the bottle from the closet floor and pulled out the stopper.

A plume of smoke, robust, edged with gold, and shot through with scarlet, rose up from the bottle's depths. The genie, when he materialized, filled the room with his presence. "*Salve,*" he said in greeting and saluted Hildy with great formality. *"Omnia vincit amor,* it seems."

"Are you being sarcastic?" Hildy said, her hands on her hips.

"It would do you well to remember that a battle isn't won alone," he said, his hand on his sword.

"Mike and I are doing just fine *without* your interference, if that's what you are suggesting," Hildy said.

"Maybe you are. And maybe you are again underestimating your opponent. She is not going to surrender the field without a fight unless—"

"Unless what?" Hildy's brows drew together; she wondered where this conversation was headed.

"Unless you have a secret weapon."

"You mean you, of course," Hildy said, waving him away and walking toward the kitchen for a glass of lemonade. "I really think Mike and I are past that point. He's breaking up with her tonight."

"As a matter of fact, I didn't mean me in this instance." The genie suddenly appeared in front of her, blocking her path. A freshly poured glass of lemonade floated before him. He handed it over to Hildy and steered her back into the dining room. "Sit. I need to show you something."

Hildy sat. The genie reached into the air and plucked his camera phone from some unseen place. He flipped it open, fiddled with the settings, then handed it to her. "Look."

Hildy glanced at the picture and promptly choked on a swallow of lemonade. "No! Oh my god! Is that you and—I can't look at this. How could you!"

"It wasn't difficult, I assure you. Kiki suggested it, not I."

"It's disgusting. Take it back." She shoved the camera phone against his chest.

Tony G. scrutinized the photo he had shown Hildy. He pressed the FORWARD button and reviewed the rest of the images he had stored there. "I don't think the pictures are at all disgusting. I did a superb job of photography. But they are incriminating. This Kiki is talented in some very surprising ways. Did you know she has a stud in her tongue?"

"I most certainly did not! Why did you take those? No, more to the point, why did you do *that* with her?"

Tony turned serious. "Ms. Caldwell, you need to know your enemy. I certainly do. She felt she had to convince me that I wasn't taking advantage of her. She explained to me, to salve my conscience, that her profession requires her to travel a lot. When she's on the road, she enjoys more than the scenery."

"No! How could she! She's engaged to Michael. Why would she insist on commitment if she wants to sleep around?"

"Oh, that. Do you know the reason she wants to marry your Michael?"

"She actually loves him?" Hildy answered, bewildered, realizing that love was now an improbable reason.

"Her behavior with me could make a prima facie case that she doesn't. But I didn't need her to, shall we say, pleasure me to know that. It was evident in the way she behaved around him. She thinks he is an idiot—a good-natured, very handsome, extremely wealthy, easily manipulated idiot."

"And that's enough reason to marry him? I don't believe it. Poor Mike." Hildy put her head on her arms. She felt shocked and terribly sad that Mike had been so misled.

"No, it's not enough reason to marry him. Her other motive is that he won't make her sign a prenuptial. He doesn't believe in them. He believes in *love*. See where that idealism gets you when the romance fades—taken to the cleaners. Ask that British singer, Paul McCartney."

Hildy looked up, her face flushed. "It doesn't matter anymore. Tony, listen to me. You cannot ever let Mike see those pictures you took. It would be cruel, and it's not necessary. He doesn't ever need to know what happened between you and Kiki. He'd be humiliated."

"Ms. Caldwell, I never intended these pictures to be seen by your Mike. They're leverage if that woman plays dirty. And I would wager she is going to."

"I tell you it won't matter what she does. Michael loves me. He asked me to trust him and that's exactly what I'm going to do."

The genie gave Hildy a pitying look. "Love is a fragile thing to put your faith in. I fear you are going to be gravely disappointed."

Hildy refused to let the genie put a damper on her good mood. She decided to take a shower and wash her hair. She felt sticky from the high humidity, which didn't show any sign of breaking. She wanted to cool off and relax.

Tony G. said the weather was like this all summer in Rome. The heat didn't bother him. It brought back fond memories. And he was incredibly bored. He'd fix them something for supper. How did she feel about a suckling pig?

Hildy had eaten enough to satisfy a bear when she was out with Mike. She requested a light salad of fresh baby greens, with perhaps some strips of grilled chicken and, naturally, dressing on the side.

The genie grunted. "Your wish is my command, but that's not my idea of a meal."

A half hour later, Hildy emerged from the bathroom smelling of citrus, her wet hair wrapped in a white cotton towel. She went over to the small television in the living room to turn on the evening news. She wanted to catch the weather report to see what to expect tomorrow. She hoped the humidity would drop. She didn't enjoy air you could wear. She almost wished the cottage had air-conditioning.

She had just begun to watch the *Evening Report* on NBC's Channel Four when her cell phone rang. She jumped up and grabbed it, hoping it was Mike calling.

It wasn't.

The minute Corrine left Mike's car she did phone Hildy. She had no quarrel with Mike's sincerity or his professed love for her little sister. But she had learned something very disturbing, and Hildy needed to know about it.

"Hildy," she snapped into the phone, "did you and Tony discuss my suggestion to eliminate your 'bug problem'?"

"Eliminate my bug problem? No, he didn't tell me anything." Hildy looked at Tony and asked him in body language what Corrine meant. He shook his head and twirled his finger alongside his temple, indicating it was a crazy idea.

"Make sure you ask him!" She was clearly irritated. "Did you tell Mike about our nearly being abducted? Did you tell him the mob is after you?"

Hildy frowned. "Of course not. I couldn't tell him about finding a genie in a bottle, now could I? Even you didn't believe me. He'd think I was out of my mind."

"How do you think he's going to react when he finds out about your having a Roman soldier living with you?"

"Corrine, he's not going to find out, now is he!" Hildy started to hyperventilate. "You didn't tell him, did you?"

"I'm offended that you would think I would,"

Corrine huffed. "But I see trouble ahead if you don't."

"Is this why you called me?" Hildy's voice went up an octave as her throat tightened. "Can't you let me feel good for five minutes before telling me how I'm going to screw everything up?" A fight between the two sisters seemed on the verge of erupting, but Corrine cut Hildy off.

"Hildy, hush. That's not why I called you. I called about a matter of life and death."

"What do you mean? Is it Mike? What's wrong?"

"Listen to me carefully. Did Mike tell you about the first case his new detective agency is tackling?"

"No. We didn't talk about it. Why?"

"He and his partner have a lead on recovering stolen construction equipment. He got a call about it while I was in the car. He and his partner have something happening tonight."

"Huh?" Hildy's confusion forestalled anything more articulate. Recovering construction equipment didn't sound dangerous, not like confronting drug dealers or anything. "I don't understand. What's the problem?"

"The problem is, Mike said the man behind the construction thefts is Jimmy the Bug. He's going after him. Ask Tony about the security at Mr. Bug's office. If Mike shows up there, he's dead, Hildy. It's a trap. He'll be killed unless you stop him."

Hildy's face turned ghostly pale and the phone slipped from her hand.

Chapter 23

The shit had also hit the fan, as the saying goes, when Jimmy the Bug's crew came staggering into the motel on Route 202, where their boss kept his office. A one-story concrete structure built in the 1950s, the Sleep-E-Z Motor Lodge had a NO VACANCY sign permanently lit out front. Adjacent to the sign, an empty swimming pool, its aqua paint peeling and its bottom filled with dead leaves, was surrounded by a faded wooden privacy fence. The high fence provided the added benefit of hiding most of the motel from anyone passing on the road.

To make things look legitimate, a few cars always sat in the numbered parking places outside the rooms of the long, low structure. But few people knew about the large parking lot behind the building. Sheltered by scrub pines and invisible from Route 202, the lot was nearly as big as a football field. One or two flatbed trailers occasionally pulled in there overnight; there was a loaded one there right now. But no truck ever stayed more than a few days.

Also, parked farthest from the motel and hugging the woods, twelve skid steers and three backhoes sat under dingy gray and mildewed tarps. Their presence was highly unusual. Jimmy never kept stolen equipment for more than a week, and even that length of time made him nervous.

The way the construction scam worked was like this: Marty got an order from a contractor who needed equipment fast and cheap. Marty or another of Jimmy's lieutenants went out and found the equipment at a construction site. Marty or one of the boys showed up with a flatbed and phony work order and took it.

Within hours of its being stolen, the equipment was delivered to its new owner, cash was paid, and the deal was done. It was lucrative. It was easy. The risk came with letting any of the machinery sit around—not that it was easily identified as stolen. It wasn't. Construction equipment didn't need license plates, it wasn't registered with any agency, the serial numbers were easily defaced or removed.

So even when Marty didn't have an order for the stolen machines, Jimmy was ready to take what fortune offered. Skid steers, in particular, which sold for $40,000 used, were routinely left parked at a building site and just begged to be taken. So Jimmy took them whenever he could. He figured it was worth the small risk involved.

Jimmy the Bug felt a lot of pride in the theft ring. It had made him rich, and it drew a lot less attention from the cops than drugs.

Having Marty out on bail with an ankle bracelet hadn't slowed down the operation yet, but Jimmy couldn't keep sending contractors up to Camden to do business. Sooner or later, they would attract the wrong kind of attention. He'd have to cut Marty out soon. Since Marty would get upset about his loss of income and might start singing to the authorities, eliminating Marty would have to be permanent.

Ordering a hit on Marty was just the way it was.

James Torelli had known Marty Biz for forty years. They went to Barringer High School together. But Jimmy the Bug wasn't sentimental, and Marty wasn't related by blood. Business was business.

Jimmy sat back in his chair and lit a cigarette. Outside of that small bit of unpleasantness, he felt pretty good today. Once he got his genie back, all would be right in his world.

But when Sal and Joey showed up, their clothes bloody and their hands empty, Jimmy knew his world had gone to hell again.

"Where's the girl?" he demanded of the twin lieutenants.

"We couldn't get her, boss," they said.

"Whadda you mean, you couldn't get her? Puggy called me. He said you three were about to grab her. How could you screw this up!" His eyes popped out of his head so far they looked like hard-boiled eggs. The veins on his neck bulged like blue ropes. "And where the hell is Puggy!"

Puggy, it turned out, was in the hospital. Neither Sal nor Joey dared to give their boss the real story. The one they made up about the casino security guards stopping them only made him curse louder. Jimmy the Bug screamed at them to get out before he shot them right in the ass. He slipped a revolver out of his desk drawer and figured he might just as well do it, but they ran out of the room so fast he didn't get a chance to pull the trigger.

Later, Jimmy figured it was better he didn't do anything hasty. Sal and Joey had to take that flat-bed to Delaware tonight. Help was hard to find. And with Puggy out of commission, he'd have to call up Newark and tell one of his other cousins to get down here to cook the ziti for him.

For a long time, Jimmy the Bug sat in his office and brooded. As soon as the twins brought the payoff from the Delaware guy tonight, he would

take care of the girl himself. He had figured out a
way to force her to return the bottle, and unlike
the morons who worked for him, he didn't intend
to screw it up.

As far as Mike was concerned, the drive back to
Atlantic City with Corrine turned out okay. He
didn't blame her for giving him a hard time. What
she said about Kiki hit home, although Mike thought
she exaggerated a little. He had been with Kiki for
a long time. The relationship didn't work out, but
he didn't feel right bad-mouthing her. They had
some good times together. He hoped things worked
out for Kiki. He wished her well.

Of course, those were Mike's thoughts *before* he
got back to the hotel, before he told Kiki they
needed to talk.

The first thing Kiki said to Mike when he walked
into their suite in Trump Plaza was that she was
going back to New York. She called to him from
the bedroom where she had her suitcases open on
the bed. He walked over to the door and stopped
without going in.

Kiki was busy packing her clothes. She was rushing, focused on the task, and didn't bother looking
at him while she folded up blouses, tucked shoes
into cloth bags, and informed him in a matter-of-
fact manner that she had a fitting for her wedding
gown tomorrow, and she had gotten a contract with
the *New York Times Magazine* to do some shoots
in the city. She'd be staying at their apartment for
the rest of the summer. He could keep this hotel
room, but only until Monday. His condo project
down here really didn't need him to be on site, did
it? She made an appointment with Armani to make
him a new tux for the wedding. By next week, he
needed to come back to New York.

Mike waited for her to finish. Slowly, deliberately, and in a calm voice he said, "I'm not coming back to New York. Kiki, we need to talk."

She whirled around, her face angry, her voice annoyed. "You're being really inconsiderate. I want you in the city."

"Kiki, I said I'm not going."

"What are you talking about?" She stopped packing and stared at him.

"I told you a while ago that I was thinking about leaving the real estate business. I am. I'm becoming a private investigator. I went into partnership with Jake Truesdale."

"You have to be joking. This is a joke, isn't it, Michael? You're just trying to test me or something."

"Kiki, I plan to sell the apartment in the city. You can buy me out if you want to. I need the money to get a place down here. This is where I'm going to be living."

"I don't understand. Do you think I'm going to commute from Manhattan? I don't want to live at the Jersey shore." Her voice was shrill.

"I know you don't. I'm not asking you to. I don't want to marry you. You went ahead with the wedding date without consulting me. You didn't tell me you were spending a lot of money on a designer dress. I'm sorry about that. Take it back. Save it for your next fiancé. I don't care." Mike wasn't going to back down. He knew what he had to do and he just wanted to get it over with.

Kiki still hadn't moved from the side of the bed. "Michael, this isn't like you. Is it because you had sex with your old girlfriend? I told you I forgave you. It was just some prewedding fling. Maybe I was too hasty about announcing the date. If you're really upset about that, it's okay. We'll postpone it until you're ready." She started to move toward him now, her arms out to him.

He backed away. "No, it's not that. There's not going to be a wedding, ever. I don't love you anymore, Kiki. I'm sorry. It didn't work out. It's over."

For a microsecond, rage crossed Kiki's beautiful face. Then she took a trembling breath and tears filled her eyes. "Michael, no!" she cried, her voice catching in a sob. "You can't do this to me!"

"Kiki, you're a beautiful woman. You'll find someone else, someone who's crazy about you. You know there's been nothing between us for a long time." He turned to go. He figured he'd come back and pack his things after she left for New York.

But before he got to the front door, Kiki launched herself at his back and was clutching his shoulders, sobbing into his neck. He gently pried her loose and turned around. "Kiki, don't do this." His voice was soft although his words were cruel. "I don't love you. I love someone else. I don't want you anymore."

Kiki glared at Mike with something like triumph in her eyes. She put her fingers around his wrist. Her red painted nails dug into his flesh. "You wanted me last night, didn't you? You wanted me enough to make love to me without any protection. So you go ahead and leave, Michael Amante. I know my body. I am pretty sure by next week I'll have proof that I'm carrying your child."

Mike felt a chilling moment of panic. His blood turned to ice in his veins. "No," he said. "No. I don't believe you. I don't believe we had sex last night. I don't believe you're carrying my child."

He pulled away from her and opened the door.

"You might not believe me. But what about your little country mouse? What's her name, Hildy? How is she going to feel when I tell her you went from her bed right back into mine?"

Mike didn't look at Kiki again. He slammed the door behind him, but he couldn't shut out the memory of her words or stop the bad feeling he had inside.

Chapter 24

Tony G. retrieved Hildy's cell phone after it had slipped from her fingers. He took a firm grip on her arm and stopped her from rushing to the door.

"I have to stop Mike! I have to get to him!" she had cried out after she dropped the phone. Her wide eyes darted left and right. The white towel fell to her shoulders. Wet strands of blond hair dangled around her face.

Tony G. held her fast. He could see she was in shock. "Get hold of yourself. Calm down. You can't go anywhere."

"Why not? I have to!" Hildy tried to pull her arm free.

"For one thing, you're wearing nothing more than a bathrobe. For another thing, whatever is wrong, we need to talk it through and decide *calmly* what to do. Running off half-cocked isn't going to help."

His words didn't seem to register. Hildy fought to get to the door. Tony surrounded her with his powerful arms, immobilizing her. "Ms. Caldwell! Ms. Caldwell, do you hear me!"

After a moment, Hildy stopped struggling. The genie released her and stepped away.

She stared unseeing at the Roman's craggy face. She blinked hard. She took a deep breath. The flood of adrenaline that had triggered her fight-or-flight response began to ebb away. "You're right," she said at last. She looked down at her bathrobe. "Damn, I wish I were already dressed."

"Certainly," the genie said and tossed some glittering dust into the air.

Hildy heard an eerie sliding tone that sounded like the opening of Led Zeppelin's "Whole Lotta Love." "Oh!" she exclaimed, as the rustling of clothes tickled her flesh. She found herself dressed in skinny black pants and a scoop-necked black tank top. She had sneakers on her feet. Her hair was dry and styled. She couldn't tell for sure, but she suspected she was also wearing makeup. She turned grateful eyes to Tony. "Thank you."

"My pleasure. Now let's sit down and discuss this." He steered her into the dining room to their usual spot at the red Formica and chrome table. "I think it would help if you started at the beginning."

Hildy wanted to plunge right in and talk about Mike, but maybe the genie was right. If she related things in order, perhaps her thoughts would become less chaotic and her fear less like a beast that was clawing at her heart. "Okay. First, my sister told me to ask what you two discussed about getting rid of my 'bug problem.' "

"About *her* idea for getting rid of Jimmy the Bug? I don't think it has any merit."

"*She* does. I hate to say it, but in the end she's usually right, so tell me."

"She said you should just think up the right kind of wish to eliminate him, that's all. I told her I couldn't bring anyone harm. She said I had no imagination." He shrugged his shoulders and held up his hands, palms skyward.

"So what kind of a wish did she mean?"

"How do I know? She's *your* sister."

"I'll have to think about it. She also said you told

her about the security at Jimmy the Bug's office. I don't understand. What were you two talking about? Why did that even come up?"

"I'm not sure how the conversation came around to that particular topic. Your sister asked a lot of questions. She wanted to know where Jimmy the Bug lived and where he worked. She made me give her a detailed description of his associates, including his girlfriend, Jennifer. You know, she wasn't even taking notes. She said she had a mind like a steel trap."

"She does, Tony. Believe me, she does," Hildy assured him. "Then what?"

"She required me to tell her all about Jimmy the Bug's criminal enterprises and if other mobsters ever tried to 'rub him out.' That kind of thing. I must tell you, she was a little scary the way she wanted all the details of some very nasty stuff. What's with this fascination with the Mafia, anyway? Is she connected?"

Hildy shook her head. "The only thing Corrine's connected with is HBO. So what did you tell her, about Jimmy the Bug's office?"

"I told her that nobody ever made a hit on him there, because they never could. Jimmy the Bug is paranoid about a rival from North Jersey moving in on his territory. His place of business is as solid as a concrete bunker. It sits off the highway in a secluded part of the Pine Barrens. Video cameras monitor anybody who comes near the place.

"Besides that, he's got an arsenal inside to use on any hit man trying to pop him. If anyone tries to sneak onto the property, he's got the place booby-trapped. Now why do you want to know?"

Hildy's face registered her growing anxiety. "Corrine said Mike and his partner have a lead on recovering stolen construction equipment. They've linked the thefts to Jimmy the Bug. She thinks

Mike may be headed to Jimmy's office tonight, and Tony—" She clutched the genie's arm. She looked at him with haunted eyes. "If that's where he's going, Mike doesn't know what he's walking into. We have to stop him before he gets killed."

A purple-hued twilight softly fell on Long Beach Island, forestalling the dark of night for another hour. The Bermuda High stayed stubbornly over the northeast, keeping temperatures high and air conditioners blasting. But fishermen casting into the surf noticed the waves were breaking farther from the shore than usual. The seabirds too felt a subtle change in the direction of the wind and winged inland, instead of roosting on the jetties.

The tropical depression called Angie had, it seemed, intensified into a category one hurricane. Still gestating in the warm Caribbean waters, it had turned ever so slightly toward the northeast, its trajectory turning away from Cuba and Miami, and taking aim at the Carolinas.

Hildy had smacked down on her alarm too quickly that morning to hear Sonny Somers reassure his listeners that the storm still posed no danger to Long Beach Island. Some computer projections had it swerving eastward to threaten Bermuda; others brought it ashore near Charleston. At worst, if it should churn up the eastern coast to New Jersey, it meant a weekend ruined by rain.

But the lowering barometer had added to Hildy's feelings of foreboding. After discussing with Tony G. what to do about the possibility that Mike was heading for a deadly rendezvous, she got into her red VW Beetle and drove off the island, west on Route 72, planning on picking up Route 202 at the Red Lion traffic circle, then turning southward.

She had tried calling Mike a dozen times. She didn't know what she could possibly say to him to keep him away from Jimmy the Bug, except to beg him to come to see her. Maybe he would put aside his plans and run to her side. It seemed like a long shot.

It was probably just as well he wasn't answering his cell phone. She guessed he had turned the power off so it wouldn't ring at an inopportune time. According to Corrine, when Hildy called her back after regaining her composure, he should be giving Kiki the bad news about their relationship right about now.

Afterwards, Mike told Corrine, he was driving to meet his partner in Delaware, which was at most ninety minutes from Atlantic City. The two of them were supposed to follow the thieves who delivered the stolen machines to the Delaware contractor. That's the point where projecting the future became uncertain.

After the thieves collected their payment, would they return with the money to Jimmy the Bug? Would they be driving to his office in the Pine Barrens? Who knew? But the likelihood existed that they would.

Hildy had to do what she felt she had to do. She figured out the driving times. She should reach the Sleep-E-Z Motor Lodge a few hours before Mike showed up. Then she had to stop him.

"Ay, there's the rub," as Hamlet had said. How could she explain her presence on Route 202, blocking Mike's arrival? How could she explain her knowledge of Jimmy the Bug's office or the arsenal inside? She'd sound insane if she told him a genie explained it all to her.

She and Tony G. tried to come up with a pretense for her presence, for her insistence that Mike proceed no farther. Outside of the truth, which wasn't an option, there was no believable explanation. Sighing, filled with misgivings, Hildy finally agreed that the only way to prevent Mike from walking into a death trap—if he did show up at the Sleep-E-Z Motor Lodge—was to use one of her two remaining wishes to save him.

And a lot could go wrong with a little magic.

Now, on her way to meet her destiny, or at least Mike's bronze Ford Fusion, she had, of course, brought the genie along to grant the wish, but she insisted he ride in his bottle. The centurion made a fuss about that, but she said she could hear his directions to the Sleep-E-Z just fine if he shouted through the glass. She wasn't driving around with Tony G., big as life in the passenger seat, any more than was necessary.

He argued she was being unfair. He promised to stop criticizing her driving skills. Nevertheless, Hildy remained silent and stubborn and refused to be swayed.

She didn't want to tell him why. She had come to realize she was getting too used to having the big Roman in her life. He had put her into harm's way, he had complicated her existence beyond anything she imagined was possible, but he had also brought her Mike. Because of Tony G., the future she longed for was within her reach. And she liked the ancient Roman, even if he was bossy, interfering, and too ready to point out her faults.

But thanks to unforeseen circumstances, she was probably about to make her second wish. If she made a third, the genie would be gone. Knowing that, she had asked him where he'd go.

He had gotten a strange look on his face and said he didn't know. He might be stuck in the bottle for a while until someone else found him.

She asked him how long "a while" could be.

The proud centurion turned his head away and wouldn't look at her. "Maybe a thousand years," he said in a quiet voice. He added that that was what had happened before. He had nearly gone mad. He looked at her and said in truth he'd rather be dead, but evidently a genie was immortal and couldn't die. It was the sorcerer's punishment, and he supposed it was what he must endure.

Deeply troubled by this, Hildy asked the genie what he'd prefer to do instead of being cast back into oblivion in his bottle, adrift on the sea or lost in the desert sands.

Tony G. didn't answer quickly but at last he said he wanted a job of work. He wanted a purpose. He did not desire to be human even if such a thing were possible. He would never willingly give up his magical powers, but he didn't want to be bored. What he needed was an existence filled with excitement, with importance, with meaning—the qualities that from the beginning of time gave substance to life.

His confession surprised her. His pain reached her soul and tore at her heart. After all, she held his future in her own hands. To wish, or not to wish, would make all the difference.

The stars were out and the moon was high when Hildy pulled her little red car onto the shoulder of the narrow, unlit two-lane highway a short distance south of the Sleep-E-Z Motor Lodge. The genie told her to move it a little farther until it was partially hidden by some holly bushes. After that, she switched off the lights and parked.

She peered into the bottle. The genie, now only about two inches high, stood on the other side of the amber glass. She asked him if he could see where Mike was right now, at this very moment.

He crossed his arms and frowned. "I am not God!" he shouted. "I am not omniscient. I'm a genie. My vision is little better than yours."

"Oh," she said. "I thought you might know."

"I don't," he yelled. "Can't you let me out of here! It's dark. We're in the middle of nowhere. No one can see me."

"Oh, all right," she conceded and pulled the cork out of the bottle.

A murky gray smoke, tinged with sulfurous yellow like a noxious fog, spilled over the sides of the bottle. A second later a decidedly grumpy genie sat in the passenger seat of the small red car. "I get cramped in there, you know."

"No, I didn't know. I thought you had rugs and cushions and all the comforts you could want."

"Not likely. I was imprisoned in there, remember. It's more like a cell."

"Oh, I'm so sorry." Hildy felt terrible. Her lip trembled.

"Oh no, not tears," he muttered under his breath. Aloud he said, "Ms. Caldwell, don't get upset. I might have been exaggerating about the austerity of my quarters. But never mind that. I wanted to be out because I think we probably have some time before Mike and his partner show up, if they're going to show up. Let's take a look around."

"I thought the place was filled with security cameras and booby-trapped." Hildy didn't sound at all enthusiastic about traipsing around in strange woods in the dark.

"It is, but the cameras are only around the perimeter of the motel, and I know where the explosives are buried. We'll be safe. Come on." One minute Tony G. sat solid as flesh and blood in the passenger seat. The next instant he simply appeared outside of the car. He tapped on Hildy's window.

"Hurry up," he urged.

"Oh, all right," she said. "But I'll get out by opening the door, thank you."

Warning her to stay close behind him, the genie led the way, slipping carefully in and out between the scrub pines. Fortunately the forest floor of the Pine Barrens is a huge basin of light golden sand, the remains of a long-vanished sea. It reflected enough moonlight to make it possible for Hildy to see where she was walking. But low branches snagged her clothing and the pine needles scratched her arms like mean children's fingernails. An owl hooted. In the underbrush, an eerie rustling came from the movement of scampering things. A rabbit darted past.

Hildy's heart beat fast. "Where are we going?" she whispered, holding on to the back of Tony's toga.

"To the rear parking lot," the genie replied. "I think what Mike hopes to find is there."

A few minutes later, Tony G. was peering under tarps. "As Archimedes once said, 'Eureka, I've found it.'"

"That's terrific. Can we go now?" Hildy's anxiety was reaching new heights.

"Wait. Look over there. See those speed bumps on the driveway into this lot?"

"Yes, I see them. Why?"

"They're filled with explosives. As soon as an intruder drives over one, ka-boom! All of Jimmy the Bug's crew know enough to avoid them."

Hildy had a vivid image of Mike innocently pulling into the Sleep-E-Z and his car exploding into a thousand burning pieces. She shuddered. "Can we get out of here?" Her teeth chattered when she spoke despite the warm night air.

"Wait, Jimmy the Bug set more booby traps. If somebody tries to walk back here, like we did, there are trip wires all over the place."

"You mean I could have stepped on one?" Hildy thought she was going to hyperventilate.

"I led you around them, but you do have to watch where you're walking."

"I really want to get out of here!" She tugged at the genie's toga.

"We should see if Jimmy the Bug is on the premises."

"I see lights on. That's good enough for me. Come on, I don't want to take a chance on Mike and his partner slipping by us."

"And I was beginning to have a good time," Tony G. sighed.

"I don't care! I just want to keep Mike from driving back here and getting blown up!"

Hurrying as much as they dared, Tony G. and Hildy returned to the car, barely in time to see a flatbed tractor trailer rumble past. It turned in at the Sleep-E-Z. The headlights of another car appeared on the highway a few moments later.

"Duck!" the genie ordered and pushed Hildy's head out of sight below the roof of the car.

The headlights passed them by and pulled into the motel's driveway. Hildy and Tony peeked out from behind the VW.

"We need to see what's going on," the genie said. "Are you ready to wish?"

"Yes, and I wish I didn't have to," she answered in a soft voice.

"Well, remember what we rehearsed and be careful what you wish for."

Hildy nodded and they raced toward the motel in time to see that two men had emerged from a bronze Ford Fusion and were moving cautiously toward the single lighted room in the motel. Hildy knew one of them was Mike. She saw him remove a gun from his waistband and hold it at his side. The tall black man with him did the same.

The genie said, "You don't have much time."

Just then the Ford exploded with a terrible bang. Gunfire went *crack, crack, crack*. The door to the motel room flew open—

"Wish, Ms. Caldwell!"

"I wish that all bullets are blanks, all explosives are duds, all weapons are useless, and Michael is unharmed," she said quickly.

Nothing else blew up, but the noise of gunfire continued. When no one fell to the ground or screamed, even when Michael and his partner were in point-blank range, the two thugs who had been driving the flatbed trailer came racing around the side of the motel. They rushed at Mike and Jake and began throwing punches. Soon all four of the men were rolling around on the ground. Hildy winced at the sound of the blows.

While the fight raged on, a third man, short and stocky, came through the open motel room door, looked around, and ran toward the woods. Hildy was too worried about what was happening to Mike to worry about the portly man's escape. Then the fighting stopped. She saw Mike stand up.

"Okay, let's go!" the genie insisted, tugging on her arm. "We've done all we can."

He and Hildy turned and ran toward her car. When they reached it, Hildy threw herself into her seat and the genie showed up instantly in his. She felt excited and exhilarated. Mike was safe. Everything was going to be okay.

She threw the Volkswagen into gear and pulled onto the highway.

It was when she had driven a few hundred feet and was about to pass by the Sleep-E-Z Motor Lodge that things went from all right to all wrong.

Chapter 25

Mike stood in the road, flagging her down.

"Oh my god!" she cried out. She snapped her head toward Tony G. "Get in your bottle. Get in there now!"

Where the genie had been sitting was suddenly simply air.

She pulled off the road and Mike ran over to the car. She rolled down her window.

"Hildy! I don't believe it! What an incredible thing. Why are you here?" His face was dirty, his shirt was torn, but he appeared otherwise unharmed.

"I—I was visiting a friend, another teacher from the high school. She lives in, in"—Hildy thought frantically for the name of a town she had seen on a nearby road sign—"in Vineland! But why are *you* here? It's the middle of nowhere."

"I'll explain later. Come on, you can help me get Jake to your car. He's hurt. My cell phone doesn't have any service out here. We need to get Jake to a hospital and get hold of the cops."

"Okay," Hildy said. "Sure. But excuse me a minute!" She smiled brightly before suddenly ducking out of sight under the dashboard.

Mike was baffled about what she was doing. Maybe she was tying her shoes, he thought.

In fact Hildy knocked the bottle on the floor and deftly stashed it under the front seat. Then she jumped out of the car. "Let's go!" she called. She joined Mike and they hurried up the long driveway together, past the empty swimming pool and toward the building.

"Why didn't you use the motel's landline to call nine-one-one?" she huffed as she ran by Mike's side.

"Can't," he said. "Look."

"Oh . . . oh my." Hildy's eyes went round as saucers. Flames leaped out of the motel's windows and through the open door where the little man had run. She guessed that the explosion of the rental car had sent debris onto the motel roof and set the place on fire. "I didn't think of this," she moaned.

"What?" Mike asked.

"Oh, nothing. Is your partner hurt badly?" Her concern was palpable. She hadn't thought to include Jake specifically in the wish either.

"No. Nothing life-threatening. He may have dislocated his shoulder and sprained an ankle. He's in some pain and he can't walk. The two guys that attacked us are out cold though. It was the weirdest damned thing. They kept shooting at us, but they couldn't hit the broad side of a barn."

"Well, did you shoot them?" she asked innocently.

"No, my gun wouldn't fire. It's brand-new. Must have been defective or something." By that time they had reached Jake, who sat on the grass; the light of the flames backlit him with an orange glow.

"Hey Jake, you'll never believe this. Guess who I flagged down. It's Hildy! She was passing right by."

Jake looked at the blond young woman dressed entirely in black who stood in front of him. He looked at Mike. "Come again?"

"I just happened to be driving by," Hildy said. "It was an amazing coincidence."

Jake gave her a funny look. "Yeah, it sure was."

"Mike," she said, staring intently at Jake, aware at once that Mike's partner didn't believe her at all. "Let me go back to my car and drive it up here as close to Jake as I can get it. It will make it easier to get him inside without him moving much." With that she whirled around and escaped from Jake's suspicious glare by running down the driveway as fast as she could.

When she got to the dark, narrow highway, she stopped. She tried to make sense of what she was seeing . . . which was nothing. The road was empty. Her car was gone, and with it, the genie in his bottle hidden under the seat was gone too.

Mike heard Hildy scream. He spun around and went running to see what had happened. He knew right away her car had been stolen and that Jimmy the Bug, who had fled the scene, must have taken it.

When he explained that to Hildy, she became hysterical, babbling about some bottle she had left in the car. He did everything he could to calm her down. He told her the police would look for her car, and if they didn't find it, he'd buy her one, he promised.

His words didn't help. She wailed louder.

He assured her that she didn't need to worry. Help was coming. He could hear fire engines in the distance.

She sniffed and calmed down, but she appeared to be thoroughly distraught. She took his outstretched hand and walked back to the burning lodge.

When they got to Jake, his partner was adamant that Mike go around to the back of the motel to see if any of the stolen construction equipment was stashed back there. Mike said sure and started to leave.

"Take a goddamn pad and pencil with you to write down the VIN numbers. I didn't go through all this bullshit for nothing," Jake shouted angrily at Mike.

Mike mouthed at Hildy, *He's in a lot of pain.* Aloud he said, "I'll be back in a couple minutes. Keep your eye on those guys." He nodded at Sal and Joey, the two unconscious men. "I don't think they're anything to worry about though." Then he trotted off.

Keeping her distance, Hildy tried to avoid Jake's probing scrutiny, but he spoke to her anyway, his anger pouring out.

"What are you really doing here, sweetheart? Don't give me whatever phony story you gave Mike. He doesn't think straight when it comes to you."

Hildy turned to Jake with stricken eyes. "You won't believe me if I tell you the truth."

"Try me."

"Okay." Hildy began talking as fast as she could. "I found a genie in a bottle that really belonged to Jimmy the Bug. And the genie knew all about this place being booby-trapped, so when I found out from my sister that you and Mike might follow those thieves back here, I thought Mike was going to be killed and I got in the car and the genie came with me and you and Mike showed up and walked right into the booby traps so I wished that your guns wouldn't work and the explosives wouldn't blow up and Mike wouldn't get hurt. Then the genie and I ran back to my car and I was going to get out of here but Mike was in the middle of the road, flagging me down. What could I do?"

"You're right," Jake said. "I don't believe you.

I don't know what you're pulling or how you got here, but I'm going to find out. I promise you that." He glared at her.

Hildy looked at him and said, "I knew you wouldn't believe me and I'm sorry you got hurt. You weren't supposed to. I didn't wish carefully enough."

At that moment a fire truck, its siren blaring, pulled up the Sleep-E-Z Motor Lodge's driveway. Firemen in heavy gear jumped off and started pulling on hoses. One of them came running over, yelling to somebody behind him, "We've got injured over here!"

Two ambulances came screaming up the driveway a little while later. Jake and Jimmy the Bug's men were scooped up and taken away. The state police had arrived as well. Mike and Hildy spent the next several hours at the local barracks, giving statements about what happened.

Hildy didn't have much to say, except that her car got stolen. They promised to put out an APB on the little red Volkswagen being driven by a notorious criminal. They told her not to get her hopes up though.

She had to hope. She had to find her car and get Tony G. back. She prayed too. She prayed that Jimmy the Bug wouldn't ever look under the front seat. She thought he might not. She couldn't bear to think what would happen if he did.

Anxiety warred with grief and worry over the genie's fate and her own future, but there wasn't anything more she could do tonight. She'd have to worry about the bottle tomorrow. Finally fatigue overtook her; all she wanted was to get back to her cottage and her cats. She wouldn't rest until she knew everything was safe and that Jimmy the Bug hadn't gone to Ship Bottom to lie in wait.

A young officer was kind enough to take Mike and Hildy all the way back to Atlantic City. She dropped them off in front of the Hertz car rental office at Midlantic Jet Aviation, out on Tilton Road, the only rental agency within a hundred miles that was open twenty-four/seven.

Mike had suggested that Hildy stay with him at the hotel, but she insisted she needed to get to Long Beach Island. She appeared fragile and distraught, in a way he had never seen her before.

Since it was close to four a.m., the baggy-eyed clerk appeared to be functioning courtesy of constant refills of his coffee cup. He told them the only vehicle available was a four-wheel-drive Chevy Suburban—at a premium price.

Beggars can't be choosers. Mike took it without a complaint.

On the drive back to Ship Bottom, neither of them talked much. Mike did tell Hildy he had broken up with Kiki. She nodded and gave him a small smile. He pulled her close to him, his left hand on the steering wheel, his right arm around her shoulders, as he did when they were teens. He suggested she put her head on his shoulder and sleep.

She felt warm and protected, but she couldn't rest. Instead she said to Mike, "Mike, you trust me, don't you?"

"Of course I do. I've never known you to lie, not to me, not to anyone."

She sighed. "Then you need to listen to me. The bottle that was in my car, I have to get it back. You're a detective now, right?"

"Yep, I'm official. I have a license and everything."

"Then I want to hire you to recover my bottle. I don't care about the car. Just get the bottle back."

He gave her a squeeze and kissed her on the temple. "Hildy, you don't need to hire me. I'll do what I can to find it. Why is it so important to you?"

"That's why I need you to trust me. I can't tell you. It's . . . it's a secret. It involves somebody else, whose life depends on finding that bottle. Mike, I mean that—a life literally depends on my getting that bottle back." Her throat closed up as she spoke. She felt close to tears and held them back. Crying would accomplish nothing. She had to be strong, not fall apart.

"I hope you trust me enough to share your secret, Hildy. Isn't that the way it has to be if we're going to spend the rest of our lives together?"

Hildy pulled back enough so she could look at Mike. "Are we going to spend the rest of our lives together?"

"If you're willing." He hugged her close again.

She reached up and held the hand he had put around her shoulder. "Mike, I've been willing for the past ten years."

"You're a funny kid, Hildy Caldwell. I still can't believe how we found each other again. It almost makes me believe in magic," Mike said.

Hildy didn't protest. She didn't comment. She didn't say a word.

When they arrived at the cottage, Mike walked her to the door. She hesitated and asked him to look around inside before she went in.

Thinking about the attempted purse snatching just days ago, he believed her apprehension about entering the dark cottage was completely normal. He flipped on the lights and walked from room to room, making sure the windows were secure and no one lurked inside.

The cats followed at his heels, then jumped up on the kitchen counter, protesting that they hadn't been fed. It was nearly dawn. Their meows clearly conveyed that they had been starved.

Mike offered to stay with Hildy, but he had mixed feelings about it. He almost hoped she'd say no. He had already decided not to go to bed; it was nearly daybreak. Although he might get a nap later, his mind was sifting through the things he had to do, from checking on Jake in the hospital to getting a truck back to the Sleep-E-Z Motor Lodge to pick up the stolen machines.

Seeing his distraction, Hildy said she needed to get some rest. She wanted him to leave more than she wanted him to stay and snuggle with her in bed. Finally, she insisted that he go, but not before she asked him again to look for her bottle as soon as he could. She clutched his hands and made him promise. He swore he would. She kissed his cheek.

He kissed her back, on the lips, not the cheek, sending her head spinning. He promised to call her, but after he knew she had gotten some rest. He'd try in the afternoon. She promised, Boy Scouts' honor, to answer the phone. They both laughed, and he left.

As she watched him pull out onto the street and drive away, Hildy noticed that the sky appeared lighter. Dawn was fast approaching.

She fed the cats. She filled the Mr. Coffee machine and set the timer for three p.m., since she was determined not to wake sooner. Then she yawned and climbed up into the sleeping loft. She turned off her clock radio alarm. She paused for a moment, then shut off the phone. She knew Corrine would be calling her first thing in the morning; she didn't want the theme song from *Gilligan's Island* waking her up. She had brain fog, she was so tired.

Her head hit the pillow. The cats dashed up the

ladder, leaped onto the bed, and curled up next to her legs. Her thoughts turned to Tony G., stashed in the bottle and still, hopefully, under the Volkswagen's front seat. She wasn't going to give up on getting him back and hoped he knew she'd be looking for him, that she'd never willingly abandon him to an uncertain fate.

Then drowsiness lulled her into a misty place between wakefulness and slumber. The last thing she remembered was a vague awareness that the air temperature must have dropped. She didn't feel the humidity anymore. Then she slept the sleep of the innocent, unconscious and insensate, more deeply asleep than she had ever been before.

When dawn did arrive it wasn't with rosy fingers or clouds edged with bands of gold. An angry splash of deep red crossed the eastern sky behind an aerial ledge of high, flat, and inky black stratus clouds. A change in the weather was coming, and it wasn't for the better.

During the island's early morning drive-time radio show, Sonny Somers gave his six a.m. forecast with an urgency in his voice he had never used on the air before. Hurricane Angie had picked up speed and now was a category three storm, he reported. It had charged forward and was raging in the South Atlantic, churning its way through the Bermuda Triangle and heading northwest.

His voice became even more excited when he reported that the first hurricane of the season was defying all the best computer projections, zigging and zagging and changing course hourly. The National Weather Center had the entire Atlantic coastline on a storm alert. This hurricane threatened to travel fast and pack a punch. Long Beach Island was not in any immediate danger, but Sonny warned listeners to stay tuned for updates. This was a storm to watch.

Hildy wasn't watching. She was sleeping unaware of anything, even the cats behind her knees.

At ten o'clock, the daytime programs on television and radio were interrupted by a National Weather Center storm warning. People living in low-lying coastal areas from Newport News, Virginia, to Sandy Hook, New Jersey, were being asked to voluntarily move to higher ground. It was a precautionary move, but a recommended one.

Old-timers in the Carolinas groused that the media turned every rain cloud into a major news story. They weren't moving for this little storm. It wasn't like Hurricane Hugo, back in 'eighty-nine, at least not yet.

By eleven o'clock Angie had become a category four hurricane that was now, unexpectedly, taking aim on southern New Jersey. Evacuation of coastal areas was being ordered, effective immediately. This was a mandatory evacuation, not a choice.

In Ship Bottom, police cruisers went block to block with loudspeakers, telling residents to take only their valuables and their pets and leave the island. But with only one road leading off the island, the evacuation was the First Responders' worst nightmare. They wanted people to begin leaving their houses immediately, not to wait even an hour.

By eleven thirty, the causeway was at a standstill with bumper-to-bumper traffic. The inbound lane had been closed, and all lanes now led in only one direction—off the island.

Hildy did not hear the bullhorns. She never noticed when the cats moved off the bed or when the gulls stopped crying overhead. She slept soundly, lost in dreams while the barometer continued to drop, and gray clouds skittered quickly across the sky. Then the wind picked up and tossed the surface of the sea into whitecaps. Hildy never stirred.

Five hundred miles to the east, Angie swirled, spun, and took aim on Long Beach Island. Forecasters did their math and looked at their computers. They began predicting that, by late afternoon, record high tides and a dangerous storm surge could sweep away every summer cottage and new McMansion built there.

At twelve o'clock noon emergency sirens began to sound from the island's southern tip in Holgate to the northern end at Barnegat Light. Their eerie wailing, echoing through the increasingly empty towns, warned of death and misery to come. In Surf City and Ship Bottom, the municipalities closest to Route 72, cars filled with children and dogs, cat carriers and bird cages lined up on the boulevard, waiting to get onto the causeway and cross the bay to higher ground.

Hildy's brain registered the sound of the sirens, but it recognized no reason for alarm. A fire somewhere in town, her unconscious mind believed. She slumbered on.

By one o'clock, the Ship Bottom police started going door-to-door on foot, making sure no foolish residents decided to ride out the storm. Ship Bottom, the widest part of the island, was only a half mile across. At the narrowest spot, in Harvey Cedars, the island shrunk to just a fifth of a mile wide.

Some of the officers were old enough to remember the Ash Wednesday storm of 1962, just a fierce nor'easter, not even a hurricane. That storm cut the island into pieces, the sea digging channels from east to west. It also left the eighteen miles that stretched from north to south mostly empty sand, the majority of the island's buildings washed away or destroyed.

Those men and women feared that once Angie, the strongest hurricane to ever come ashore, struck the Jersey coast, there would be nothing here except the black waves that would roll with deadly force across the island to Barnegat Bay.

When two Ship Bottom police officers reached Twenty-fifth Street, no vehicle sat in front of the little gray cottage with the cutout whales cavorting over the door. One of the officers knocked hard and listened. Nothing stirred inside. The place appeared as deserted as Mrs. Baier's house next door. He had no reason to knock again. He had dozens of houses to check. He caught up with his partner and they moved on.

Hildy turned over in her bed, briefly stirring. Her eyelids fluttered. She nearly woke, but her eyes felt so heavy, she stopped trying. She needed more rest. She buried her face in the pillow and slept on.

Chapter 26

In Atlantic City, Mike began phoning Hildy shortly after he heard about the mandatory evacuation. He was surprised when she didn't answer, and he was concerned. He had left her there without a car. She'd have to find a ride with someone willing to take her and a carrier containing two cats. After repeated attempts to reach her without success, he thought he had better drive to Ship Bottom to get her.

Mike kept phoning Hildy as he drove northward up the parkway. She still wasn't picking up. Once his phone rang just after he had gotten her voice mail for probably the fifteenth time.

The caller was Hildy's sister, Corrine. She had panic in her voice. "Is Hildy with you?" she asked.

Mike answered no, that he had left Hildy out on the island late last night. But he was going to get her and not to worry.

"Not worry!" Corrine's voice was only a shade below a scream. "She's the only sister I have."

An intermittent rain had started to fall. The wind had picked up. The eye of the hurricane was still hundreds of miles away. This was just a taste of things to come.

Once Mike got to Exit 63, he discovered that New Jersey state troopers had closed the exit ramp that connected the parkway with Route 72 going east toward Long Beach Island. Without slowing down very much, Mike put the Chevy Suburban in four-wheel drive and went around the barricade and across the triangle of green lawn.

He quickly discovered why the off-ramp was blocked. Route 72 now had all lanes marked to travel west. Hoping no one would stop him, Mike went east anyway, riding down the shoulder as fast as he dared.

Going against the traffic and avoiding the shouts of drivers telling him the road was closed, he covered the five miles to the first bridge at the start of the causeway. This was the longest span of four that leapfrogged from Manahawkin to each of the three small islands in Barnegat Bay before reaching Long Beach Island.

He went no farther. An angry Manahawkin police officer, a plastic shower cap on his hat and a long oilcloth raincoat covering him from shoulder to ankle, flagged him down.

Striding over to the Chevy Suburban, the cop gestured for Mike to roll down his window. He stuck a beefy red face toward Mike and threatened to issue a citation for driving on the shoulder. Mike waited out the tirade, and then tried to talk his way onto the bridge. He frantically explained that he had left his girlfriend on the island; she had no car; she wasn't answering her phone.

Hearing the urgency in Mike's voice, the Manahawkin officer became more sympathetic. He told Mike no one was being allowed back on the island. As soon as the civilians were cleared, all but a skeleton crew of First Responders were leaving too.

After reassuring Mike that everyone was being evacuated and no one left behind, the cop actually called over to Ship Bottom and gave the officer on duty Hildy's address. He had reached the same officer who had knocked on Hildy's door. The young man affirmed that the house was empty. No, he didn't see any cats in the window. No one responded to the loud knocking on the door. The guy's girlfriend must have left with a neighbor.

At that point, the Manahawkin officer had other things to do than deal with a panicky boyfriend. He gruffly told Mike to turn his vehicle around and get out of the area or he'd throw him in jail.

Mike obediently made a U-turn and briefly got into the line of traffic heading west. But as soon as he was out of sight of the police officer, he pulled off the highway into a strip mall's parking lot. He left the Suburban there and began walking back to the bridge. Once he got near enough to see the span packed with cars filling all lanes, he realized he'd never get onto the bridge, even on foot. Cops were everywhere.

The wind pushed at his clothes and the rain soaked him through. He shoved his hands in his pants pockets and looked around, trying to figure out what to do. To his left, across the waving salt grasses along the channel, he spotted a sign saying WAVE RUNNER AND KAYAK RENTALS about two hundred yards off the highway. He hunkered down against the wind and headed for it.

On his way, he studied the water. This channel was narrow, no more than a quarter of a mile across. The sheltered bay water was choppy, but not yet impassable, the current running south at a good rate.

Mike approached the boat rental office. He peered through the window. It was dark inside. He tried the door. It was locked. He glanced around. The Wave Runners and kayaks had been dragged out of the water. Most of them were chained together up on high racks. A few older kayaks, abandoned in haste and left to their fate, lay on the ground.

Mike had spent his summers canoeing and kay-aking on the Susquehanna River. His arms were brawny and his back was strong. He didn't hesitate. He left on his sneakers but rolled up his pant legs. He grabbed one of the kayaks, checked to make sure it had its paddle, and put it in the water, where it rocked with a terrible madness. He got in and managed to stay upright. He dipped the paddle in the water and stroked hard, determined to cross this narrow channel to the island beyond.

The wind, coming hard from the north, and the rushing current pushed him southward. He knew not to fight against it but to use its power. He paddled a diagonal course that took him right under the first causeway bridge. He kept clear of the abutments by using his paddle, but he had a few bad moments when he thought he was going to turn over.

Once he was out on the other side of the cause-way bridge, he could see that the island, the small-est of the three in the channel, jutted out beyond the bridge for only a short way. He was swept past its tip, too far to be able to paddle there and land. Actually that was a good thing, he decided. Now he aimed for the second island, which was just a few hundred feet beyond.

He approached shore within minutes. As soon as his paddle hit bottom, he jumped out into the muck of the salt marsh. The wind tore at his shirt as he waded ashore and slowed him down. He pulled the kayak with him until he got it up onto dry land. He didn't know why he did that. There was little chance it would be of any use on the return trip if Hildy was along.

He looked around. He was halfway to Long Beach Island, but it was taking time, a lot of time.

Once he abandoned the kayak, he walked toward the highway which ran on pylons above the ground. On it, Mike could see cars still fleeing eastward, but moving at a good rate. He thought these must be the stragglers and emergency workers, some of the last people to leave.

He ducked under the elevated causeway and found an unpaved road leading north to a cluster of summer cottages. There another street intersected with it and went eastward. He trotted along it. Except for the sound of the wind, everything was silent. No cars remained in the driveways. The houses were empty. All the people had fled.

A few minutes later he reached the water's edge again. The far shore was only fifty feet away, but the current was running too fast to risk swimming. He wiped the rain from his eyes and looked around. Another Wave Runner and kayak rentals dock lay on his left. Again he ran over to find the office shut tight, but as before some kayaks had been left lying on the ground, unchained.

He quickly got one in the water, feeling positive and certain he was going to make it. He aimed for the Dutchman's Brauhaus restaurant across the narrow channel and was able to ride his kayak right onto their dock. The water had already washed over the wooden boards with the rising tide.

He climbed some stairs, then dashed through the restaurant's parking lot to a house-lined street next to the causeway. He glanced upward. He stood there a minute watching. No cars traveled the highway now. He ran on. When he reached the last channel of water before Long Beach Island, he simply pulled himself up onto the bridge and jogged on the empty highway, coming out at the CVS Pharmacy, where Jimmy the Bug's man had waited for Hildy at another time.

Running through the deserted streets of Ship

Bottom, Mike finally began to think about what he should do when he got to Hildy's. The wind was increasing by the minute. Would they have time to run back across the causeway on foot? If they did, would they be caught in the open with debris flying everywhere and the wind threatening to sweep them into the churning water below? He decided they'd have to listen to the latest reports to find out when the storm was set to hit, then decide.

All the time he was running toward Twenty-fifth Street, he assumed Hildy was still in the little cottage and still on the island. It never occurred to him that she might not be there. He knew in his heart, and he knew with the certainty that links those who love, that she was.

Chapter 27

The howling wind roused Hildy from her slumber at around three in the afternoon. She lay in bed, disoriented. A staccato beat of raindrops pattered on the roof above her, and the daylight she could glimpse outside the small window under the roof's peak seemed extraordinarily dim for a summer afternoon. She wondered why.

She sat up and rubbed her eyes. The air felt cool against her skin. She was beginning to think something was definitely peculiar when she heard a pounding at the front door. Then she heard Mike's voice calling her name.

She scurried over to the ladder and lowered herself down as quickly as she could. Then she raced for the door, where Mike's fists seemed intent on breaking it down. She flung it open. Mike stood with dripping hair and drenched clothes.

"Mike? What's—"

"Hildy!" he cried and grabbed her in his arms, holding her close. "Are you all right?"

Hildy said something like "Oooof," as he squeezed tight. "Mike, what's the matter? Of course I'm all right."

He let go and looked at her. "For God's sake, why didn't you answer your phone!" he was shouting, the relief of seeing her giving way to exasperation.

Hildy backed into the sunporch, surprised at his anger and hearing her own voice getting loud in response to his outburst. "I'm sorry, Mike, but I was sleeping after being up all night. I turned it off. What time is it, anyway? You did say you wouldn't call until this afternoon."

"That was before this goddamn island was going to get washed away in a hurricane!" he bellowed.

Hildy looked at him, stunned. "What? What are you talking about?"

Mike tried to calm down. He wasn't angry at Hildy. He had been scared to death on her account. He said in a more reasonable tone, "Hildy, haven't you seen a weather report?"

"Well, no. I just woke up when I heard you at the door."

"Well, look outside!" Mike stepped away from the door. Hildy peeked out at the rain blowing sideways in the gusts of wind. She looked up the street. She looked down the street.

"Where is everyone?"

"The island's been evacuated. There's a category four hurricane coming right at it. Once the storm surge hits, anything at sea level will be washed away."

"Noooo!"

"Yes, we have to get out of here, and soon."

"Oh, Mike! Oh, where are my cats! Shelley! Keats!" Hildy turned and ran toward the kitchen calling their names. No cats came when she called.

Increasingly upset, she cried out, "Maybe they're scared. Maybe they're hiding somewhere. Shelley! Keats!" She got down on her hands and knees and began looking under the furniture. "Mike, please, help me look!"

Mike went into the dining room to search there, and he saw a note lying on the red Formica table. He picked it up and read it. Then he called out, "Hildy, stop! Stop looking! Come here."

She appeared in the doorway. "Did you find them?"

"No. They're not here. They're already gone."

"What! Jimmy the Bug's kidnapped them again and I don't have a wish to get them back!" she wailed and looked about ready to cry.

"Hildy, you aren't making any sense. Why would Jimmy the Bug take your cats?"

Hildy ran over and ripped the note out of his hands. She looked at it and said, "Oh! Mrs. Baier took them."

When the evacuation order was first given, Hildy's elderly neighbor looked outside and didn't see Hildy's car. Thinking Hildy couldn't get back to the island, she used the key Hildy had given her to come in and put the two cats in a carrier. They would be safe with her Henry at Mrs. Baier's sister's house in Princeton. She had left a phone number where Hildy could reach her.

Hildy's legs were trembling. She sat down on one of the plastic-covered chairs, hung her head down, and took some deep breaths. "I was so scared."

Mike came over and stooped down next to her so he could see her face. "I can see that. It's okay. Your cats are all right. But, Hildy, we're not. We need to get to higher ground."

He stood up. "Listen to me for a minute. The electricity is still on. I'm going to check the weather on TV and see how much time we have before the storm hits. You get dressed."

Hildy nodded. She went over to the closet and started pulling out some clothes.

"I think you better hurry," he said more calmly than he felt and walked into the living room. He switched on the TV. Every channel was covering the storm. The news wasn't good. The outer rim of the hurricane was not more than fifty miles off the coast, with gusts up to seventy miles an hour. Winds of up to a hundred and twenty miles an hour were expected when the body of the storm hit. People were warned to stay indoors or go to a designated storm shelter. The eye should make landfall somewhere between Long Beach Island and Atlantic City by six p.m.

It was three fifteen.

"I don't know what we should do," Mike called to Hildy, who was now in the bathroom brushing her teeth. "I don't think we can risk going up on the causeway to get off the island. Is there anywhere to take shelter near here?"

Hildy came into the living room. She had on a shirt, jeans, and sneakers; she carried a clear plastic rain slicker in her hand. "Here, you take this one. I have another in my backpack. Thunderstorms blow up so quickly off that ocean that I always carry rain gear when I'm out for a ride or hike. We can take a couple of garbage bags with us too. You know, you can make a rain poncho with them."

"Okay, but about the shelter. Do you know of any?"

Hildy looked at him, her eyes clear and unafraid. "Not near here, no. But I do know where we'll be safe."

"Where's that?"

"Old Barney."

"The lighthouse?" Mike asked.

"Yes. It's stood for a hundred and fifty years. It can withstand the storm."

Mike quickly pointed out to Hildy the problem with her idea. They didn't have a car. The lighthouse was nearly nine miles away at the tip of the island. They'd never reach it on foot before the wind caught them in the open. They would die out there, if not from the storm surge, then from flying debris.

Hildy shook her head. "No, we won't be caught in the open. I figure we can make it to the lighthouse in about twenty minutes, a little bit faster maybe if we really try."

"How?"

"We'll take the bikes. I bought a new one last week and I still have the rental one I had leased for the summer. We can do it. We've done it before."

And they had, when they were twelve years old.

Mike smiled for the first time since he had arrived. "It was nine miles around Harveys Lake."

"We did it in—"

"Nineteen minutes and thirty-five seconds," he said at once. "This island is as flat as the shore of the lake. We only have to average maybe twenty, twenty-five miles an hour."

Hildy thought for a moment. "But hurricane winds move in a counterclockwise direction and we're on the front edge. We'll be pedaling against the wind as the hurricane approaches," she added.

"Shoot, I forgot about that." He looked worried again.

"We can do it, Mike. I'm going to fill the thermos and put some food and bottled water in my backpack. You check the air in the bike tires. There's an air pump on the chassis of the rental if you need it. I'll put a blanket in a garbage bag. It can go in the bike basket. Then we better get out of here."

Five minutes later they were out on Island Beach Boulevard pedaling north. Mike wore the heavily laden backpack and rode the old bike with the basket. Hildy had her new trail bike. At first, the trek was almost fun; then the going got a lot tougher than either of them thought it would be.

Hildy's rain parka kept tangling around her legs and the hood slipped down over her face so it was hard to see. The rain had intensified and the gusts of wind seemed to come from all directions, which was almost worse than a steady gale. At one point, a strong blast hit Hildy sideways and blew her over. She went down hard into the street. Mike stopped his bike and ran to help. Fortunately, the only damage was her badly scraped hands.

When they pedaled through Harvey Cedars, Hildy felt her first frisson of deep fear. She could actually see the spray of the waves breaking to her right, beyond the houses that lined the beach just a block away.

Nearly forty minutes had passed from the time they left Ship Bottom until they arrived in the town of Barnegat Light. The edge of the storm had arrived, as well. On this exposed point, sitting on Barnegat Inlet and surrounded on three sides by water, the wind was so strong it made it difficult to stand, let alone pedal.

Just ahead was the state park's parking lot, already covered with water. They had to get off the bikes and push them through the ankle-deep flood. At the far end of the parking lot, they came through some hedges onto an asphalt path leading to the lighthouse. There they got their first real look at the huge waves that were crashing up onto the jetty from the ocean side. Some breakers washed right over the huge black rocks. They were also smashing into the rocks right below the lighthouse with such force that white spray arced up to hit the lighthouse's sides.

Hildy stopped, reluctant to go on. "The visitor center is away from the beach, and it's all concrete block," she said. "Maybe we should go there."

"No, it's on too low ground," Mike said. "It won't wash away, but chances are it will get flooded. We can make it to the lighthouse. The door's on the side away from the water. As soon as a wave hits and begins to recede we'll run for it."

"What if the door is locked?" she asked.

"Then I'll break it down."

Hildy nodded okay, pushing away a terrifying vision of being swept into the roiling sea. Fear wasn't going to stop her. She steadied her nerves and got ready to push her bicycle hard and run.

Chapter 28

Mike went first, moving quickly toward the lighthouse through the screaming winds and punishing rain. He found the door unlocked. He flung it open and beckoned Hildy to come. She waited for a wave to strike the seawall and fall back into the dark ocean. Then she dashed forward, going as quickly as she could with a bicycle at her side. At the doorway, Mike was waiting to grab the bike and pull her in.

After the din of the roaring sea and unremitting winds, all seemed still, quiet, and safe within the solid brick walls of their sanctuary. The sounds outside had become muted and hushed. Not even the lighthouse's small windows rattled. The shadows under the stairs were thick; the light was dim. A sense of the sacred overcame Hildy, as if she had entered a cathedral. She felt reverent and immensely thankful for this magnificent structure that now gave them shelter from the storm.

They peeled off their dripping rain gear and hung it over the stair rail. In case the storm surge reached as high as the knoll where the lighthouse stood, they decided to hoist their bikes up the winding stairs to the first landing. They tried a light switch; there was no response. Power must have gone out. They might be left in absolute darkness for hours.

Then they had some discussion about where to wait out the hurricane, whether to wait on another landing or make the long, arduous climb to the top.

Ultimately they decided to do both. They ascended twenty steps to the next landing and sat on the floor. Mike handed over the backpack and Hildy pulled out the thermos of hot coffee, a box of Little Debbie Swiss Cake Rolls, and two of the ham sandwiches she had packed. They shared the thermos-top cup. They quickly demolished the sandwiches. They gave each other knowing smiles when they downed the Little Debbie snack cakes, since they, like almost every kid in northeast Pennsylvania, had grown up on them. A feast made by Brillat-Savarin could not have tasted better.

Then, refreshed, they made their way up the seemingly endless winding staircase to the small round room at the very top of the lighthouse. A murky twilight had fallen outside the windows that encircled the room. Rain lashed the reinforced glass. But the tower didn't sway or tremble or acknowledge the winds except with a faint rattling of the small door that led to the widow's walk.

Hildy and Mike made a nest of sorts on the wooden floor. They took off their wet shoes and Hildy hung her sodden socks on a railing. No matter how bad the storm outside, Hildy had never been happier. She took out the small battery-powered radio she had included with their supplies. She turned it on and found a weather broadcast—and the news was good.

While the outer edge of the storm still battered the Atlantic coast, Angie itself had zigzagged once more and changed course. It was moving away, not toward them, heading northeast. The hurricane might endanger the Hamptons at the end of Long

Island, but South Jersey had been spared from a direct hit. Once power was restored and damage assessed, people would be allowed to return to their homes, even as soon as the coming morning.

Immediately Hildy tried to use her cell phone, wanting to tell Corrine she was okay. The OUT OF SERVICE notice continued to appear on the screen. The call, like so many other things, would have to wait. But neither Mike nor Hildy minded their seclusion. One kiss led to two, and two kisses led to other things.

During the hours that followed, they had all the time in the world to enjoy each other's company, explore each other's bodies, whisper of the past, and spin scenarios of their future. And as Hildy learned to her satisfaction and delight, the second and third times making love with Mike far surpassed the first.

The second time they made love, which was the first time on this night, Mike took his time and took advantage of this private, secluded place, which was theirs alone. He kissed Hildy and stroked her; then he asked her what she liked. She giggled and said she didn't know. He laughed and said he'd give her some options. After she tried them, he said, she could tell him what gave her the most pleasure.

Hildy soon discovered there wasn't anything she didn't like. Mike made her squeal, he made her moan, he made her squirm. But she finally told him, as she lay on her back, her hands buried in his auburn hair, her legs spread wide, her voice very low, and her breath coming fast, that she thought she liked what he was doing with his tongue at that moment the best.

The third time, which was the second time as the storm raged outside and the rain sent water cascading down the windows, started out with Hildy asking Mike what *he* liked. Even if he had to show her how to do it, she insisted she really wanted to please him. He laughed again and said he appreciated her attitude, and he'd be glad to be her tutor in the art of love.

So for the next half hour, he gave her some lessons that she would never forget, although she did tell him she was looking forward to more practice in using her hands and her mouth, her teeth, and her tongue. But she was very glad he seemed to like the position the French call *soixante-neuf* the best, because she did too. So they did it for as long as they could before neither of them could hold back, and Hildy cried out in pleasure again and again.

Then happily sated with each other, they drank the bottled water. They snacked on trail mix and bananas. They finished off two more sandwiches, and finally, Mike being especially tired, they fell asleep in each other's arms.

Bright sunlight woke them shortly after dawn. Looking through the windows, they could see the sea was green, flat, and calm. White seabirds wheeled around in an aquamarine sky. The rhythms of everyday life had returned.

They picked up their things, ran down the steps, and burst out the door into a world washed clean and filled with promise. They found the park's restrooms open and usable. They came back to the lighthouse and lowered their bikes down the stairs. Making sure they left Old Barney tidy, they began the ride back to Ship Bottom, avoiding debris and drifted sand, but seeing only minor damage to homes.

When they approached the Dark Star Café, they were surprised to see Chef Salzarulo outside setting up tables with carafes of coffee and trays of pastries. The café's jovial owner waved to Mike and

Hildy, more shocked at their appearance than they were at his.

They stopped their bikes and told their story. He shook his head, and then winked. The lighthouse would have more secrets to keep now, he said.

As for him, he had left with everyone else, but as soon as the winds died down during the night, he had come back to the island on a motorbike. He had slipped past the barricades before the utility workers and cleanup crews came across the bridge, but they were on the island now.

He shrugged. He had his wood oven going. He could boil water without electric power. People needed their morning coffee, right? Hildy, who didn't function well without caffeine, agreed and thankfully took the take-out cups he offered to her and Mike.

Webster's Unabridged Dictionary describes an interlude as anything that fills the time between two events, as in the interval between the arrival of two trains. The interlude for Hildy and Mike began with the dying out of the storm. Neither of them could have foreseen where it would end.

In the sparkling daylight, it seemed as if nothing could go wrong. The bike ride was exhilarating. They felt optimistic and so much in love. They stopped at the cottage for Hildy to change; then they rode the bikes across the causeway to the rented Chevy Suburban that Mike had left in the strip mall on the far side.

After loading the bikes in the back of the vehicle, Hildy discovered cell phone service had been restored. She reached Corrine and calmed her down.

"But what about the St. Vlad's bus? Are the parishioners okay?"

"Corrine, I don't know what you're talking about."

"The St. Vlad's bus made another excursion right before the storm. They never made it back. It was a big story up here. We're hoping the whole bus-load had to bunk down in the casino and ride out the storm. Imagine that! I missed all the excitement."

"Corrine, I don't want to think what would have happened if you spent twenty-four hours at a slot machine," Hildy said.

"I might have hit the jackpot, you know. Hildy, if you go down to the casino, check to see if everybody's okay. We've all been worried. We think they're headed back here tonight."

"Sure. I'm pretty sure I'll be back in AC soon," Hildy said, and looked at Mike with glowing eyes.

"Love you," Corrine said.

"Love you too," Hildy echoed, and ended the call. Then Hildy checked her voice mail and after deleting twenty messages from Mike and about the same number from Corrine, she found one from the state police. Her red Volkswagen had been recovered; it had been abandoned on Collings Road in Camden. They left a number to call and an officer to contact so that she could pick it up.

Hildy's spirits soared. Perhaps the bottle remained under the seat, perhaps Jimmy the Bug was on the run, perhaps Kiki was out of Mike's life, and perhaps the course of true love would run smooth. As she was to discover, one out of four improbabilities coming to fruition was probably better than average.

"It's here! It's here! It's here!" Euphoric, Hildy pulled the pretty amber glass bottle from under the front seat. She held it up for Mike to see.

"That's great, Hildy. I wish you'd tell me why finding it was a matter of life and death," he said.

She got quiet, then softly replied that one day

soon she hoped she could. Then she asked him to please check under the hood to see if the brake lines were cut or if a bomb was planted there.

Mike raised his eyebrows and gave her a puzzled look. "Why in the world would Jimmy the Bug have booby-trapped *your* car?" he asked quite reasonably.

She stared at him, tongue-tied. She wanted to tell him all the reasons why the Mafia boss might want to blow her up or blow her away. But she couldn't, since if she blurted out the truth and he didn't believe her, he'd think she had delusions— a woman destined for the booby hatch, not for a major role in his life.

On, the other hand, in the unlikely case he said, "Sure you found a genie in a bottle and Jimmy the Bug is ready to kill you for it," he would soon be aware of the lies she had told and the trickery she had used since she first met him, not at all accidentally, on the beach.

"Oh, what a tangled web we weave, when first we practice to deceive," she thought. She opened her eyes very wide. She hoped to look very innocent. "Oh, Michael," she exclaimed, trying for the ditzy blonde effect, "the awful man who took my little car was that Mafia person, wasn't he? Maybe he wants to destroy the evidence or something. Please, Mike, I'm afraid to drive it unless you check it out."

Mike had never known Hildy to be the least bit irrational. She didn't even get upset by spiders or snakes. He chalked up her strange request to the tumultuous events of the past forty-eight hours. He humored her and opened the hood. He saw nothing whatsoever amiss. He pronounced it safe.

She stood on tiptoe and kissed him on the cheek. "Oh, thank you *soooo* much. Now I'll just go on back to the cottage and, and. . . . chill until I hear from you." She attempted to flutter her eyelashes at him.

"Do you have something in your eye?" he asked.

"I'm fine, forget that. Anyway, I'll be at the cottage in Ship Bottom. I want to be there when Mrs. Baier brings back my cats."

"Okay, I've got a ton of things to take care of. I'll call you later." Mentally, Mike was already focusing on other things besides cats and cottages. He needed to recover stolen machinery and get his business going. He never gave a single thought to Kiki. He wasn't thinking about his ex-girlfriend, his current girlfriend, or romance.

No doubt some hours from now Mike's body would encourage him to think of sex and the woman he wished to engage in it with, as any normal under-thirty male would. But for now, he kissed Hildy on the tip of her nose, gave her a pat on the fanny when she turned around to get in her car, and waved absentmindedly at her as she drove off alone . . . or at least he believed she was alone.

Meanwhile Hildy had already begun an excited conversation with the bottle on the passenger seat.

"Tony G.? Can you hear me in there? I can't let you out yet, but I wanted you to know how terrific it is to see you again," she called out, nearly giddy with relief.

The voice coming from behind the amber glass said, "I wasn't aware that you could actually see me. You appear to be looking out at traffic."

Hildy frowned. She *was* in city traffic. She couldn't possibly stare at the bottle right now. "Are you annoyed? Why in the world would you be mad at me? I was frantic with worry."

"*You* were frantic with worry? *I'm* the one you left under the seat for nearly forty-eight hours. Since the last thing I saw was your boyfriend flagging down the car, I have a pretty good idea what you were doing all that time. You could have taken a break to let me out to stretch my legs. Some friend you are."

"But I wasn't— Don't you know that Jimmy the Bug stole this car? He drove it all the way to Camden with you right there under the seat." Hildy was incredulous.

"Oh!" The genie's surprise gave way to a snicker. "That explains it. I heard some muttering, cursing, and a lot of grunting. The dashboard got smacked hard a couple of times. I tried to close my ears. I thought maybe you were fooling around in the car."

Hildy's cheeks instantly turned cherry red. "How could you think such a thing!"

"I've lived for two thousand years. Nothing surprises me. There was this time in Greece . . . a woman who made her living in the oldest profession, she had this snake and she was famous for—"

"Stop! I don't want to know! Listen, I'm going to pull off the road and let you out of the bottle. We have a lot to talk about." And she did.

Battered and bruised, his arm in a sling, Jake Truesdale sat behind his desk in his Atlantic City office. He was a very unhappy man. His partner had just walked in, and they too had a lot to talk about.

"Are you still in pain?" Mike asked, seeing the frown on Jake's face. "This should make you feel better. I recovered a dozen skid steers and two backhoes at the Sleep-E-Z along with a bulldozer, three skid steers, and, would you believe, a cherry picker down in Delaware."

He reached over and grabbed a calculator off the desk. Jake continued to glower at him as he punched in some numbers. Then he turned the calculator around to show Jake the total. "That's roughly a million dollars' worth of equipment and at twenty percent, we stand to collect around two hundred thousand. Pretty good, huh?"

Jake shifted uncomfortably in his chair. His shoulder was killing him. His ankle felt like there was a red-hot iron poking it. But his injuries weren't what was bothering him. "Yeah, pretty good. But we have a problem, which I hate to bring up, but you need to know."

"What kind of a problem?" Mike asked, totally in the dark.

"A blond, five foot four, female problem."

"Hildy? Why in the world is she a problem? Everything is great with us. Better than great. I haven't felt this good in years."

"You're not making this easy for me, Mike. Why don't you stop running your mouth and let me get it out."

Mike leaned back in his chair, wondering what in the world had his partner so riled up. "Sure, go ahead."

"First off, I couldn't buy that this girlfriend of yours just happened to be passing by the Sleep-E-Z Motor Lodge at the exact moment you were out in the road trying to get help."

"It's a weird coincidence, sure, but we always did have this special connection—"

"Mike, shut up. It wasn't a coincidence. I talked to the cops who interrogated the two guys we beat up. They work for Jimmy the Bug, no surprise there. The big surprise was that those same two thugs were also caught on videotape trying to abduct two women in the bus docking area of Caesar's a couple of days ago.

"The cops confronted them with the tape. They said they were after one woman because she had stolen something really valuable from their boss. The other woman was her sister."

"So what does this have to do with Hildy?"

"I'm coming to that. Mike, I saw the security tape. The woman they were trying to abduct was Hildy. I don't know what her connection is to Jimmy the Bug, but there is one. I don't know what she was doing at his office in that motel, but she sure as hell had to have been there. Something's wrong, buddy, really wrong. She's not who you think she is. I think you've got your dick caught between a rock and a hard place."

Mike looked confused. "I've known Hildy since I was in kindergarten. I don't understand this at all."

"Well, how much have you seen her lately? You've been with Kiki for as long as I've known you."

"Well, yeah, but still. Are you sure you're talking about Hildy Caldwell?"

"Mike, I checked. I double-checked. I wanted to be sure. This chick is into something with Jimmy the Bug up to her baby blue eyes. And you're being played. I don't know how, I don't know why, but whatever's going on, it's not kosher."

Mike couldn't get his mind around what Jake was saying. But yet, so many things that had happened involving Hildy didn't quite add up. Then there were the odd things she had said about Jimmy the Bug, and her making him check for a bomb in her car. Jake had a point, but he knew Hildy. She was a straight arrow.

"Look, Jake, I'll go talk to her. I'll get it straightened out. There's got to be some simple explanation for all this. Maybe she's working undercover for the FBI."

"For your sake, I hope so. But I think that's as likely as me being J. Edgar Hoover in blackface."

Chapter 29

Another serious conversation had taken place in the Volkswagen. It continued after Hildy reached Ship Bottom, after she and Tony G. entered the cottage.

Hildy had filled the genie in about all that had happened since Mike flagged her down at the Sleep-E-Z Motor Lodge. She told him about Jimmy the Bug's men being caught and about the motel catching fire. She told him Mike now had proof that Jimmy the Bug was behind this really huge construction equipment theft ring. She emphasized that she believed Jimmy the Bug was now on the run, and therefore, she said, she believed their troubles with the mobster were over.

Tony G. disagreed. Finally, he gave up trying to convince her and said he supposed they'd find out one way or another. There was no sense arguing about it.

Hildy grinned. She was sure she was right.

They stopped talking while Hildy thoroughly checked the cottage for damage. Then she phoned the number Mrs. Baier had left. She wanted to thank her and to find out when Shelley and Keats would be coming home.

Hildy was delighted to discover that Mrs. Baier was on the verge of leaving Princeton to return to

Long Beach Island. Poor little Henry didn't care for her sister's Chihuahua, although Hildy's cats didn't seem to mind the ankle-biter at all.

Heartened to hear that she'd soon be reunited with her cats, Hildy felt the time had come to tell the genie what she had decided to do. "Tony G., Antonius Eugenius, I have done a lot of thinking and I have something very important to discuss with you."

Tony G. didn't like the sound of this pronouncement. He hoped Hildy wasn't going to use her third wish to turn Jimmy the Bug's criminal empire into the largest cat rescue operation in the world, or something equally as difficult, like peace in the Middle East. "It sounds quite weighty and may be better put on the table after a meal. It's only midafternoon. It's not supper yet. Would you care for some tea and cucumber sandwiches?"

"No way!" Hildy burst out. "I haven't had anything but coffee since very early this morning. I want a steak, medium rare, French fries, and a salad. Remember, dressing—make it Thousand Island—on the side."

"Your wish is my command," Tony G. said with just a hint of sarcasm. Hildy heard a snippet of something familiar being sung by Annie Lennox, a wisp of glitter fluttered by, and the genie pointed to the dining room. "Shall we eat?" he asked.

The table was set and laden with all the food that Hildy requested. She sat. She dug in. She discovered she was really famished. The steak was excellent; she enjoyed her meal. The genie seemed to be quite pleased with his cuisine too. And although Hildy hadn't requested wine, two glasses of a nice dark red Pinot Noir sat by their plates. In a way, she thought, she and the genie had something to celebrate.

"I'd like to propose a toast," she said and picked up her glass.

Clearly surprised, Tony G. lifted his too. "What are we toasting?"

"To your future," she said. "I've figured it all out."

Hildy went on to explain that she had decided that she would never use her third wish. The punishment the sorcerer had inflicted on the genie must stop, and stop now. The way she saw it, if she never wished again, the genie could start to take control of his own destiny.

"Do you mean you wish to employ me as your domestic—for the next sixty or so years?" he asked, not sounding particularly enthusiastic.

Hildy choked on the wine she was sipping. "No! I want you to have your own life, doing that 'job of work' you spoke of. You will remain out of your bottle. Get your own residence—you can't stay with me and Mike. It would be awkward, worse than awkward. Impossible! But those are details we can work out. What do you think of the principle?"

For once, Tony G. was at a loss for words. When he finally spoke, he said, "Thank you for the thought. But something may happen where you need to use your third wish. You have every right to do so. I won't hold it against you. However, if until that time I can enjoy some freedom, be my own man again, I would be eternally grateful—and grateful for eternity that I had the chance."

Tears came into Hildy's eyes. "Tony G., I swear to you, I promise you, I give you my word, I will never use that wish. I understand the challenges life brings, its joys and its sorrows. I might not want to face the bad things, but using magic to avoid painful consequences or to get what I want isn't right. In the end, it's how each of us deals with our fate that determines who we are. You see?"

"I think that was a pretty speech, and I know you think you mean it—"

"I know I mean it," Hildy interrupted. "That's the end to this discussion. You know, I feel so much better. Now you can have a life, and my life can get back to normal. No more abracadabra." She stood up, did a neck roll, shook out her beautifully razor-cut hair. Then she winked at Tony G. "But some of this has been fun, hasn't it? Now let's take what's left of this genie-brewed wine into the sunporch, toss around some ideas about what you can do with your life, and wait for Mrs. Baier to bring back my cats."

Hildy and Tony G. finished off their glasses of wine and newly filled glasses replaced the empty ones. Hildy had gotten a slight buzz and felt totally relaxed. She hadn't realized how deeply stressed she had been until now, when the wine did its own kind of magic. It was making her sleepy too.

"You know, I've been up since dawn. I think as soon as Mrs. Baier comes, I'll take a short nap," she announced. "I'm going to put on an old T-shirt and some shorts. As soon as that carrier arrives, Shelley, Keats, and I are hitting the sack."

Hildy went into the other room, rummaged around in her closet, and changed. She came back into the sunporch with her feet bare and her shorts hidden by her oversized, favorite threadbare and faded Nittany Lions shirt. She felt almost like her old self again—a bit of a tipsy old self, she thought, and smiled.

She looked at her wineglass. She noticed there was just a swallow left in the bottom. *Why waste perfectly good wine?* she thought. She picked it up to take the last swallow.

Meanwhile Tony G. stood motionless, his thoughts far away, one of his huge hands on the sword at his side, the other holding his wineglass. Uncharacteristically he had a goofy smile on his face. He had gotten his own wish, at least for a while, and he couldn't believe his luck.

The doorbell rang.

"My cats!" Hildy cried, and still holding the wineglass, she ran to the door. She flung it open.

It wasn't Mrs. Baier. Mike stood there on the doorstep.

"Mike? I didn't think it was you," she cried.

Mike looked at the wineglass in her hand. He smelled the alcohol on her breath. He glared at the smarmy Italian Count Arigento, as he knew him, standing large as life behind her in the room—in what looked like nightwear. "Evidently not. Your boyfriend is still wearing his bathrobe." He spun around and stomped toward the Chevy Suburban he had just left.

"Wait!" Hildy cried. "You're wrong. It's not what you think it is!"

Mike stopped at the driver's door and turned. He looked at her with eyes of pain. "No, Hildy. *You're* not what I thought you were." He got in and without looking back, drove away.

Hildy stood there in shock. Her first frantic, desperate thought was that she had to stop Mike. She had to catch up with him and explain. But her second thought was more a feeling, of being terribly, utterly let down.

She shut the door and walked back into the sunporch. She realized that sure, seeing Tony G. here looked bad, but Mike should have let her explain. If he loved her, he should have trusted her. If he loved her, he should have believed her. If he loved her, he should not have walked away.

"I'll go speak with him," Tony G. offered. "I'll give him the old razzle-dazzle. He'll see what I really am."

Hildy shook her head. "No. Let him go. He

should know me better than that. If he loves me, he'll come back. He'll want to talk this out. He won't leave things like this. If he doesn't really love me, then it's better I found out now. I can put the past behind me and finally move on."

Tony G. didn't really agree. He figured the guy acted like any normal guy would in the same situation.

"Hey, Tony," Hildy said in a quiet little voice as she started to walk out of the room. "Would you mind waiting for Mrs. Baier? I'm going to lie down and take a nap."

The genie nodded and said he'd be glad to. He felt terrible about what had happened. He thought someone like Hildy, who had the softest heart of any human he had ever encountered, deserved better luck.

Hildy went up the ladder to her sleeping loft. She really wasn't tired anymore. She just didn't want Tony G. to see her cry.

Chapter 30

Hildy was about to find out that her sister, always older and mostly wiser, had an entirely different view of the whole situation.

After lying up in the loft sobbing her eyes out for maybe ten minutes, Hildy decided that crying wasn't making her feel any better. Talking with Corrine might give her some much-needed sympathy and emotional support. After all, nobody understood her better than her own sister.

Hildy called Corrine, who had just turned off Oprah, and relayed the whole miserable scenario, word for word, minute by minute. Then Hildy got to the part when she said to Tony G., "And if Mike really loved me, he would have let me explain—"

At that point Corrine's patience totally evaporated. "Are you nuts? What was there to explain? He found you drinking with a guy, who he thought you were dating, who was wearing a toga, which not unreasonably Mike thought was a bathrobe. What was he supposed to think?"

"But he was wrong," Hildy insisted. "You know that. I'm not dating Count Arigento. Count Arigento doesn't even exist."

"Exactly! And Count Arigento is really Tony G.—who is a *genie*. Not a guy. *A genie who lives in a bottle!* What is the matter with you, Hildy?

This is not rocket science. You take the bottle, with Tony G. in it. You go to Mike's hotel room. You knock on the door, and when he answers, you say, 'Watch!' You pull out the cork. Bam! Smoke comes pouring out of the bottle and turns into Tony G. You say, 'See, he's not a guy, he's a two-thousand-year-old genie.' It worked for me, didn't it? And that's the end of the misunderstanding."

"Cor-reeeene. It's the end of the misunderstanding, but Mike is going to call security to have me put in the loony bin."

"Hildy, trust me, he's not. Once he regains consciousness, because he's going to faint dead away on the floor same as I did, you can explain the whole thing right from the beginning. And you know how you end the conversation? You said Tony wants a job? Ask Mike to hire him. I mean, who could be a better detective than a genie? Hildy, are you listening to me?"

Hildy let out a deep sigh. "I guess it can't hurt to try."

Actually, Corrine's idea might have worked, if Mike had been in the hotel room after Hildy managed to get the room number and find the floor and knock on the right door. She had the genie's bottle in her hand, and she was all ready to pull out the cork.

But Mike didn't answer the door. Kiki did.

Something like a snarl came out of Kiki's mouth. "What do you want?"

"I came to see Mike. Is he here?" Hildy said, trying to peer around Kiki to see for herself whether Mike was lurking inside. She would have been angry if he was, but it would have leveled the playing field in a way.

"He's out. He'll be back though—to be here with me." She gave Hildy a smirk.

Hildy heard a muffled voice from inside the bottle say, "Don't fall for it. She's full of crap."

So Hildy said, "I don't think so. He told me he had broken things off with you the day before yesterday."

"It was just a lover's quarrel. I mean, he had just screwed me every which way to Sunday that same morning . . . and honey, he was a tiger. He didn't even put a condom on because he wanted this to be the time he gave me a child."

The muffled voice said, "Didn't happen. Bet on it."

"I don't believe you. Look, I thought Mike was here. He's not. I'm going to go."

Kiki's hand darted out and held Hildy's arm, her red nails digging into Hildy's flesh. "Wait just a minute. You think I don't know he slept with you? Well, he told me all about it *and I forgave him.* He was so grateful. I mean, what would he want with a country bumpkin like you? And he's going to be so thrilled when I tell him I'm pregnant."

She gave Hildy another smirk.

Hildy shook her arm loose from this shrew's grip. She stood up as tall as all five feet four inches in Teva sandals would allow. She squared her shoulders. She looked Kiki in the eye and said, "If you're pregnant, it's not Mike's. And if you try to pretend it is, I'll make sure he knows you slept with Count Arigento . . . without a condom."

Kiki's mouth fell open; then she shut it fast. "The count told you that? Well, it's my word against his, now isn't it."

"No, it isn't. Count Arigento was kind enough to let me see the photos he took with his camera phone of your . . . your performance. And as they say, a picture is worth a thousand words, now isn't it?"

"Oh, the hell with it!" Kiki screeched. "You want Mike, you can keep him! He wasn't ever any good in bed anyway!" And she slammed the door in Hildy's face.

"Maybe not with you, he wasn't," Hildy said to herself and smiled.

Jimmy the Bug had returned to Ocean City an angry man. His best-laid plans had been flushed down the crapper. The construction machine thefts, the best scam he had ever devised, had been busted. His most loyal henchmen had landed either in the slammer or the hospital. But was he dispirited? Was he depressed?

Hell no. That was not Jimmy the Bug's style. He wanted vengeance. An eye for an eye. And he knew if he got the genie back, the reversals of fortune that had occurred in the last few days wouldn't matter. He'd be on top of the world, where he always dreamed he'd be.

So he picked up the phone and put the order out, through his family in Scranton: Grab Hildy Caldwell's sister Corrine. He needed her alive for a while, but as soon as he had what he wanted, he would send word to have her killed.

Then he got into his white Cadillac CTS, put a cat carrier in the trunk, and began part two of his twisted but foolproof plan.

Mike Amante drove back to Atlantic City a sorely troubled young man. He knew what he had seen. He knew what Jake had told him. But he couldn't make sense of any of it. It didn't matter that he hadn't seen Hildy in years. Through his mother, he had kept tabs on everything she did. Which wasn't much. Until this summer, she had lived with her cats and led a modest, if terribly dull, uneventful life.

The Hildy Caldwell he knew did not cavort with gangsters. She didn't have illicit affairs. She never told a lie. And she loved him; he had no doubts that she did.

Maybe he should have waited for her explanation. But seeing her with Count Arigento split his heart with white-hot pain.

Now, his mind in turmoil and his emotions trampled, he wasn't sure what to do, but finally he felt a tug inside telling him to return to Trump Plaza. He needed to get his stuff out of the hotel room. Then maybe he'd make a decision. He parked the rental car in the hotel's garage. He went through the casino, arrived at the elevators, and pushed the call button. The light over one of the closed doors flicked on. The brushed steel doors slid open.

Hildy stood there in the elevator car, a stunned look on her face, the weird bottle she cared about so much in her hand.

"Hildy? What are you doing here?" Mike asked, incredulous. This was still another coincidence, and he just couldn't explain them anymore.

"Mike! I went to your hotel room, to talk to you. Please, I can explain everything. It may sound hard to believe. But I need you to trust me." Her eyes pleaded, but her voice held firm.

The elevator doors started to shut. Mike stuck his foot in them and they opened again. But he was determined not to stick that same foot in his mouth. He entered the elevator. He hit the button for his floor. He took Hildy in his arms. "I'm sorry. I shouldn't have walked away without hearing you out."

"And I should have told you everything earlier," she said.

"Yes, I think you should have. But whatever it is, it's okay. Let's go to my room and we can talk, really talk." He glanced up at the floor indicator. "We're almost there."

"Ah, I don't think going to your room is a good idea," Hildy said.

Mike laughed. "I promise to behave."

"It's not that." Hildy smiled. She really wouldn't have minded.

"What then?" he asked.

"Kiki's there, and she's not taking the breakup very well."

Mike couldn't help himself. He grinned. "I take it you spoke to her."

"Sort of. She called me a country bumpkin and then said—well, she screamed it actually—that if I wanted you, I could have you."

Mike gazed down at Hildy. He couldn't think straight again, but now he knew why with utter certainty. He loved this woman—it wasn't enchantment or magic. It was true love plain and simple. He didn't care about counts or Mafia bosses or anything. "Do you want me, Hildy?"

"Yes, yes, Mike, I do." She stood on tiptoe and kissed him quickly. "But I have to get some things off my chest. And I've been thinking. It should be done in front of your partner. Can we go to your office instead of into the dragon lady's lair?"

"If that's what you want," Mike answered.

Hildy saw the surprise on his face. "Look, Mike, your partner doesn't trust me. At some point, you'd have to choose between him and me. I don't want that. So let's go clear the air."

Jake Truesdale downed some more Tylenol. He looked at the clock. Mike had phoned to say he'd be there in ten minutes to clear things up. He sounded jumpy and a little strange. Maybe this partnership wasn't such a great idea. He liked Mike, but the guy was young and paid more attention to his little head than the one on his shoulders.

Jake understood that, but Mike's choice of women could be an ongoing problem.

All right, he'd give him ten minutes. He'd listen to what Mike had to say, then make a decision on whether to stick with his partner or go it alone.

Ten minutes later, on the dot, the door to the office opened. Mike and Hildy stood there.

"You didn't say you were bringing company." Jake wasn't putting out the welcome mat.

"I asked to come here with Mike." Hildy strode into the room. "I think it's time to lay all the cards on the table. That's how you detectives talk, right?"

"Not really, but why don't you say what you came to say." Jake's expression was sour.

Mike clenched his fists. He thought Jake should have more respect. Jake noticed. He was in no condition to get in a fight and maybe he was out of line. He decided to give it another try. "Why don't you have a seat and tell me your story," he said to Hildy and nodded at a nearby chair. His voice was less hostile, but wary.

Hildy felt no intimidation. Compared to standing in front of a class of hormone-crazed fifteen-year-olds, facing Jake Truesdale didn't even faze her. She tipped up her chin; her voice was crisp. "I'll stand and show you, rather than tell you. But to give you some background for what you are about to witness, let me say that I found this bottle in Caesar's, next to a slot machine." She held it up as any teacher did in show-and-tell.

"However," she continued, "as I tried to explain to you at the motor lodge, I soon found out it had previously been in the possession of the Mafia boss, James Torelli, known as Jimmy the Bug. To be succinct: He wanted it back. He attempted to steal it from me. He attempted to extort it from me. He attempted to abduct me. I'm happy to say that he did not succeed."

"Why didn't you just give him the bottle? You said it was his." Jake wasn't impressed. He wondered where this cock-and-bull story was going.

"I said it had been in his possession. But I assure you, he must never regain ownership. And it's time to show you why."

Hildy pulled the cork out of the bottle with a dramatic flair. "Antonius Eugenius, come out here." She appeared to be speaking to the bottle. Jake, thinking that this was one crazy lady, looked at Mike. Mike shrugged.

A wisp of smoke slithered out of the neck of the bottle. It trailed upward toward the ceiling where it quickly became a bright white shining cloud, edged in gold and shot through with silver. Suddenly the cloud sank to the floor and shimmered. A second later a Roman soldier stood where the cloud had been. Mike was a big guy. Jake was a little taller. This guy dwarfed them both.

He also looked very familiar to Mike. "Count Arigento?" Mike asked.

Hildy blushed. "I'm sorry, Mike, but there is no such person. I'm embarrassed to say that we dreamed up a phony Italian count to make you jealous. I apologize. Let me introduce Antonius Eugenius, also known as Tony G., a centurion in the army of Caesar Augustus—or he was in 6 BC when he was bewitched and made into what he is today. A genie in a bottle."

"What is this, a parlor trick? Didn't that magician David Copperfield do something like this?" Jake scoffed at what he witnessed, a skeptic to the core, or perhaps a doubting Thomas.

"I realize it strains credulity," Hildy said in her best schoolteacher voice. "Therefore Tony G. has

consented to give a demonstration. I yield the floor."
Hildy sat down.

Tony G. nodded. "I understand, Mr. Truesdale,
you have suffered some recent injuries. Let me help
them heal." Tony G. opened his hand to show it
was empty, then made a tossing motion and a spray
of sparkling glitter floated through the air. The first
line of "I Heard It Through the Grapevine" played.
Jake looked surprised, then stunned.

"Huh? What just happened?" He rubbed his dislocated shoulder. It didn't hurt.

"You can stand up if you'd like, but I guarantee
your ankle is quite healed."

"What the hell are you?" Jake bellowed, being
the type of man who became belligerent when worried or scared.

"As Ms. Caldwell mentioned, I am a genie who
has been riding around in that amber glass bottle
for two thousand years."

"Oh, bullshit," Jake said.

"Wait," Mike interjected. "Don't be so fast to
dismiss this. Hildy, is this really true?"

"Yes, Mike, it is. I know it sounds impossible,
but, if I may quote Shakespeare, 'There are more
things in heaven and earth, Horatio, than are
dreamt of in your philosophy.' Perhaps another
demonstration would help. Tony?"

Tony G. grinned. He reached inside his tunic and
pulled out a piece of papyrus, with angular writing
on it. He moved as if he owned the room. He
stopped, he bowed, he put the papyrus on Jake's
desk.

"What's this?" Jake said, picking it up and trying
to read it. All the Us looked like Vs.

"A list of Jimmy the Bug's customers," Tony G.
answered. "Those are the guys who bought stolen
equipment from him. I understand you're trying to
recover it."

"How did you get this?"

In truth, Tony G. just sat down and wrote the list out from memory, having overheard plenty when he belonged to Jimmy the Bug. What he said was, "Magic. I'm a genie. It's what I do."

Mike cut in. "Jake, if that's for real, it's worth a million dollars to us."

"Let's see if it checks out before we start counting our chickens." Jake scowled, although he was beginning to have an uneasy feeling. Maybe the guy who looked like he worked for Caesar's was a real genie, or not a real person, depending on how you looked at the situation.

"So you see," Hildy said, "it's been a big misunderstanding, Mr. Truesdale. I was telling you the truth when I told you I had gone to the Sleep-E-Z Motor Lodge the other night because my sister said you and Mike were headed there. Tony G., here, knew it was booby-trapped. I was just trying to save your life. So I wished that the bombs and bullets couldn't hurt anybody."

Jake looked at the short blonde with the earnest face. He looked at the guy who called himself a genie. He felt a little light-headed all of a sudden. His eyes rolled back in his head and he fainted dead away.

While Mike pulled Jake out from under the desk and sat him up until he started to come to, the momentous meeting was further interrupted by a call on Hildy's cell phone. She looked at it and saw Corrine's number on the screen. She answered and heard her brother-in-law Jack's voice. "Hildy, we have a problem."

"What's wrong?" Hildy was immediately worried.

"Corrine—" He stopped for a minute, unable to speak. "Corrine has been kidnapped. Someone broke into the house and took her. I've had instructions from her abductor."

"Oh no!" she cried out.

"Listen to me, Hildy. This is what I've been told to tell you. This guy wants you to meet him on the street near Caesar's, on the corner of Pacific Avenue and South Arkansas Avenue in one hour. He'll be driving a late-model white Cadillac. He says to bring the bottle. He says to forget about wishing for Corrine's release. He also has your cats, and he said that you don't have enough wishes to save them all. If you want to see them alive again, you need to go there and give back the bottle. Hildy, do you understand?" Jack's voice shook while he talked.

"Yes, Jack, I'll go right away." Hildy clutched the cell phone so hard that her knuckles turned white.

"Wait! One more thing—the caller was insistent. You have to go alone. Just you and the bottle."

"Okay, Jack. Don't worry, I'll get Corrine back. I'll contact you as soon as it's done." She ended the call.

"What's wrong?" Mike said, seeing Hildy's face.

"Jimmy the Bug has my sister and my cats." Then she told him the rest.

"Hildy, it's okay. Jake and I will be there. We'll grab Jimmy the Bug when you go to hand him the bottle."

At that point the deep, authoritative voice of a two-thousand-year-old genie interrupted. *"No!"*

They all turned their heads to look at Tony G. He put his hand on his sword and spoke as a centurion who had once issued orders to a hundred and sixty men. "Jimmy the Bug had one of his henchmen grab Hildy's sister. If he doesn't call in, chances are—" He hesitated, reluctant to speak the obvious.

"Oh," Hildy said. "You're right. What am I going to do?"

"Ms. Caldwell. You know exactly what you must do. Wish for your sister's release; then Jake and Mike can try to snatch the cats from Jimmy the Bug on the street."

Hildy gave Tony G. a steely-eyed look. "But you'll be gone. Forever. No. I won't do it."

Tony G.'s face looked immensely sad. "You must. I know you gave your word, but your sister's life is at stake."

Hildy shook her head. "I've done a lot of thinking about what my sister said, about the kind of wish that would solve everything. I'm pretty sure I know what she meant. I believe it will work."

"But you'll still be making your third wish, Ms. Caldwell, if I might be so bold as to point that out," Tony G. said. "I will vanish in any event."

"No, that will not happen. There is a small risk involved, but I'm willing to take the risk if you're willing to give me a little help . . . without my wishing for your help, that is."

"Your wish is my command," he said, completely sincere for the first time.

First she made a call to Caesar's and requested a page of the casino floor. She got the person she needed to speak with. She talked for quite a while. Then she told Tony G., Mike, and Jake her plan.

Chapter 31

Hildy stood on the corner of Pacific Avenue and South Arkansas Avenue, making sure to stand back from the curb, the genie's bottle in her hand. Butterflies chased around inside her stomach. She took a deep breath to steady her nerves. The timing had to be exact on this, and it was the one thing that worried her.

A moment later, a late-model white Cadillac CTS approached, coming from the south on Pacific Avenue. Hildy looked nervously around. Jake and Mike sat inside the Chevy Suburban on Arkansas Avenue, there for backup mainly, in case things went wrong. They weren't what she was looking for.

The Cadillac stopped at the light. Hildy glanced behind her again, trying not to be too obvious about it.

The Cadillac began to move, crossing the intersection and pulling up where Hildy stood. The passenger-side window went down. A man's voice yelled out, "Bring the bottle over here."

Hildy shook her head. She held up the bottle. "You bring my cats over here! Then I'll give you the bottle."

Hildy heard some cursing. She also saw out of her peripheral vision a Martz Trailways tour bus approaching the corner on South Arkansas after exiting the bus stalls at Caesar's.

Jimmy the Bug popped the trunk release and got out of the Cadillac. He walked to the back of his car and lifted the carrier out of the trunk.

The tour bus stopped at the corner even with Hildy at about the same time.

"I need to make sure they're safe," Hildy yelled. "Put the carrier on the curb and push it toward me so I can see them."

Jimmy the Bug kept his eye on the bottle. It was only about ten feet away. He'd have it in his hands in seconds. His blood raced. He didn't care about these damned cats. Let her have them. She'd have plenty to grieve. So he did what that crazy dame asked him and shoved the carrier toward her. Shelley and Keats began to howl.

Then Hildy made her move. The doorway of the bus opened. She threw the bottle. Spinning end over end, catching the light and shining brilliantly, it sailed into the bus, where Father John caught it with perfect ease.

Jimmy the Bug shouted, "Hey!" At the same time Hildy grabbed the carrier and ran to the tour bus, taking the steps in one jump and landing in Father John's arms.

The driver slammed the door shut just as Jimmy the Bug reached it. The enraged man grabbed the door handles and started to tug.

"Move move move!" everybody on the bus yelled out. The bus driver floored the accelerator, and the bus rumbled into the intersection, dragging Jimmy the Bug with it.

Jimmy the Bug finally let go. He ran back to his Cadillac. He threw himself inside and stomped on the gas, doing an illegal U-turn through the intersection to follow the bus, which was clearly headed for the Atlantic City Expressway.

Hildy's cat carrier got passed from hand to hand until it rested on an empty seat next to Annie. She held it tightly. Hildy stood in the front of the bus, next to Father John. They both clung to the front seats as the driver drove as fast as he could to try to elude the Cadillac chasing them.

Then there was a hard bump in the back of the bus.

"He's ramming us!" Hildy's former rescuer, Roger Samuels, called out. *"Floor it!"*

Hildy turned to Father John. "Father, you need to do something for me—it's terribly important. I need you to hold that bottle I threw to you—it's . . . it's filled with holy water—and recite this prayer." She handed him a piece of notepaper. "It's a matter of life and death!"

The bus swayed and lurched. Jimmy the Bug smashed into its rear again.

Father John remained unruffled. "Of course, my child. In fact, let me ask the entire bus to recite it with me." He began to read.

"In the spirit of goodness, mercy, and love . . ." Father John paused for the members of St. Vlad's to repeat his words.

"In the spirit of goodness, mercy, and love," they chanted in unison.

"I wish—are you sure you want me to use the word *wish*?"

"Yes, Father, please, hurry, it's very important."

"All right then. I wish that the criminal named James Torelli, also known as Jimmy the Bug—"

The bus of elderly people solemnly repeated the words. As if he could hear their words, Jimmy the Bug began ramming the back of the bus repeatedly, his fury evident. The bumping and jolting sorely tested the bus driver's skills, but he stayed the course.

"—be struck with remorse, repentance, and an overwhelming desire to make amends."

"—be struck with remorse, repentance, and an overwhelming desire to make amends," the parishioners intoned.

Father John continued, "Specifically, he must guarantee the safe return of Corrine Gannon—"

The parishioners nodded enthusiastically and echoed the words. Jimmy the Bug smashed into the bus again.

"He must become a vegan and be unable to harm a living soul, *not even a bug.* He must right the wrongs he has perpetrated, and spend the rest of his days in meditation and prayer, in a monastery, in some faraway mountains, for the rest of his born days. Amen."

The banging of the Cadillac hitting the bus abruptly ceased.

"Is that it, my dear?" Father John asked and went to hand the bottle back.

"Actually, I would like you to make one more wish—I mean prayer. Would you mind?"

"Prayer has been a bedrock of my calling for sixty years. Why would I mind?" he asked, his eyes twinkling.

"All right, Father. This one is for you." She looked out at the bus full of gray-haired passengers. "All of you."

"All of us?" Irene Samuels asked.

"You bet," Hildy said and handed another slip of paper to Father John. He began to read aloud:

"In the spirit of goodness, mercy, and love, I wish that the St. Vladimir's dome shine as brightly and beautifully as it did when it was first built a hundred years ago, gilded with real gold, and should this miracle be granted, that people come from far and wide to see and believe . . . and that

the Roman saint named Antonius Eugenius—I've
never heard of that one, my dear," he whispered,
"—be remembered for this miracle. Amen."

After he had finished, Father John turned kindly
eyes to Hildy, an odd look on his face. He handed
her back the bottle, and this time she took it.

"The dome will be golden again when we get
back, won't it?" he said quietly to her.

"Yes, Father, I believe it will."

"And people will hear of the miracle?"

"Yes, Father, I'm sure they will."

"And they will come to St. Vlad's to worship?"

"You'll need a huge shrine to accommodate
them, I'm sure."

"And the church will be saved?"

"Yes, Father, I believe it will."

"Then I say again that God moves in mysterious ways."

"Amen to that," Hildy said. And she knew without a doubt that the Cadillac CTS that had been
closing in on the lumbering St. Vlad's bus was gone,
that her sister was safe, and that all was right in
her world.

After asking the bus driver to pull over and re-
trieving her cat carrier from Annie, Hildy got off
the bus. She waved to everyone and walked back
to the blue Chevy Suburban that had followed the
Cadillac that was following the bus.

Mike was already out of the SUV, waiting to
embrace her. He hugged her hard, gave her a quick
kiss, and took the cat carrier from her hands. Then
he opened the back gate of the Chevy and put the
protesting cats inside. Hildy began to climb into
the backseat.

Mike stopped her. "No, not there. Jake, would
you mind switching seats with my bride-to-be?"

"No problem," he said and exited the passenger

seat. He got in the back. Hildy got in the front, but she left the bottle next to Jake.

"Would you pull out that cork, please?" she asked once everyone was in and Mike prepared to drive off.

Jake looked a little uneasy, but he opened the bottle. A tendril of bright white smoke began to emerge.

"Now I think," she said, "that Tony G. wants to discuss something with you."

"Yeah, what's that?" Jake asked.

"A job."

Mike held the steering wheel with his left hand and pulled Hildy close with his right, just like he used to.

He looked at her and said, "If I may quote—"

"You may," she said and kissed his cheek.

"As Shakespeare also said, " 'All's well that ends well.' "

And so it did.

Chapter 32

High in the mountains of the Himalayas, the country of Nepal sits at the very top of the world. There the Jainist monk known as Brother James began his morning prayers. A small circle of followers and admirers gathered to listen and be near the holy man, so revered by so many.

Brother James, also known as Brother James of the Bug, had dedicated his life to the protection of all creatures with an exoskeleton. He was unfailingly kind to insects, and was particularly fond of a pet cricket he called Jennifer, although he didn't know why he had named it that.

Some of the faithful called him the Jainist version of St. Francis, a saint for modern times.

The stone floor of the chapel was cold. His feet were bare. His robes were not very warm. But his needs were simple, and he didn't mind. Brother James began his chants. He prayed for repentance, he expressed remorse, he asked for forgiveness for every wrong he had ever done. He couldn't remember exactly what wrongs they were, but sometimes he dreamed that long ago and far away he had been a bad, bad man.

Epilogue

" 'The frost is on the punkin,' " Hildy quoted, and shivered when she and Mike arrived at Gus Genetti's Hotel and Conference Center in Wilkes-Barre for Lake Lehman High School's tenth class reunion.

"Frost? It feels like there's snow in the air," Mike observed as he helped Hildy climb out of the Prius. Hildy wore her copper-colored Donna Karan original and strappy sandals—and she was freezing as they dashed across the street hand in hand from the parking lot. Laughing and in high spirits, they ducked into the building right off the old-fashioned town square in the center of the aging city built a century ago by railroads and coal.

Hildy and Mike were Jerseyites now and both had overlooked how quickly the temperatures could plummet at the end of October in northeast Pennsylvania. In fact, a few shining snowflakes drifted down and briefly settled on Hildy's hair.

Once inside, warm and snug, Hildy with Mike right behind her stopped at a long table to collect their name tags, which included their yearbook picture, so people would remember how they looked *then.* As she pinned hers on, Hildy surveyed the crowded room where men and women stood around sipping wine or drinking beer. She waved at a few of her former classmates, noticing that the biggest change for the women of her class was the added pounds. For the men, it was the loss of hair. But all in all, she recognized everyone right away.

After an hour of squealing, hugging, and reminiscing with old friends, Hildy was herded into a line of former classmates waiting to go into the banquet room for dinner. As each person entered, he or she was introduced with some wit and great enthusiasm by Jay, who had gone from class clown to class celebrity after he had become the last fashion designer standing on a reality television show.

When Hildy reached the door, with Mike at her side, the DJ changed the music from Queen's "We Will Rock You" to Erasure's rendition of "Magic Moments."

"And now," Jay said from the raised stage at the end of the room, wielding the microphone like the MC at a wedding, "here comes the prom king and queen, back in each other's arms—Mike Amante and his new bride, Hildy Caldwell Amante! Let's hear it for the lovers!"

With their arms around each other, Hildy and Mike walked into the room to the sound of applause. The lights dimmed and a shower of silver glitter fell from someplace near the ceiling like a thousand tiny stars. Undulating waves of sparkling light danced and spun around the couple as those watching oohed and aahed at the spectacle.

"Wow!" Jay yelled into the microphone. "We always said you two were so hot that you lit up the place." Then he twisted his head around and said to a thin, brittle woman behind him on the stage, "Nice touch, Darla!"

Darla—who had never ever gotten back with her high school sweetheart Frank the fullback—had headed the decoration committee for the reunion. She had been busy shooting dirty looks at Frank's very pregnant wife when the twinkling stars began to fall on Genetti's. "I didn't order *that*," she hissed to Jay. "I bet Hildy paid somebody to throw glitter all over the place. She'll have to pay for the clean-up too."

But the glitter had gone as quickly as it came, fading away softly into a rose glow before vanishing without a trace—just as the genie's laughter went unheard, like the sound of one hand clapping, lost in the music and the din of the applause.

Acknowledgments

I would like to express my deep gratitude to two friends who inspired me to write this book—

A big thank you to Hildy Morgan, who told me how it was to grow up being named Hildegard. She generously allowed me to use her name for my heroine, as well as the story of how she came to be called Hildy. I admit to giving my character some of her spunk, generous spirit, and compassion too.

Another huge thank you goes to Brynda Huntley, who met her high school sweetheart, Mike, after *forty years*—and yes, they fell in love all over again. When she told me what had happened—and Mike later shared with me how he adored her then and now—I felt I had to write a romance about a woman who reunites with her first love, her true love, again across years and miles. Hildy Caldwell and Mike Amante's story is my fictional version of Brynda and Mike's real-life dream come true.

I would also like to remember Mrs. Benson, my high school Latin teacher, long dead but not forgotten. Her passion for language and Roman history instilled a lifelong enthusiasm in me for them too. I could not have imagined Antonius Eugenius without my four years in her class.

And so, dear readers, *amo, amas, amat*—"I love, you love, he or she loves." After all, what else is really important in life?

Hugs and kisses to you all,
Lucy Finn

ALSO AVAILABLE FROM

LUCY FINN

CAREFUL WHAT YOU WISH FOR

Back in her tiny hometown with a new baby to care for,
successful attorney Ravine Patton thought her life had
gone up in smoke. Then her Diaper Genie went
haywire, and out popped a handsome pilot who'd been
trapped inside. Gene—who, it turns out, is her genie—
has granted her three wishes.

Lucky Ravine now has the gorgeous hunk scrubbing her
entire house. But it isn't long before she starts falling for
Gene, which means big trouble. Because once her third
wish is fulfilled, he'll vanish from her life forever. And
Ravine realizes she's going to have to be very careful
about what she wishes for next.

**Available wherever books are sold or at
penguin.com**

Don't Talk Back
to Your Vampire
by Michele Bardsley

*Sometimes it's hard to take your own advice—
or pulse.*

Ever since a master vampire became possessed and bit a
bunch of parents, the town of Broken Heart, OK, has
catered to those of us who don't rise until sunset—even if
that means PTA meetings at midnight.

As for me, Eva LeRoy, town librarian and single
mother to a teenage daughter, I'm pretty much used to
being "vampified." You can't beat the great side effects:
no crow's-feet or cellulite! But books still make my
undead heart beat—and, strangely enough, so does Lorcán
the Loner. My mama always told me everyone deserves a
second chance. Still, it's one thing to deal with the usual
undead hassles: rival vamps, rambunctious kids adjusting
to night school, and my daughter's new boyfriend, who's a
vampire hunter, for heaven's sake. It's quite another to fall
for the vampire who killed you….

"The paranormal romance of the year."
—MaryJanice Davidson

"Hot, hilarious, one helluva ride."
—L.A. Banks

**Available wherever books are sold or at
penguin.com**

Now Available
From Vicki Lewis Thompson

OVER HEXED

Dorcas and Ambrose, former matchmaking sex therapists for
witches and warlocks, are now working for mere mortals—
although the handsome Sean Madigan is kind of an Adonis.
That is, until Dorcas and Ambrose strip him of his sex appeal
and introduce him to his destiny, Maggie Grady. This time
winning a girl's heart won't be so easy for Sean. It means
rediscovering the charms buried beneath the surface.
But what a surface!

"A snappy, funny, romantic novel."
—*New York Times* bestselling author Carly Phillips

Available wherever books are sold
or at penguin.com